CIRCLE OF
BLOOD

THOMAS M. MALAFARINA

HELLBENDER BOOKS

an imprint of Sunbury Press, Inc.
Mechanicsburg, PA USA

HELLBENDER BOOKS

an imprint of Sunbury Press, Inc.
Mechanicsburg, PA USA

For information about special discounts for bulk purchases, please contact Sunbury Press Orders Dept. at (855) 338-8359 or orders@sunburypress.com.

To request one of our authors for speaking engagements or book signings, please contact Sunbury Press Publicity Dept. at publicity@sunburypress.com.

ISBN: 978-1-62006-129-9 (Trade paperback)

Library of Congress Control Number: Application in Process

FIRST HELLBENDER BOOKS EDITION: May 2019

Product of the United States of America
0 1 1 2 3 5 8 13 21 34 55

Set in Bookman Old Style
Designed by Crystal Devine
Cover by Amber Rendon
Edited by Lawrence Knorr

Continue the Enlightenment!

FOR MY INCREDIBLE WIFE, JoAnne, who wishes I would stop dedicating all of my books to her. In my opinion, it's the least I can do for all the years she has tolerated my involvement in the strange world of the horror genre.

INTRODUCTION

N EARLY 2011 my publisher, Lawrence Knorr of Sunbury Press contacted me and asked if I would have an interest in co-writing a book with him sometime. He had a very rough concept for a ghost story. I was finishing a short story collection and was hoping to start another novel, so his timing was perfect.

I told Larry I'd be willing to put off starting anything else and work with him. He provided me with an 11-line summary. Little did I realize I'd be working on the book for more than a year and a half and would end up hijacking the novel and writing the entire thing myself.

I should point out the reason why this happened. It wasn't because of any lack of desire to participate on Larry's part; when it comes to my creative endeavors, I can be a bit of a control freak. Also, once my juices start flowing, I tend to write like a maniac and can't stop. This leaves little time for, as they say, "playing well with others." Fortunately for me, Larry was extremely magnanimous in allowing me to take his crux of an idea and carry on by myself.

This was the first time I had ever worked with any form of outline let alone one created by someone else. I admit it was challenging for me. I prefer to start writing and see where the story takes me.

In the back of this book, you will find Larry's original 11-line overview. I would suggest you wait to read it until after completing the book. From these lines, an entire novel of over 155,000 words eventually evolved.

In 2012, I completed the original manuscript and we titled it *Fallen Stones*. Several months later it was published by Sunbury Press. I'd like to think that in the years since my writing has improved and I've always wanted to take the time to rewrite the book.

Toward the end of 2016, I decided it was time I take a fresh look at the novel and see what I could do to make it flow more freely (and be a much shorter 89,000 words) without changing the story. I also decided to rename the book.

I was more than pleased with the results and I hope you will be as well. Here is *Circle of Blood* for your reading pleasure and thank you as always for your continued support.

Thomas M. Malafarina
March 2019

PROLOGUE

SCARCELY A SOUND could be heard in the dimly lit chamber save for the gentle rustling of papers, the almost-silent breathing of the room's sole occupant, and the occasional dripping of water from the faucet, a noise which seemed to echo loudly in the otherwise soundless space. The quiet was both serene yet ominous, suggesting an evil presence might be lurking just beneath the all-encompassing cloak of stillness.

The time was just after midnight on a cloudy April night. Even if the moon had been full and bright the antique Italian glass windows along the ceiling wouldn't have allowed sufficient illumination to enter from the world outside. What meager light was present came from the centermost section of the room where numerous tapered candles, perhaps twenty or more, surrounded the rim of a pearl-white claw-foot bathtub. The four claws were representative of an eagle's talons grasping firmly onto a ball, a typical design used in many tubs of the early twentieth century period.

The tub was elevated atop a three-foot-high polished marble platform with a set of three stairs surrounding it on all four sides. This made it appear as an ancient sacrificial altar.

Reclining, a man soaked in steaming water filled to chest level. He appeared to rest even though relaxing was the furthest thing from his mind. His thin right leg bent to provide a surface for his reading material. He stared at the paper through red-rimmed, dark-circled, sunken eyes for a few minutes at a time occasionally turning the pages with an absent mind. He was much too preoccupied to comprehend its contents.

He appeared not to be acting completely of his own volition. The skeleton-thin man looked exhausted, beaten as if he had finally lost a long, futile battle and had simply surrendered to an inevitable conclusion. His eyes left the document yet again and locked onto one of the flickering candle flames dancing peculiarly on its wick.

He had fastened each of the blood-red candles to the rim of the tub with melted wax. As they burned, more of the substance dripped slowly down their dwindling lengths. They were now half of their original size, an indication of how long he had been waiting. Although the man had no recollection of doing so, he had refreshed his continuously cooling bath on several occasions.

The wax of many of the candles had dribbled down past the surface of the water resembling rivulets of coagulating blood.

A cell phone and a straight razor lie on the floor next to the tub. The gleaming silver blade of the razor shone in the candlelight. It was an antique perhaps eighty or more years old, encased in an ivory handle, engraved with three initials: D.C.L. He had found the razor in an old wooden cigar box in the cellar of the main farmhouse shortly after moving in along with several other trinkets including a set of gold cufflinks bearing the same monogram.

He had carefully sharpened and used the blade often since then. Had he been able to think more rationally, he might have realized most of his current problems had coincided with the discovery of the razor. But his days of thinking clearly had long gone by the wayside.

Emerson Charles Washburn broke his transfixed stare away from the dancing candle flame and looked absently about the room. He still held the document in his hand but paid little attention to it. He had no need to read it. He knew its contents verbatim since he had written it himself. He had later handed it over to his local attorney for rewriting so that the lawyer could add the mandatory legalese or "mumbo jumbo" as Emerson was fond of referring to it.

In his heyday, Emerson Washburn had beaten and killed many men with his own bare hands. If enemies from his former life could see what a wretched wreck he had become, they'd take great pleasure in his decline. Some might seize the opportunity to repay him for his past misdeeds.

He looked slowly around the room absorbing the essence of the space and marveling at the fine craftsmanship of the contractors he had employed to turn what was once a dilapidated, hexagonal shaped out-building into a luxurious spa retreat. Emerson had spared no expense as was typical of the man who had acquired his fortune from past illegal enterprises.

A large stone fireplace had been rebuilt into the wall behind him. When he had purchased the property, the fireplace was in ruins. It now was luxurious with a thick, highly-polished, handcrafted mahogany mantel.

Surrounding the tub area on four of the remaining five walls were large mirrors. Above the mirrored walls weathered varnished boards of varying lengths were placed at angles to form a series of repeating triangular patterns, which served to draw the viewer's eyes toward the vaulted cathedral-like ceiling with arches of heavy timbers. Most of these amazing aesthetic features were scarcely visible in the gloominess of the shadowy room but the simple knowledge of their presence helped Emerson relax, preparing him for the unwanted visitor he knew would arrive soon.

Through extensive research, Washburn had learned the original owners of the property were his maternal grandparents, Dwight and Marie Livingston. He hadn't known much about his grandparents, but after hiring a private investigator Emerson discovered the Livingstons had been quite wealthy with significant land holdings as well as owning several coal companies. They had purchased the land and built the house in the early 1900s.

He had also learned his grandparents weren't the first settlers to build on the property. Houses of one sort or another had existed on the land for several hundred years. However, when his grandparents bought the land no buildings were present. As a result, they started with a clean slate.

Emerson knew his grandparents had both died young, in their early thirties. He had always suspected they might have done something horrendous because none of their living decedents ever spoke of them.

On several occasions as a young boy, Emerson would catch his mother or father discussing something in hushed voices, wearing looks of disapproval. He might hear the occasional snippet of a phrase or the occasional word such as "mother," "father" or even words like "tragic" and "horrendous," and he knew they were speaking about his mother's parents.

This often confused Emerson as he had also heard his grandparents had died when his mother was only about two years old. He couldn't comprehend how she could feel such hatred for people she never really knew and certainly couldn't recall.

His imagination often ran wild trying to determine what his grandparents had done to warrant such a family shunning. If his parents caught him eavesdropping, they'd immediately cease their conversation and order him outside to play. They had no intention for him to learn the mysterious family secret.

Then years later, after Emerson had found his way into a life of crime, he often wondered if he had chosen the lifestyle because of some genetic predisposition. What sort of evil had his grandparents perpetrated that was so vile as to have them banished from all family discussions? As a child, he often thought he would give anything to learn the horrible family secret, but now that he knew everything, he wished to God he didn't.

Whatever "bad blood" had coursed through his grandparents' veins obviously ran through his own. His criminal empire had dealt in virtually every known vice modern man could desire from stolen goods to drugs to prostitution.

As he soaked in the tub Emerson recalled the life-changing event which made him cast aside his life of crime and had brought him home. Many years earlier during one of his "business trips" to Pennsylvania –Berks County to be specific–an incident occurred spurring him not only to become interested in his heritage but also to have it become an obsession for him.

He had read an account in the local newspaper about the tragic death of a couple in a car accident. A drunk driver had plowed into the couple's vehicle head-on as they were driving home from a movie. To Emerson's surprise, the names of the couple were those of his estranged brother Nathan and his wife, Mary. Because of his brother's opposition to Emerson's lifestyle they hadn't spoken in many years. Despite their lack of closeness, he felt a deep sadness knowing he was now alone in the world.

Perhaps he had been overcome with melancholy finding himself growing older without either a wife or children. His brother's death became the catalyst for him to embark on a ten-year search for any living relatives.

During the investigation, he learned about the existence of a farmette for sale in Schuylkill County that had originally been his ancestors' family homestead. He immediately bought it sight unseen. This wasn't how Emerson Washburn normally conducted his business, but the idea seemed so right.

The farmhouse and outbuildings had been abandoned for more than thirty years and had fallen into disrepair. The buildings were uninhabitable shells, which had been vandalized over the years. Previous owners never kept the property for more than a few months. Emerson now understood the reason why.

He suddenly felt a slight prickling sensation at the back of his neck and knew from previous encounters what was happening. He reached down over the side of the huge tub and allowed the document he was holding to fall to the floor with a slap, echoing loudly in the silent empty chamber.

The cover of the document read "Last Will and Testament of Emerson Charles Washburn."

As he slowly returned to a sitting position in the tub, he noticed a familiar change occurring to the wall-sized mirror located directly in front of him. It was a change he had seen many times, but it still disturbed him to the very core of his soul. The mirrored glass shimmered and then rippled outward like a pebble dropped into a pond. Emerson smelled the familiar foul odor like that of rotting vegetation and the stench of decomposition.

The candles surrounding the tub flickered as a breeze suddenly blew across them. The visage in the glass was a man dressed in the style of clothing an early twentieth-century gentleman of wealth would have worn. His form was translucent and moved with the jerky spastic motion one would see if watching an old silent movie.

However, Emerson knew the likeness which had visited him many times before wasn't an illusion but was the spirit of his long-dead grandfather, Dwight Charles Livingston. The ghost was tall and thin perhaps gaunt would have been a better description and appeared to be in his early thirties with dark brown hair and stylish mustache. He wore wire-rimmed glasses and carried a cane with an ivory handle fashioned in the shape of an animal's head, a wolf. Washburn had seen a similar cane in a large portrait of Dwight and Marie Livingston which currently hung in the living room of the main farmhouse.

One sight he never failed to notice but always wished he didn't have to endure, was the long gash sliced across the specter's throat. It was like a giant gaping toothless mouth of tattered flesh hanging in a flap across the wretched creature's neck. Several times Emerson thought he had seen some sort of insects, perhaps worms or maggots crawling about inside the cavernous slash.

Over the previous year, the specter had haunted and tormented Emerson relentlessly. He had first seen the image shortly after discovering the straight razor. Since then he had been forced against his ever-weakening will to do whatever the spirit commanded, including soaking in the tub that very night.

For a time he had managed to resist the spirit's demands. But after countless hours of torment, sleep deprivation, weight loss, and declining health, he found he had to either bend to the will of his long-dead grandfather or be driven mad. Now that he had met the creature's latest and hopefully final demand, Emerson prayed the spirit would be satisfied, would return to whatever corner of Hell it had arisen from, and would leave him at peace.

Emerson often wondered why he simply hadn't just cut his losses and fled. But that wasn't his way. Anyone who knew Emerson Washburn understood the man would never give up a fight.

However, there was more to his remaining than simple stubbornness. Unknown to Emerson there was another force controlling his destiny keeping him in the game. He was being manipulated at a point far below the flesh, far below even the cellular level. His very soul was lost and was being directed and not just by the ghost of his grandfather, but by another spirit in the house, his grandmother Marie. The pair of specters had set into motion a plan, which would not only affect him but also another unsuspecting group of Livingston descendants.

The apparition looming before him had a face as white as chalk. Its blood-red eyes were sunken deep in dark-rimmed sockets. If Washburn had looked at his own sickly reflection in the surrounding mirrors, he would have been shocked at how his countenance was almost as deplorable as the long-dead being before him. The creature's fine garments were soiled and smelled as musty as a tomb. What once had been the man's white linen shirt now hung askew, yellowed and covered with blood and filth. The ghost appeared to be much younger than Washburn's own sixty-three years because Livingston and his wife had both died tragically at such an early age.

Emerson sat in the rapidly chilling bath water feeling especially vulnerable in his nakedness. He had reluctantly agreed to read the agreement from the confines of the tub because the spirit had demanded it. He no longer had the willpower to oppose the specter's orders. He no longer understood his own actions, nor could he seem to control them.

The image emerged from the mirror slowly floating through the air and hovering near the document resting on the marble floor. With a wave of its ghostly hand the pages flipped open turning rapidly until they stopped at the desired page. Livingston stared down and a look of satisfaction spread over the specter's withered face. It had seen what it had come to see; the blood circle would soon be closed. What had happened before would happen again.

Emerson hadn't taken his eyes off the spirit and with caution said, "Dwight, Grandfather. I've done what you asked. I've named her as my heir; the one you specified. Will you now please go and leave me in peace?" The creature didn't speak but simply floated, staring blankly.

Washburn asked once again, "What more can you possibly want from me? I've done as you ordered. I always do what you wish. I've left my property, my money, and all of my earthly possessions to a niece I never knew existed. Isn't that enough? Please, I'm begging you. I'm a sick and tormented soul. Go now and leave me in peace."

The image didn't fade, didn't leave, nor did it melt back into the glass as Emerson had hoped. Instead, it stared silently.

Then the translucent image began to dissolve before Emerson's eyes, breaking down into a mass of millions of tiny, sparkling particles. It had never done any such transformation in his presence before. He was transfixed. A moment later the cloud of iridescent white specks floated toward Emerson, surrounding his head like a throng of flying insects. The collection then began to grip tightly against his skull absorbing into his pores. Washburn sat motionless in the tub his eyes glazing over in a trance. Then like a mindless robot, he slowly reached his right arm down over the side of the tub grasping the handle of the straight razor.

Sitting upright in the bathtub the creature inhabiting Emerson's body looked down at the blade of the razor glimmering in the candlelight. The creature noticed the blood-red candle wax dripping down the sides of the bathtub and a sly smile appeared on his lips. Calmly looking down at his chest, the man methodically began cutting a series of diagonal wounds into his flesh making a number of "V" shapes.

Emerson's body neither flinched nor cried out even though he felt the burning agony as every nerve ending in his body seemed to explode. Instead, he sat calmly as the blood streamed down from one "V" to the next like thick, muddy water. It began to turn the bathwater a hideous shade of crimson. He looked upward amused at how the newly sliced furrows in his chest matched the patterns of the wood surrounding the upper walls of the spa.

Next, he made a series of incisions across his face, his forehead and cheeks before reaching up and slicing off his left ear, which fell into the water with a moist, sickening plopping sound. He then made a number of deep incisions across his left arm and wrist allowing the arm to hang limply in the bloody water. As the spirit felt Emerson's body becoming weak with blood loss the phantom reached down into the water where it systematically began to hack at Emerson's testicles and penis, castrating them from his body and allowing them to float almost comically in the ruby water like some perverse bath toys.

The glowing mass of glittering elements left Emerson's body and seconds later the specter was once again standing next to the tub looking down at the bloody carnage it had left behind. The ghost floated calmly toward the mirror wall and was absorbed into whatever world existed beyond the glass.

Emerson's eyes suddenly opened filled with shock, pain, and terror upon the realization of the irreparable damage inflicted on his dying body. Too weak to help himself and unable to move, the ravaged man moaned and cried with agony as the last of his lifeblood flowed into the tub.

Seconds before his body finally shut down Emerson noticed more faces watching him from one of the other mirrored walls. It appeared to be the image of two young boys hovering in the glass. Washburn could see no bodies just floating faces. Although he had never seen the pair before they looked familiar to him. The one boy looked about six years old while the other was perhaps a year or two younger. Then he realized who they were.

The two didn't seem to have the same sort of evil countenance as Dwight Livingston but instead appeared filled with sorrow. There was an almost angelic aura about the pair as they watched sadly while the last few moments of Emerson Washburn's life trickle away.

Washburn lay dead in the bloody cauldron his head tilted to the right against the back of the tub, his right arm dangling limply over the side of the tub resembling the familiar pose in the famous painting "The Death of Marat" by Jacques-Louis David. The bloody straight razor had fallen to the floor and the tips of his fingers rested against the face of his cell phone, which lay near his last will and testament. Suddenly the phone sprang to life and began dialing a number. After a series of rings, a man's deep voice answered. After several minutes amid the faint echoes of an unintelligible conversation, the phone went dead.

As Emerson's spirit left his body it was immediately sucked into the still undulating glass. Then the surface of the mirror returned to its normal appearance and the room was once again silent. Inside the mirror, the emaciated, naked, genital-less image of Emerson Washburn appeared looking distraught, beaten, tormented, yet sadly accepting of his fate.

The floating faces of the two young boys looked on from the adjacent mirror wall as they slowly shook their heads in sad resignation. A sudden cold wind swept through the room as the candles were extinguished and the room plummeted into total darkness. A slight glow appeared at the center of the wall of mirrors and wild, maniacal laughter echoed through the pitch-black space.

1

THE YOUNG WOMAN sat at her kitchen table feeling be-wildered staring down at the sealed envelope she held tightly in her trembling hands. She assumed the mys-terious packet contained an important letter of some sort. It had arrived as a certified registered letter. Never before had Stephanie needed to sign for a letter. She felt a strange hollow sensation in the pit of her stomach suggest-ing any such letter couldn't possibly be good news.

She tried to think of any bills she might have forgotten to pay recently. Perhaps one had gone delinquent and been turned over to a collection agency. She didn't believe so as she was fastidious about her record keeping and bill paying.

She looked apprehensively at the return address twist-ing her longish brown hair in circles as was her habit. The name printed in an ornate, calligraphic gold script read, "H. Mason Armstrong, Attorney at Law." Stephanie's lips moved silently as she read the name, one of those childhood habits she had never been able to overcome.

"H. Mason Armstrong, Attorney at Law," she finally said aloud. "Sounds a bit pretentious to me."

For Stephanie, it suggested the owner of the name per-ceived it to be a powerful moniker for a lawyer whereas he might feel his first name, which could be Harold, or maybe Henry, wasn't strong enough. She always noticed things like that. She believed she could tell when people were "putting on airs" as her mother used to say.

The address for the law firm was in the town of Ashton, Pennsylvania in Schuylkill County. She couldn't imagine what an attorney from Schuylkill County could possibly want with her. Stephanie was only marginally familiar with that area, having lived her life in Western Berks County some fifty-plus miles south of Ashton. Once again, she looked down at the ornate lettering of the return address and was convinced this lawyer was trying to appear like he was some big city law firm when in fact, he was more likely simply a small-time storefront solicitor from a small coal region town.

Stephanie recalled reading somewhere that Ashton had a tourist attraction, a coal mine called the Miner's Tunnel where visitors could ride in coal cars down inside what was once a working coal mine. She had been meaning to take her family on the tour before Jeremy was too old and too "cool" to appreciate it. But they just hadn't been able to find the time. Perhaps they could get there this year over the summer.

The manufacturing company where her husband, Jason worked as an engineer had a sister facility just outside of Ashton. On occasion, Jason made business trips to the facility.

He'd always return from his visits to the small community with stories of how that plant was one of the few places in the area anyone could hope to earn an adequate wage. He'd often describe how hard the local people had to struggle to make ends meet. He'd often joke saying if they could live in Ashton while still earning his higher Berks County salary they could live like royalty. However, they both had spent their lives among the rolling farmlands of western Berks County and believed they could never be happy living anywhere else.

As a young girl, Stephanie had also heard stories of how some of her ancestors had once lived in Schuylkill County. She knew her grandmother had moved to Berks County as a young woman seeking employment opportunities and had met her grandfather. Once in passing, Jason had mentioned one of his grandmothers was originally from Schuylkill County as well.

Stephanie turned the letter over in her moist hands, unsure if she should open it or wait until Jason got home. It might be easier to face whatever potential bad news awaited her with Jason by her side. Having him with her always made everything easier.

Then she realized by the time Jason got home from work her stepson Jeremy and her daughter Cindy would be home from school as well and the house would be thrust into the type of chaos only a twelve- and ten-year-old could create. Not to mention the fact that eighteen-month-old Samuel would soon wake up from his afternoon nap adding to the pandemonium. No, she supposed she'd have to open the letter now while the house was quiet, and she had the time to give it her full attention.

She thought about how much she treasured these quiet times when the two older kids were at school and the baby was asleep. She was free to get some housework done or perhaps work on her book or just sit around and contemplate life. She knew such precious moments would be available less and less when little Sammy eventually grew out of his need for afternoon naps. Plus, it was the end of May and school would soon be letting out for summer vacation. She had no idea how she'd ever find time to work on her book when that happened.

She knew Jason did what he could to help give her the time she so desperately required, but there was always so much to do and she seemed to be pulled constantly in so many different directions. Stephanie feared her writing might once again fall by the wayside as it had done before. She had resumed writing for the first time in over ten years when school started last fall and she had only agreed to do so because Jason had talked her into it.

He had found one of her earlier children's books while he was unpacking a box. She had written it several years before they met. Jason was amazed to discover his new wife was a published author and he encouraged her to return to her obvious passion. He learned how she'd all but given up writing and illustrating children's books when her daughter Cindy was born.

At that time she had still been married to her first husband Bill Sanders. Bill hadn't been in any way supportive of her writing and there had always been so much tension in their lives in the form of constant bickering.

After her divorce, Stephanie was a single mom with primary custody of an infant daughter and no time to consider working on books. As a result, she simply stopped, promising herself she'd get back to her work if things ever settled down.

Then Jason Wright came into her life.

Stephanie and Jason met at a bar. After shy introductions Stephanie's outgoing friend Cheryl kept the conversation going. Six months later Stephanie and Jason were married and a little over a year after that they discovered she was pregnant with Sammy. Stephanie often joked affectionately with Jason how when she met him she had finally found "Mr. Wright."

Financially things were a bit tough for the young couple as they were rebuilding their new lives together. Fortunately, Jason earned enough money for them to afford to buy a small townhouse with just enough room for both kids and a small nursery for the baby. This also meant Stephanie could quit her job and stay home. Then Jason encouraged her to start writing again.

She had completed the story portion of her book before Sammy was born and was struggling with the illustrations. Her old publisher was so happy to learn she was back in the game, that he signed her to a contract without her even having to pitch the book. Stephanie had never made any significant money with her books but still got the occasional ten or twenty-dollar royalty check every six months.

Her publisher believed she had what it took to create a bestseller and hoped this latest book would be the one to make her a household name. Stephanie didn't care about wealth or fame but did hope her books might be successful.

She didn't want to let her publisher or Jason down so she worked whenever she could find time to complete what she hoped would be her best children's book yet.

Unfortunately, that wouldn't happen today. Today she sat holding the strange envelope. She slid her finger under the flap and carefully tore it open revealing a single off-white sheet of paper adorned across the top with the letterhead of the lawyer in the same pretentious gold-leaf calligraphy as the envelope.

Stephanie began reading the letter. After completing the three short paragraphs she read it in its entirety once again and then a third, then a fourth time. The first time she read it she didn't fully comprehend its meaning. She felt like she'd been reading a letter meant for someone else. The second time she read the letter was to make sure she truly read what she thought she had read the first time. The third time she read it was to get all the facts straight and the last time was simply to read it calmly and to completely understand what it might mean to her and her family.

According to the letter, a previously unknown uncle by the name of Emerson Washburn had recently passed away. His last will and testament had been probated a few days earlier and he had named her as the sole heir to his estate. This man was apparently her late father's brother. Neither he nor her mother had ever mentioned him having a brother. And since they had both died in a tragic car accident shortly after Stephanie's eighteenth birthday any opportunity to learn of his existence had died with them. Washburn apparently owned some sort of farm in a rural area outside of the town of Ashton.

"Ashton?" she wondered. She found it strange how she had just been thinking of the town a few moments earlier and suddenly that same town now appeared as a focal point of her inheritance. The letter said she was to contact the lawyer at a suitable time to arrange to collect her inheritance and take possession of the property.

Stephanie sat with her mouth hanging slack-jawed in disbelief. She had no idea if the mysterious Uncle Emerson had been a wealthy man or if he had just been a man of average means. Did he have a substantial insurance policy?

She recalled how when her parents were killed, between the lawsuit and the money from their own life insurance, her older brother Chuck had been able to finish his last year of college and there was enough money for Stephanie to get her degree as well. It seemed strange how someone she had never known had been kind enough to name her as his heir. However, she had to admit living on a single income with three kids made money very tight and every penny would help no matter how small the inheritance might be.

She was already thinking far into the future, about selling the inherited Schuylkill County farm as soon as she was able for whatever she could get and then using the proceeds to buy a nice single home on a large lot in western Berks County with a big backyard for the kids to enjoy.

She felt guilty about spending money she didn't even have yet especially when she considered its origin. Suddenly she experienced a second cold chill race down her spine and the fine hairs on the back of her neck seemed to stand on end. She felt like someone was watching her. She quickly glanced around the room but saw no one. For the briefest of moments, she thought she saw something out of the corner of her eye. But when she turned to look, all she could see was the large oval mirror out in the hall leading to the front door. She gave a nervous laugh, thinking about how she had managed to spook herself. Stephanie shook her head and read the letter several more times.

She decided not to call Jason at work to tell him but instead to surprise him with the news after dinner. It was Friday afternoon, the start of a weekend. His work had been so very stressful lately that this good news might be just what he needed.

2

JASON SAT AT his desk running his fingers through his tousled brown hair. He was certain this project would be the death of him even at his young age. Jason Wright was an engineer for a high-tech manufacturing company called Technofacture International. This latest project was beginning to work on the very last of his already frayed nerves.

He was currently reviewing a financial justification for the purchase of a state-of-the-art half-million-dollar computer-controlled machining center. According to his estimates, the automated machining cell would easily pay for itself in less than two years, which was an incredible return on investment. But the whole justification process was out of his comfort zone and he was certain no matter how many times he checked and rechecked his figures, something would be wrong which might endanger the project's approval.

And that was just the tip of the stress-inducing iceberg for him. Even if the project was approved, he still had to arrange for the purchase of the machine as well as the related components and subcomponents of the manufacturing cell. Plus he had to see to the design and purchase of work-holding devices, an overhead crane, cabinets, utility carts, and so forth. Then he had to coordinate the machine installation as well as learn to write programs to control the machine, train the machine operators, prepare operator manuals, and about a thousand other incidental items.

During more prosperous economic times, a project of this size would have been handled by a team of at least two or possibly three different engineers. But in the lean, mean world of twenty-first century manufacturing the sole responsibility fell on his young shoulders. In addition, he had to keep up with his normal shop floor support duties.

The success of this project was paramount. It had been eight years since his facility had been given capital funds for the purchase of new equipment. If this project wasn't a resounding, knock-one-out-of-the-ballpark success it might be the end for his facility.

Most of the other machines in the plant were so old and so antiquated just keeping them running was a daunting task for their maintenance department. His company was falling far behind in their productivity, so much so he feared if things didn't soon turn around he and many others might be losing their well-paid jobs.

The facility where he worked was in Lancaster County, Pennsylvania and was just one of the dozens of plants the company owned around the world. Jason's site was also one of the few sites to still have a labor union. The company's once-cooperative relationship with their bargaining unit had been damaged over the previous years and it seemed to continue to degenerate almost weekly. Most of the grievances filed by union members ended up being resolved by the corporate lawyers. This brought a great deal of unwanted attention by corporate management to the plant's labor-relations problems.

As the company's productivity figures fell more and more of the manufacturing work was being shipped to other Technofacture facilities around the world. With the dirt-cheap labor rates in China and India, this had the potential of becoming a major problem for his plant.

To make matters worse, his company also had a manufacturing plant some sixty miles northeast of Lancaster outside of the small town of Ashton. It was a non-union facility with a highly skilled and motivated workforce, more modern machinery, and a much lower labor rate than at the Lancaster site. In addition, the workforce was known throughout the corporation for their strong work ethic, high productivity, low absenteeism, and general dedication to getting the job done.

Jason felt like the weight of the world was pressing down on his shoulders. It was like the fate of his small manufacturing plant might very well be spelled out by the direction this single project would take. He had no idea at that moment just how justified his concerns were.

As Jason sat staring at the computer screen reviewing his spreadsheet his phone rang startling him and breaking his concentration. Jason assumed it might be the shop supervisor with a problem. It seemed lately his days were filled with nothing but interruptions in the form of one crisis or another. Jason took a deep breath, composing himself then answered the phone.

"Jason Wright, Manufacturing Engineering," he said in his typical cheerful greeting preparing himself for the noisy background sounds of manufacturing machinery to resonate through the phone; but there were no such sounds.

"Jason," the voice said, "this is Walt. Can you come to my office?"

Walter Williams was Jason's department manager. He was a kind, even-tempered man just a year or so from retirement. He had been grooming Jason to take his place whenever he chose to finally leave the workforce. And although Jason was flattered by the vote of confidence, he had a lot of concerns about eventually moving into the role of the department manager.

As Jason approached his boss's office he was filled with a surprising and overwhelming sense of dread. But Jason had never believed in omens, precognitions, or any such things. Taking another deep cleansing breath and forcing the odd sensation from his body, Jason gripped the knob and began to turn it as the door slowly opened inward.

"What's wrong, Walt?" Jason asked, seeing the uncertainty and displeasure on the man's face. Walter wasn't just

Jason's boss but over the years he had become his close friend and mentor as well.

"Well," Walt said reluctantly, "It's about the justification you wrote for the new machine."

"Oh, no. Did I screw something up? Did they reject it? I've been going over my calculations today to make sure everything was right on the money and I'm confident it was fine. At least I was confident until now."

"No, it's not that, Jason. Everything in your justification was succinct, well written, and to the point. In fact, the corporate controller said he wished every request he received for capital funds was as well written as yours was. Lord knows in all the years I've been in this job I've never seen one written so well."

"Then what's the problem?" Jason asked too concerned about his project to acknowledge the compliment.

"Let me cut to the chase here, Jason," Walter said, and Jason knew he was definitely in for bad news. Whenever Walter used clichés like "cut to the chase" or "the bottom line is" Jason understood the man was about to deliver some bad news.

"They like the project and are going to approve the machine's purchase for manufacturing all of the families of parts you planned on running across it." Then with more hesitation, he said, "But the machine won't be installed at this facility. It'll be in Ashton," Walter explained. "The boys at corporate are in love with that operation."

"But what about us? What about all of us here?" Jason asked, leaning forward in his seat. "How can we be expected to keep manufacturing parts competitively with outdated equipment which is practically being held together with a few bolts and chicken wire?"

"We won't have to for much longer."

Jason felt like he'd been hit in the face with a baseball bat. He sat stunned looking at Walter. He already assumed what the man was about to say but didn't think he could tolerate hearing the words.

"By the end of July this year, Lancaster will cease all machining. From that point on all manufacturing operations will be transferred to the Ashton facility."

Jason was staggered. He had expected bad news, and perhaps somewhere deep down inside he had even anticipated hearing it for a long time, for months, maybe for years. But the finality of the statement and the reality it brought with it was almost beyond his comprehension.

"What I just told you and what I'm about to tell you is extremely confidential. It can't leave this office. Is that clear?" Jason numbly nodded his head. "All right then. Next Monday and Tuesday, a delegation from the Ashton organization will be visiting our facility to evaluate our machinery to determine which, if any, machines they might want to take to their facility. And whatever machines they choose not to transfer to Ashton will eventually be scrapped."

"But what about the union?" Jason asked, not particularly caring about the members of the rank and file but perhaps more worried about their reaction to such shocking news. He could feel a bead of sweat trickling down his back.

"Jason, when I said none of this must leave this office it wasn't just the salaried employees I was concerned about. In fact, the bargaining unit is my primary concern. They won't be told about any of this until a week before the secession of operations is to take place. Until that time, we'll be putting the shop on mandatory overtime and will be working round the clock to build inventory to allow for whatever time it takes to complete the transfer. They absolutely can't know about our plans or about the purpose of the delegation coming down here on Monday. When the group from Ashton is touring the shop next week if anyone from the shop asks you anything, you're to say you aren't sure who the people are or why they're here. You have got to play dumb about all of this."

"Wa . . . wa . . ." Jason stammered suddenly unable to put two words together to form a cohesive thought. For a moment Jason continued to look on dumbfounded and then he finally managed to speak, "What about the other engineers? Hell, what about you? What about me?"

"Well," Walter said, "let's start with me. They offered me an early retirement package, you know, a golden handshake as they call it. The way it looks I'll be retiring sometime before the end of July."

Jason replied sarcastically, "Let me guess. You get the golden handshake and the rest of us get the golden shower. Right?"

Walter smiled knowingly understanding Jason was simply letting off a bit of steam with his off-color accurate assessment.

"Jason, I've been grooming you to fill my shoes when I retired. I've always spoken highly about you not only to the management here in Lancaster but to the managers at our other facilities as well as to the boys at corporate. As a result, they're prepared to offer you the manager of manufacturing engineering position at the facility in Ashton."

"Ashton?" Jason said in disbelief, "But what about Jim Dodson? Isn't he still the manager at the Ashton facility?"

"He is, or I should say he was," Walter replied, "but he too was offered a chance to take early retirement and he jumped at the opportunity even faster than I did."

Jason asked with concern, "But wasn't he grooming someone in Ashton to take his place? I'd hate to go up there and walk into a hornets' nest knowing I stepped on someone's toes."

"To be honest, I don't know if he had someone in mind and I really don't care. And neither should you. You'll be getting a significant increase in salary, a chance to earn corporate bonuses, and become part of the management team. It's an important rung on the ladder for someone with your potential. You'll get a relocation package and help with finding a house."

A new house? He was going to have to uproot and relocate his family; a new place to live and a new school for the kids in the fall.

From the times Jason had visited the facility Ashton seemed like a small, economically-depressed area with old-fashioned, neglected neighborhoods.

He and his family were accustomed to seeing the lush, rolling hills of western Berks County. Although his small townhouse may not have had any thriving lawn to speak of, it did have a nice backyard and the place was only a few years old with all new appliances. Some of the houses he had seen in Ashton had to be a hundred years old.

He recalled many of the engineers and managers at the Ashton facility had built new homes in subdivisions in the more suburban area of Mountain Springs not too far from Ashton. Perhaps with the bump in pay and the difference in the cost of living he might be able to buy a single house and still be able to let Stephanie stay home to work on her books. Jason was surprised to discover he was starting to warm up to the idea.

"Jason," Walter said interrupting his thoughts, "I realize you have a major decision to make here. I'd like you to take the weekend and talk it over with Stephanie. Maybe you two can take the kids and drive up through the area around Ashton and see what sort of house you might want to buy. You can get a lot more for your dollar up there and your salary will be substantially higher so I see no reason why you wouldn't be able to buy or even build a much bigger home.

"And I'll tell you what. I'm going to need you here the early part of next week for a few days until the Ashton group is finished, but if you decide to take the offer you can take off next Wednesday through Friday to meet with some realtors. I'll speak with the personnel folks at Ashton to see who they recommend."

Jason was literally overwhelmed. "I, wow . . . I just don't know what to say. I'm shocked and at the same time very grateful to you, but still quite confused."

"Why don't you head out for the weekend? It's a great opportunity but it definitely requires some thought."

Jason stood on wobbly legs his mind reeling. He had so many things to consider so much to think about. He thanked

Walter once again and headed for the door. As he passed a large mirror hanging on the wall behind the office door, he thought he saw a strange man staring out at him. Although he only got a split-second glimpse, the image made his breath catch in his throat. Jason swore the man appeared to have wild and insane eyes. His face was a mass of bloody cuts and his left ear appeared to have been severed from his head as well. Jason blinked and the image was gone.

Walter noticed Jason's reaction and asked "Are you all right, Jason? You look like you just saw the devil himself."

Jason realized he must have had one of those strange moments when you see something out of the corner of your eye, something you swear you actually saw only to discover it was all an illusion or a trick of light, shadow, and imagination.

"It's a lot to take in, that's all," he replied. "I could use a drink."

"Well, that's probably not a bad idea. The best advice I can give is to do whatever it takes to relax and then figure out what you think is best. I'll be right here whenever you make up your mind. And if you have questions you know you can call me anytime."

On his drive home, Jason tried to figure out how he was going to break the news to Stephanie. They'd have to give it some serious thought as his only other option would be to try and find another job locally. He had enough severance and vacation to carry him for a few months at best, but regardless, he'd have to try to land another position right away. He was the only source of income for his family.

He hated the idea of introducing more change to his kids' lives. It was only a few years earlier Jason had gotten divorced from his unfaithful first wife. And when his ex-wife and her new husband moved to Ohio, his son, Jeremy had to get used to living with Jason alone. Jeremy had only seen his mother once since the divorce.

To complicate matters further, two years later the young boy then had to adjust to Jason's marriage to Stephanie as well as moving into their new townhouse and getting to know his new younger stepsister, Cindy. And then when Stephanie became pregnant the two stepsiblings, formerly only children, suddenly found themselves with a new baby brother. Jason realized it was quite an adjustment for them to make and was pleased with how despite everything they seemed to have adapted.

Jason knew moving would definitely impact the children to an even greater extent. The two kids had been in the same school system since preschool and at ten and twelve years old they had a large network of close friends. Jason decided neither he nor Stephanie should mention anything to the kids until they both had at least an initial chance to discuss their limited alternatives.

He was seriously considering the possibility of commuting the fifty plus miles every day. He already had a forty-five-minute drive to work. So what would another fifteen or twenty-five minutes matter? But he knew it would eventually begin to take its toll physically and mentally not to mention the wear and tear on his car.

If he commuted Jason knew much of his raise would end up in his gas tank. Jason realized this was going to be one of the toughest weekends of his life and he and Stephanie would have to do a lot of soul searching before making their final decision.

Suddenly he felt a prickling sensation on the back of his neck and felt like someone was watching him. Jason looked in the rearview mirror and was certain a man was sitting in the back seat of his car. The man appeared to be in his sixties, rail thin and shirtless. He had long slashes down his chest forming a series of V-shapes from which blood flowed freely. The man's face was likewise slashed as with a razor and one of his ears was missing. It appeared to be the same tortured man who he thought he had seen in Walt's mirror.

Startled he blinked his eyes and just as quickly as it had appeared the horrific vision in the back seat was gone. Jason felt a steady rough bumping and realized his car was heading off the highway and was riding the rumble strips. He got the car back under control and looked again into the rearview mirror. To his gratitude, the unspeakable creature was gone.

"Wow," Jason said aloud, "I really have to find some way to relieve this stress. It must really be getting to me."

The rest of the way home Jason's eyes darted between the highway and the rearview mirror wondering if the horrible vision would return. Despite the mild May temperature and the fact his air conditioning was running full blast, Jason was drenched with a cold sweat beneath his clothing.

3

Forty-eight hours earlier . . .

A **DARKLY CLAD** man hunched in the shadows feeling the tumblers of the lock gradually give way beneath the pressure of the lock pick held tightly in his right hand. He had practiced this task many times during the past several weeks honing his technique for this special moment. Soon he heard the familiar click indicating the locking mechanism had released. Opening the door ever so slowly, he waited a moment, listening for an alarm system. He was pleased to be greeted with nothing but wonderful silence.

The lack of security wasn't the smartest move on the homeowner's part but perhaps in this area of the country locals didn't deem such countermeasures necessary. Or maybe the owner simply never got around to installing one.

He opened the back door of the house and slid quickly into the darkened rear kitchen shutting the door behind him. He stood silently in the room. His back pressed tightly against the door. He felt the cool glass of the small window-panes against the back of his head. The only sound in the kitchen was his shallow breath escaping in barely audible puffs.

He waited, giving his eyes time to adjust to the near total darkness. Jack thought about how long he had searched to find his enemy and all the years he had planned to exact his revenge. He looked down at his left hand which he stretched open palm up, fingers extended, appearing as nothing more than a black-silhouetted form. But in that charcoal shadow, he could see the one missing element of the shape, the place where his ring finger had once been. It was the finger which had once held his precious wedding ring but now both the ring and the finger were long gone, taken years ago by his enemy; taken by the rotten black-hearted bastard known as Emerson Washburn.

Jack Moran had spent six months tracking Emerson Washburn, and when he finally learned of his whereabouts, he discovered the man was dead.

"Suicide was too good for that rotten pig," Moran had thought. "He saved himself from the hell on earth I was gonna bring down on him."

Jack turned slightly to look out through the window in kitchen door making sure the five-gallon can of gasoline he brought was still readily available. Jack placed the lock pick into his jacket pocket and felt for his lighter. Then he reached around to touch the thirty-eight-caliber revolver he had loaded and tucked into his jeans at the small of his back. He didn't actually believe he'd need the weapon, but it never hurt to be prepared.

Standing in the darkness he thought back to that unforgettable night when he had been knocked unconscious by several of Washburn's goons. Jack had been a compulsive gambler and a chronic liar which, when combined always seemed to bring negative consequences. That was how he found himself owing Washburn over fifty large.

About a year earlier Jack's wife Christina, to whom he had been married for seventeen years and their only child, a lovely fifteen-year-old beauty named Samantha, died in a tragic automobile accident. Prior to the accident Jack had been attending Gamblers Anonymous meetings regularly trying to get his head straight and was doing quite well at fighting his addiction. He always wore his wedding ring proudly rededicating himself to his wife and daughter. His ring became more than just a symbol of his love; it became a talisman and a source of strength which he used to battle the war raging daily inside him.

However, once his wife and daughter were taken from him he fell into an uncontrollable downward spiral of drinking, followed by reckless gambling. He still treasured the ring, what it symbolized for him, and always would. But it no longer seemed to hold any of its original power to help him fight his inner demons. The accident left him a broken, empty husk of a man and killed any desire to refrain from acting on his impulses. Jack fell off the gambling wagon in a big way and headed full speed down the road to self-destruction.

Whenever someone was as far in debt as Jack Moran had been, Emerson often found it critical he take care of such situations personally. It was a matter of his need to command the respect of his crew. Emerson wanted his boys to know he was not opposed to getting his own hands dirty.

That was how one night almost thirteen years earlier Jack Moran had been brought before him, bleeding, beaten, gagged and silently pleading for his life through tear filled eyes.

Washburn felt something meaningful was needed to drive home the fact he wouldn't tolerate any more impudent actions on the man's part. So, with two of his goons holding Jack down Washburn pulled out a short tin shear and without showing the slightest bit of emotion he methodically cut off Moran's ring finger, ring and all.

"I know how much this ring means to you Jack not to mention I suppose, the finger it was attached to," Emerson said.

The goons holding Jack began to chuckle until Washburn gave them a hard look. "I know about the accident which took your wife and daughter. I'm afraid it's obviously too late for the finger but I may be willing to give you back your ring and spare your life."

"I'll tell you what," Washburn said. "You seem like a reasonable, level-headed young man. I think I'll give you one more opportunity to make restitution."

Moran's look of defiance disappeared, quickly replaced by one of hope, of acquiescence to whatever demands Washburn might make.

Washburn said, "I hope you realize what I'm about to suggest to you is going to make my associate Gino over there quite angry since he'd like nothing better than to make you suffer long and hard. Isn't that right, Gino?" Emerson looked over Jack's shoulder toward a mountain of a man standing in the shadows. From his vantage point and because of the poor lighting in the room, Jack couldn't determine if the figure was a man or if it were some sort of horrible inhuman creature. The shadowed figure said nothing but instead made an unintelligible grunting sound.

"You see, Jack," Washburn explained, "He's simply one of those special individuals who enjoys hurting people. He's very serious about his work and tends to be disappointed when I take away his playthings. But sadly I'm afraid he'll have to live with his disappointment for now and wait for another opportunity."

Washburn hesitated for a beat then said, "So then, let's get down to business. I realize you're not really an experienced thief but simply an out of control gambler who's had a few bad breaks. But I think I've come up with a unique way for you to get me the money you owe me by tomorrow night and still manage to keep yourself alive in the process."

Jack mumbled beneath his gag and Washburn nodded his head to one of the henchmen to remove the obstruction. Then he took a deep breath and asked. "But, but what can I do? How can I possibly get that much money?"

Washburn said condescendingly, "Now, don't worry about that Jack. With the assistance of my two associates Johnny and Santo, I have a strategy for you. How do you feel about armed robbery, Jack?"

"But I never robbed anyone before. I wouldn't even know where to start," Moran said terrified.

"Well, lucky for you both of these gentlemen have a great deal of experience in that line of work and they're going to help you become quite proficient very quickly. This is what we call O.J.T.; you know on-the-job-training. I certainly hope you are a quick study for your sake. First, I'm going to have them take you to a doctor friend of ours who will get your hand stitched up and give you some medication for the pain. Then they'll take you to a number of choice places where we know the proprietors keep large supplies of cash. They'll give you a huge, scary-looking gun, unloaded of course and you'll simply walk into these various establishments and relieve them of all of their money at gunpoint. Then you'll bring that money out to Johnny and Santo and move onto the next chosen target. By the end of the night providing you're not caught or killed, you'll have brought me more than enough money to pay your debt as well as to get your precious ring back."

"But, but . . ."

"No buts, Jack," Washburn warned. Then he signaled to the dark figure in the back of the room and the massive man-beast walked slowly to toward Jack. The hulking creature was beyond huge and was rippling with muscles. His enormous Neanderthal head was colossal with a low hanging furry brow and deep-set dark eyes. His eyes appeared to be void of any emotion. The man's face was covered with scars and his nose was broken and twisted. He wore a tight black tee shirt and dark pants served to magnify his already intimidating massive muscles.

The huge ape-man's eyes began to sparkle with obvious pleasure at the thought of having Jack to himself as a sinister smile curled up on his thick simian lips. The term "sub-human" came to mind but that didn't feel quite right to Jack. Perhaps "non-human" or "other-than-human" would be a more accurate way to describe the heinous creature.

Jack quickly turned back to Washburn unable to keep looking at the monster of a man. "Alright. I'll do it. I'll get you your money. But after I've done what you ask will you keep your word and let me go?"

Washburn shouted, "I always keep my word! You should know that!"

Then Washburn seemed to push his anger aside and return to his calm demeanor. He said with confidence, "Besides, we both know it'll only be a matter of time until you're in this same pitiful situation. When that day comes maybe I'll let Gino work on your remaining fingers or some other choice part of your body instead."

Jack felt a cold chill run down his spine as he realized just how true Washburn's words were.

As Jack Moran stood in the dark kitchen of the now dead Emerson Washburn's home looking down at the space which was once his finger, he recalled how he had dutifully done his best to rob the various businesses as Washburn's goons had designated.

The first several attempts had all gone surprisingly well with little or no resistance; everything had been going so smoothly. That was until he got to the sixth target of the night, a convenience store where everything suddenly went wrong. In the middle of the robbery, he had been overpowered by an off-duty policeman resulting in the twelve long years of an original fifteen-year sentence he had spent in prison paying for his failed crime.

Washburn's men had fled the scene at the first sign of trouble. Revenge against Washburn was what Jack Moran thought about every day of his sentence while fighting off rapists, perverts, and psychos. Each day he managed to stay alive, he thought of nothing but vengeance and reclaiming his precious wedding ring. For all he knew, Washburn might have flushed his most treasured memento down the nearest toilet. But he didn't believe so. He had a suspicion Washburn would have kept it as some form of perverse leverage to hold over him, in the event they crossed paths again someday.

Jack put aside his thoughts of the past and tried to focus on the business at hand. He believed somewhere in the house his ring was still hidden. If it was there, he'd find it. He was prepared to search all night if necessary to do just that.

He switched on his flashlight, cupping his hand over the front to keep the brightness to a minimum. Jack looked down along the hallway to determine which direction to head next.

He could see a large handcrafted front door with its beautiful stained-glass sidelight looming in the distance at the end of the long hallway. He also saw a wooden banister traveling up along what had to be a flight of steps leading to the upstairs bedrooms. He sensed the ring he so desperately desired was in one of those bedrooms.

Walking up the long stairway to the upstairs hall, he shone his light into several open bedrooms hoping to find Emerson Washburn's private sleeping quarters. At the far end of the hall, he came to Washburn's bedroom. Unlike the rest of the house, the room was dismal in appearance, filled with heavy, antique furnishings and some of the most thread-bear carpeting Jack had ever seen. It was as if the room existed in another period in time. Jack had no idea how the man could have slept in a place which smelled so dank, musty, and old.

Guided by some force he didn't understand Jack immediately went straight toward a large well-worn dresser where he found an ornately decorated man's jewelry box sitting on top. He lifted the lid and was astounded by the number of fine pieces of jewelry inside the box. He decided he'd help himself to pockets full of the treasures once he had found what he was looking for. He pulled handfuls of rings, gold chains, expensive watches and medallions from inside of the box as well as what appeared to be gold collector's coins, haphazardly dropping them on the top of the dresser.

When the box was almost empty, he lifted it up, turned it at an angle and dumped the remainder of the items on the dresser. Jack sat the flashlight on the dresser and began sifting through the mounds of jewelry searching for his precious wedding band. After several minutes he realized his search was futile and the ring wasn't among the treasures. Angrily Jack picked up the jewelry box and threw it to the floor. It struck hard against the worn carpeting raising a small plume of dust.

The box was now damaged, and Jack noticed the bottom jutting out at a strange angle where it had broken away. Upon closer examination, he discovered there was a false bottom in the box. He picked up the box and pulled hard prying the bottom free. It suddenly tore away, and both parts flew from Jack's hand. As they did, a cylindrical wad of yellowed, brown-stained tissues fell from the compartment landing on the dirty torn cover of the bed next to the dresser.

Jack walked slowly toward the rolled-up tissues knowing what he'd find inside. He unraveled the tissues and saw the skeletal remains of his own severed finger its flesh mummified and shriveled. And at the center of the decayed mass, he found his ring; his precious wedding ring still attached to the boney remnant.

He suddenly felt a sharp pain in his left hand at the place where his ring finger had once been. He knew it as a ghost pain, a phantom ache which he had not felt for years. But now in the presence of his long-missing digit, the pain felt almost a real as the night Washburn had taken his finger from him.

Struggling desperately to maintain his composure, Jack took a piece of the tissue, wrapped it around the back end of the finger so he wouldn't have to come into contact with the dead appendage and slowly slid the ring off the rotted tip with his other hand. Still using the tissue, he tossed the hideous finger bone across the room where it clacked against the face of a large full-length antique dressing mirror. The sickening bone-on-glass clattering sound sent chills through Jack's body.

He took more tissues and wiped some of the tarnish and fleshy remnants from the ring attempting to bring back enough of its original luster to be able to read its inscription. Then he saw what he had been waiting almost thirteen years to see. The inscription on the inside of the ring read *Jack and Christina 7/14/1979*, the date he and his wife had been married.

Jack's eyes fill with tears for the loss of his wife and daughter so many years earlier, for the misdeeds leading to his encounter with Washburn, for the loss of his finger, and finally his landing in prison. Perhaps some of the tears were for the happiness he now felt at regaining his special treasure. So many different emotions seemed to flood through Jack simultaneously; thoughts of happier times with his wife and daughter, sadness at their loss and thoughts of hatred for what Emerson Washburn had cost him.

He looked down at the expensive jewelry on the dresser and realized he no longer was interested in the stupid trinkets. He had gotten what he came for and now it was time to exact his revenge. Even in death, Emerson Washburn would pay for what he did to Jack. If he had any living heirs, then they could suffer the loss in his stead. Jack didn't particularly care. The anger was much too strong within him. He knew exactly what he had to do next.

Jack slid the ring onto the third finger of his right hand, picked up the flashlight and headed toward the doorway. He was going downstairs to retrieve the can of gasoline. Then starting at the top floor he'd saturate Washburn's precious rugs and custom draperies with the flammable fluid and subsequently burn the place to the ground. After more than a decade he'd finally get his revenge on the man responsible for ruining his life.

As Jack approached the doorway, he heard a strange noise, a whisper coming from somewhere behind him. It seemed to call his name in a quiet, drawn-out breathy sigh, "Jaaaaaaaakkkk." The cold chill he had felt several times earlier returned to crawl its way down his tingling spine on invisible icy spider-legs. A cold sweat formed on the back of his neck and his upper lip. His stomach clenched as his natural internal warning system began screaming to him telling him something was about to go very, very wrong.

4

ON THE EVENING Stephanie received the letter dinner was an odd event. There was little conversation between the couple as both Stephanie and Jason were mulling over the best way to tell each other their potentially life-changing news. If it weren't for the kids talking about their respective days at school and the baby yelling for either food or attention the change in atmosphere would have been much more noticeable.

As far as Stephanie could tell her news was of the good variety. After all, some relative she had never known had died and left her an inheritance, hopefully a substantial one. Although at first it seemed unbelievable and unlikely, she was finally starting to realize it actually was true.

For a while that afternoon as she waited for the kids to come home from school she wondered about the mysterious unknown relative, this Emerson Washburn character. What sort of man had he been? Why had her father never mentioned his having a brother before? And more importantly why had he named her as his sole heir to his estate? Why hadn't he included her brother Chuck as well? Didn't Emerson have any children or family of his own?

She decided when things settled down she might want to learn more not only about Emerson Washburn but about her family history in general. She had never really had much interest in such things but the discovery of this missing relative seemed to spark a sudden curiosity in finding out more.

Yes, she decided she'd definitely do some research into her own family tree and maybe even look into Jason's as well.

Across the table, Jason was similarly struggling with how best to present his news to Stephanie. What he had to tell her was for the most part bad news and yet this particular dark cloud seemed to have something of a silver lining. That was assuming they were both willing to uproot and relocate their family.

Both Stephanie and Jason sat in silence picking absently at their dinner. As the mealtime wound down, Jeremy and Cindy got up from the table said a quick "Bye, Mom" and "Bye, Dad" before racing off to the living room to either watch TV or play video games. Eighteen-month-old Sammy was caught up in the excitement and began banging on the tray of his highchair chanting, "Down, down, down." He always wanted to do whatever his older siblings were doing.

Stephanie wiped the baby's face and hands clean and then lifted Sammy down. No sooner had his feet touched the kitchen floor then like two tiny rapid-firing pistons they carried him scurrying into the living room in search of his brother and sister. After a few seconds, the parents both heard the two older children complaining loudly, "No, Sammy! Don't touch that! No, no, no! Mom! Dad!"

This was followed promptly by a halfhearted admonishment from Jason shouting from the kitchen, "Be nice and play with your brother." He looked over at Stephanie and smiled lovingly but she seemed to be preoccupied with other thoughts.

Stephanie and Jason loved all of their children and tried to never show any favoritism between them but there was something so very special about Sammy. He was their common bond, the glue helping to bind them all together. Jason and Stephanie often referred to their family as a "Yours, Mine, and Ours" family.

When things sounded like they were under control in the living room Stephanie returned to the kitchen table and put her hands on the back of the chair with a sigh, allowing all the concerns of the day to flow out with that single stress-relieving breath. It was then she noticed for the first time Jason didn't appear to be quite himself either. She had been so busy worrying about her news; she hadn't noticed the cloud of worry which seemed to envelop Jason like a dark shroud.

"Jason, honey?" Stephanie asked. "What's the matter? I can see something's wrong."

Jason looked up and as he eyes met Stephanie's he felt the all-familiar pangs of love he experienced every time their eyes met. She was the one true love of his life. He realized it the day they met and sometimes just thinking about just how precious she was to him was overwhelming. This only made the news he was about to deliver all the more difficult.

"Well," Jason hesitated, taking a deep breath, "I have some unpleasant news." Stephanie visibly tensed her fingers felt as though they would dig into the back of the chair. "Walt called me into his office. You remember the project I've been talking about for months, that new machine tool?"

"Oh no!" Stephanie said with audible concern. "Don't tell me they didn't agree to give you the money. Not after all the work you put into it!"

Jason shook his head and explained, "No, that's not quite it. The project had too good payback for them not to approve it."

"Well, then what happened? What's the problem?"

Jason replied, "The project itself was definitely accepted. But corporate doesn't want the machine to be located in our plant. They want to send it to the Ashton facility, up north in Schuylkill County."

"What? You know more about the project than anyone up there. How can they do that?"

"Unfortunately, they can and will do whatever they choose, Steph. The Ashton factory is a non-union facility with a great track record for quality, productivity, and management-shop employee relations, while our place has a strong and radical union with a history of a confrontation with management. And our production numbers are in the toilet too. Remember three years ago when the union went on strike for several weeks?"

"Yes. How could I forget? You had to go out in the shop with your other office coworkers and run the machines. That was a bad one and the company almost closed the plant over the strike. But I thought they both came to an agreement and everything worked out."

Jason explained, "Well, not quite. You see, the company agreed to many of the union's demands just because they felt shutting down the plant in the middle of a strike was bad public relations. Plus, they needed to keep producing product. However, it seems corporate has a very long memory. While the union was bragging to the media about how they brought the company to its knees the suits must have been planning a way to get what they wanted. They always get what they want in the end. And here is the really bad part of the story. Not only are they putting the new machine in Ashton but they're also moving our entire manufacturing operation up to that facility. Lancaster will be closing down."

"What will happen to you; to us? Are they going to let you go?" She pulled out the chair and carefully walked around it and decided to sit down for the news, which she was certain, would follow.

Jason took another deep breath and said, "Well, that's up to me, or I should say up to us." Stephanie said nothing, just stared at Jason with some confusion. "Bottom line is I can either take the layoff and got try to find another job somewhere else." He hesitated for a moment and then with as much enthusiasm as he could muster said, "Or I can take a promotion and be the manager of manufacturing engineering at the Ashton Plant."

"What?" Stephanie asked again, her face beaming with surprise and pleasure.

"Yep," Jason said obvious pride. "More money, more responsibility. It's a definite promotion."

Suddenly Stephanie began to shake and for a moment Jason was afraid she was crying until he realized she was chuckling. This wasn't the reaction he had expected. He could have understood anger, frustration, sadness, and worry but laughter wasn't at all what he would have anticipated.

"Steph, are you OK? I mean there are many ways we can approach this. I could commute back and forth for a while, and then in a year or so if the job works out, we could find a place to live either up in Schuylkill County or even somewhere in northern Berks County. I mean if that's what you, I mean we want to do. And if it didn't work out, I could continue to commute until I find another job closer to home."

Stephanie leaned back in her chair not looking at Jason but staring at the floor while shaking her head in amazement. She said, "Well, honey. It looks like you're not the only one with a surprise today."

Jason suddenly got a concerned look and asked "What? You're not . . . not pregnant again, are you?" He slapped his hand against his forehead in surprise. He assumed Stephanie's strange out of place laughter might be attributed to some hormonal pregnancy thing.

The question caused Stephanie to burst into fresh fits of deep belly laughter. When she calmed somewhat, she said, "No, silly, I'm not pregnant. Here look at this."

She handed him the manila envelope with its ornate gold-leaf return address. She had been laughing so hard tears came to her eyes. She dabbed them with the sleeve of her shirt.

"What's this?" Jason asked. "H. Mason Armstrong? A lawyer? I hope we aren't being sued. I don't get it."

"You will. Just read it," Stephanie said still chuckling.

"Why are you laughing?" he asked. "This wasn't exactly the greatest news I just dumped on you."

She replied, "I'm not really sure why I'm laughing. I think I'm either just amazed by the strange turn of events today or I'm simply relieved. This has been a really bizarre day. Please, read the letter. You know how I always say things happen for a reason, even things that seem to be bad at first? Read the letter and you'll understand."

Jason gave her a quizzical look and then read the letter first by quickly skimming then after looking up wide-eyed at his wife; he read it again just to make sure he had read it correctly.

"Inheritance? How much?" It was the first thought he had, and he had blurted out the words without even thinking. "I mean, I know it's probably in bad taste to ask something like that, but I assume you didn't even know this guy, this Emerson Washburn, right?"

"No, I never heard of him. Apparently, he was my father's estranged brother and I assume he was single with no kids. He must have thought I was his only living relative. So it looks like he must have either known about me or learned about me somehow, and for some reason chose to leave his estate whatever that might be, to me."

"Speaking of which, what about your brother, Chuck? I wonder why he wasn't named in the will."

"Good question. Maybe Washburn didn't know about him or for some reason chose to exclude him. I might have assumed Chuck had gotten a similar letter if this one didn't specify I was the sole heir to his estate. Maybe we'll find out more later."

"This is so weird," Jason said. "I mean the whole strange series of coincidences. First, I almost got canned from my job, and the only spot available for me is with the division in Ashton. Then you get this inheritance letter from some unknown relative also from Ashton and you're left an estate with property in the area."

Jason then had a new thought. "Do you realize depending upon how much money or property is involved, this could change everything?"

"Yes. I've spent all afternoon thinking about the letter, the inheritance, and what I was going to say to you. And now I realize depending upon how this turns out all of our worries might have been for nothing and our troubles may be over." She laughed again but then suddenly her face took on a more serious expression.

"I hope you realize it might not be worth much, maybe not much at all," she cautioned. "I mean who knows what land or property is worth up there. I suspect a lot less than here. But if by some miracle it's a lot of money oh my, just imagine. Then we'd have the financial freedom to do whatever we want. You could simply take the layoff maybe even start that private consulting firm you've been dreaming about. Who knows?"

"I have to wonder how much is actually involved in the estate," Jason said. "I mean is it land, is it property, money jewelry, cash, whatever? Have you spoken with the lawyer yet?"

"Heavens no! I'd never consider calling him until after we spoke."

"Well then, we have to give this Armstrong guy a call and see what's what. You know this could be really big."

"I was going to try to call tomorrow but then I was thinking tomorrow's Saturday and he may not be in the office until Monday."

"Monday?" Jason exclaimed. "There's no way we can wait until Monday! We have to try him first thing tomorrow and at the very least leave a voicemail. If he checks his messages, he might get back to us sooner. Hey. What about email?"

Jason again skimmed the document looking for an email address and with a disappointed look said, "Crap! No email. I just got another idea. What time is it?"

Stephanie looked at the wall clock behind Jason and replied, "It's about 5:45."

"I know its Friday night, but he could be still in the office," Jason suggested. "It wouldn't hurt to try, would it?"

"Yes, I suppose you're right." Stephanie agreed. "It wouldn't hurt to give him a call, introduce ourselves and see what we have to do next."

Jason handed the letter with the lawyer's phone number to Stephanie who already had her cell phone in hand. She quickly dialed the number and told Jason excitedly. "It's ringing."

After only two rings the phone was picked up, and Stephanie was stunned to hear a man's deep baritone voice, "Good evening, Mrs. Wright, this is H. Mason Armstrong. I've been expecting your call."

5

"**JAAAAAAAAKKKK**," Moran heard the mysterious voice calling again. He wanted to run but his feet felt frozen in place as they often did in horrible nightmares. He laboriously turned in slow motion feeling like he was doing so in an atmosphere thick with fluid.

As he looked into the darkness his eyes focused in the direction of a tall wood-framed oval dressing mirror across the room. Halfway up the weathered frame, two rusted iron mechanisms were present to allow the mirror to tilt. It was now slowly moving into a vertical position. Jack reached around to the small of his back and carefully removed his revolver ready to use on whoever might be lurking behind the mirror.

The surface of the mirror suddenly changed before his eyes; looking less mirror-like and more like the surface of a reflecting pond. From a point in the center of the mirror, a series of ever-growing concentric circles emanated, resembling ripples in water.

"Jaaaaaaakkk," a voice called louder and more distinct than previously. To Jack's surprise, the liquidy voice was coming from deep inside the mirror itself.

Along the undulating water-like ripples in the mirror, Jack saw a form begin to take shape and to his dismay and horror, he realized it was the face of Emerson Washburn. However, it was a Washburn-like incarnation born of some accursed corner of Hell. Its face blurred in and out of focus twitching spasmodically leaving Jack uncertain of what he was actually seeing.

The mirror creature was skeleton-thin, and its mottled rotting flesh hung in folds, sloughing off in places to reveal glistening white bone beneath. Small white insects, maggots of some sort crawled in and out of holes they had bored about the specter's decaying face. The mouth of the hideous being hung slack-jawed and when it once again whispered his name Jack could smell a vile and nauseating odor coming from the mirror like that of a dead animal carcass baking in the broiling summer sun.

Mustering all of his strength Jack lifted his hand pointing the revolver directly at the mirror. He hoped shooting the glass would send the Washburn-like thing back to whatever torturous pit it was trying to crawl from. However, he discovered his ability to will his finger to pull the trigger was gone. The gun suddenly weighed a ton as his right hand dropped back to his side hanging uselessly at the end of a dangling dead arm.

"I see you found your precious ring," the image in the watery mirror hissed. The water-like film on the face of the mirror began to ripple more rapidly as the thing emerged from within the mirror. Jack wanted to turn and run screaming from this unbelievable nightmare but found he was paralyzed. The specter drifted across the room until it loomed just a few inches in front of Jack.

"Oh, Jack, you didn't really think you could get the better of me, did you? Even in death, I'm your superior. I see everything. I know everything. I'm aware of your scheme to burn my lovely house to the ground. But sadly for you, you'll never have that opportunity. You see, I've left this house and all my possessions to my long-lost niece. And I must keep it safe for her. The others have commanded it. They have very special plans for her and her family."

Then suddenly the phantom began to dissolve, breaking into billions of tiny glowing particles. For a moment Jack thought the repulsive thing would vanish when abruptly the mass of glowing specks flew toward him encircling his head like honeybees swarming to protect their queen.

The luminous flecks tightened around his skull slithered into his nostrils and crept between his tightly closed lips. His eyes burned as the particles worked their way through his tear ducts. Then the entire swarm seemed to melt in through the very pores of his flesh. Jack could feel a tingling sensation all around his skull as each microscopic glowing element passed into his body.

Within a few seconds, he felt an incredible cold spreading throughout his body starting with his head, creeping down along his spine into his chest, down to the pit of his stomach and eventually all the way to the tips of his toes. Whatever the Washburn-thing had been Jack understood it had now somehow become part of him. He could sense the very consciousness of Emerson Washburn inside his mind and his body and could tell Washburn was now in physical control of him, operating his body like a puppet master with a marionette.

Jack felt his right-hand reach around and tuck the revolver back into his pants. He still held the flashlight in his left hand and felt Washburn position the hand downward to provide light for him to see ahead. In the mirror across the room, Jack could see his own reflection. For the briefest of moments, Jack looked at his own face in the mirror at his own eyes but no longer recognized the look they held. His eyes now reflected the violent and deranged soul of Emerson Washburn.

Jack's body turned as he staggered out of the bedroom traveling along the upstairs hall toward the stairs. He was terrified Washburn might throw his helpless body down the stairs, not necessarily to kill him but to make him suffer. Washburn might cripple him and leave his body to die alone, helpless and in agony.

He made it safely down the stairway and then continued shuffling along the downstairs hall, into the kitchen and finally out the back door onto the deck. After the door was closed and locked Jack's left hand clicked off the flashlight and tucked it into his pants pocket while his right hand reached down and picked up the gasoline can.

He trudged around to the front of the house then down the long moonlit driveway. The stolen car Jack had used to get to the property was parked and hidden a few hundred feet along the main road.

When Jack reached the sedan, Washburn commanded his arm to open the driver's door as well as the door to the back seat. He dumped the gasoline inside the car allowing it to soak into the cloth carpeting in both the front and back. He then had Jack take what was left in the can and lift it high over his own head having it trickle down over his face completely saturating his clothing. Jack's eyes burned unmercifully as the gasoline streamed over and into them. His sinuses were likewise singed by the caustic vapors emanating from the flowing fuel and Jack's lungs burned from the fumes.

Washburn commanded Jack's helpless body to sit in the front driver's seat and start the engine while leaving the door open. Jack looked into the rearview mirror and at first saw only his own blurry, reddened, and terrified eyes looking back at him. After a moment, Jack once again saw Washburn looking at him through those same eyes as they changed to reflect a much more hateful and sinister appearance. At that moment Jack heard Washburn's voice speaking to him inside his own head.

"Too bad you just couldn't let things go, Jack, too bad for you indeed."

Jack sat in the car smelling the pungent odor of gasoline permeating the air in the close confines of the sedan. He felt dizzy and nauseous. Suddenly his body revolted, and he vomited involuntarily down the front of his shirt and onto his lap. Jack sat smelling the sickening, sour stench of his own puke mixed with the gasoline fumes.

Washburn said in Jack's mind, "Well, I suppose we had better get on with this."

Then Jack's right hand reached into his pocket and grasped his cigarette lighter; the same lighter he had brought with him with the intention of burning down Washburn's home.

"Oh, my Lord in Heaven, no!" Jack's thoughts screamed in his mind, "Please, please don't do this." But Jack realized Washburn's plan was irreversibly set in motion and no power could do anything to stop it.

"I suppose I'll see you in Hell someday, Jack, my boy," he heard Washburn say as his right hand flicked the thumbwheel on the lighter. It didn't light or even spark and for a moment and Jack thought he might be spared the horrible fate he saw ahead of him. Then two clicks later it sparked to life and the car was engulfed in a flaming inferno.

The sparkling particles streamed from Jack's body and rapidly reassemble themselves outside the fiery conflagration. Then the specter of Emerson Washburn having completed its task, floated back through the darkness toward his home to prepare for the coming of the new homeowners: the Wright family.

Jack sat helpless in the car, paralyzed but still able to feel every element of the searing pain. Washburn didn't want the man to miss a single moment of his flaming death. Jack Moran experienced unfathomable agony as his flesh bubbled, boiled and melted from his body while every one of his nerve endings fired electronic impulses to his brain synapses. Inside his mind, Moran discovered he was now alone inside of his burning shell of a body and in his dying misery. He mentally howled a final death shriek. He could smell his own skin and hair burning from his body as the world around him eventually, mercifully faded to blackness.

6

"**E**XCUSE ME?" STEPHANIE questioned discomforted by the way the lawyer had answered his phone. Suddenly she felt a squirming centipede scooting across the back of her neck with its feather-light legs as an icy chill shivered down her spine. She had been taken completely by surprise and she asked, "What? Mr. Armstrong? Yes, um, yes, this is Stephanie Wright but how did you know it was me?"

"Good evening, Mrs. Wright," the lawyer repeated in his deep baritone voice; one which sounded accustomed to public speaking. "Well, I assumed you'd be calling me sometime today after receiving your registered letter. And since you hadn't called yet I deduced you would do so after speaking with your husband when he got home from work. Secondly, I'm not expecting calls from any of my other clients this evening. Third, and perhaps most important, is that I have caller ID on my phone and your name came up." He gave a bit of a chuckle.

"Oh," she said with surprise feeling a bit foolish. "I suppose, I guess I didn't think you, I mean I didn't realize, you know. Ashton's such a small town. I mean, you're way up there." Stephanie was fumbling to find the right words. However, the harder she tried to get out of the embarrassing hole she had dug herself into the deeper it got.

Armstrong seemed to understand her dilemma and chose to have a bit of pleasure from her obvious discomfort suggesting, "Believe it or not, way up here in the coal region we actually have such modern conveniences as running water, electricity, and even flushing indoor toilets. Not to mention other amenities such as cable TV, cell phones, the Internet and yes, even caller ID.

"I'm so terribly sorry, Mr. Armstrong," Stephanie said when she heard the obvious sarcasm in his reply. The truth was she hadn't expected Armstrong to be in his office and was caught by surprise not only when he answered the phone but also when he did so by using her name. She hoped the man had a good sense of humor and had been simply offering the self-deprecating comment to break the ice.

"You just caught me by surprise, is all," she said in a feeble attempt at explanation.

He replied, "No need to apologize, Mrs. Wright. I understand completely. You see I have to admit, I'm actually a transplant to the area. I moved to Ashton some thirty years ago when I married my late wife, Margaret and have been living here ever since. We met back when we were in college. She was born and raised in Ashton. After we moved here, I realized there was something so inherently special about this area I found very appealing and still do lo these many years later." He hesitated for a beat and said, "But, then again you didn't call to hear my life story. No doubt you called regarding the inheritance you were bequeathed by my client, the late Mr. Emerson Charles Washburn."

For a moment, this statement also caught Stephanie off guard. The document she had received listed the deceased man as Emerson C. Washburn. For some reason, she had never considered his middle name might have been Charles. Her older brother Chuck had been given the name Charles David Washburn. She wondered for a moment if Chuck's name might have come from the same family source as Emerson's middle name perhaps an ancestor several generations removed. Once again, she found herself thinking about her genealogy.

After a moment Stephanie replied distractedly, "Um, yes. That's exactly why I called. Sorry, I'm a bit confused by all of this. You see, I've never inherited anything before, and I didn't even know this Emerson Washburn existed. I guess it's just I have so many questions and absolutely no idea where to begin."

"Not a problem at all, Mrs. Wright," he said, "That's why I'm here. If I do my job correctly, I should be able to make all of this flow smoothly for you. I suppose the first thing we need to do is to get you and your husband up here to get started on the paperwork at your earliest convenience."

Stephanie held the phone against her chest and said to Jason, "He wants us to get started on the paperwork for the estate as soon as possible."

Jason said, "Tell him we can come up tomorrow morning if he would like us to."

"I can't ask him that. He may not work on Saturday." But she spoke into the cell phone again. "Mr. Armstrong?"

"Please, Mrs. Wright. Call me Mason," the attorney corrected.

"Very well," she said, "then you can call me Stephanie, and my husband's name is Jason. We were wondering if tomorrow would be too soon for us to stop up to see you."

The lawyer replied, "That's not a problem at all. In fact, I was hoping you might be available tomorrow sometime. I set my own hours so if you both would like to stop by tomorrow that'll be perfectly fine with me. What time can I expect you?"

She asked Jason, "What time can we be up there tomorrow morning?"

"Ask him if eleven is a good time. It takes about an hour or so to get up there so we should be able to have everyone awake, dressed and ready to go by nine forty-five," Jason quickly calculated.

Stephanie asked, "Mr. Armstr . . . I mean, Mason. Would eleven o'clock be a good time?"

"Eleven o'clock will be just fine. That'll allow me to sleep in tomorrow then head down to the office after a brief stop at Maggie's for a hearty breakfast."

At first, Stephanie wondered if perhaps Maggie might be a lady friend of Armstrong's then she recalled something

Jason had once told here. There was a small eatery at the top end of Ashton called Maggie's Restaurant which he described as a quaint local gathering place especially for breakfast.

"By the way," she mentioned, "we'll have to bring our kids along with us. I hope that won't be a problem."

"Absolutely no problem whatsoever. On the contrary, I was hoping you'd bring them along. After we take care of all the legal paperwork I plan to take you all out to show you around the Washburn property, which will shortly become your property. I think it'd be great if your kids could see it as well."

"Property?" Stephanie asked, "What sort of property is it?"

"Well, I prefer not to get into too much detail over the phone as there are a number of things we'll need to discuss first tomorrow but I can tell you the property is a forty-acre farmette."

Stephanie said slightly stunned, "Alright then. We'll see you tomorrow morning at eleven at your office. Is there anything special we need to bring along with us?"

The lawyer replied, "Your driver's license and birth certificate for official proof of your identity. But honestly all you have to do is show up and we should be able to get our paperwork completed by noon. I'd offer to buy you all lunch, but I have another appointment at three o'clock and have to get you out to the property and back before then. Besides, I assume with three young children you'll likely be stopping for fast food on the way here. Lord knows I've used a similar tactic many years ago on long trips with my own kids."

Stephanie saw Jason leave the kitchen, she assumed to check on the children in the living room. Things had become quiet in the room and the only thing parents feared more than kids noisily misbehaving and getting into trouble was when they were quiet.

"But I'll make a deal with you," he insisted. "After we finish our business, you and your family can take an hour or so to become familiar with the area. I'll have a set of complimentary tickets to Ashton's main tourist attraction here for you. We have a steam train ride, a coal mine tour, and a state-run coal museum. I think you and your family will enjoy all three; especially the mine tour. Then when you're finished if you'd consider staying around a bit longer, I'll be more than happy to take you and your family out to dinner at one of our local fine dining establishments."

"Thank you very much, Mr. Arms . . . I mean, Mason. I greatly appreciate it. I think the mine tour is a great idea. And coincidently I was thinking about that very tourist attraction earlier this morning. It's almost like you were able to read my mind," Stephanie said quietly not wanting the kids to hear.

Then she realized that Armstrong's offer for dinner was one she'd have to decline. She apologized and told the lawyer, "Unfortunately, we will have to pass on the dinner invitation as I'm certain the baby will be ready for a nap after the long day and will likely be getting cranky around dinner time. In fact, I suspect all three kids will likely sleep on the way home."

"Not a problem at all," the lawyer replied. "Whatever works best for you and your family is fine with me."

Stephanie said, "Thanks again. But come to think of it, maybe we should be buying you dinner sometime since we're the ones getting the inheritance."

"That's certainly a generous offer," Armstrong said, "but keep in mind I'm not only a lawyer but also a businessman and I've been well compensated for carrying out the wishes of your late uncle. And I'm always looking for the next potential client. Since I hope you and your family will consider hiring me to continue to handle your legal needs in the future, the least I can do is to attempt to make a positive impression."

"Well, if it's any consolation you've already made a very fine impression. So we'll see you tomorrow morning then."

"Oh, by the way, please remember to dress casually. Feel free to wear jeans and sneakers or comfortable shoes. We'll likely be walking around out at the farmette and dress shoes won't cut it once we get off the walkways to look about the property."

"Farmette." Stephanie tossed the word around in her head. She thought about the rolling fields of Western Berks County and wondered if such land existed in Schuylkill County. Although she hadn't considered it before she suddenly realized it must. After all, it was only fifty or so miles north and the area couldn't be all small towns and coal dirt. There had to be the possibility of at least some outlying rural farm area.

As she had just told Jason she believed things in life happen for a reason. And now she was beginning to wonder if all of the situations which had occurred that day and been some sort of serendipitous cosmic assemblage, the sum total of which was pointing her and her family in the direction of Schuylkill County; more specifically in the direction of Ashton and her family's history.

She had originally been thinking of its potential resale value but now resale was no longer the main thing on her mind. Learning more about the property was. The property apparently wasn't the rundown disaster she had feared it might be. Instead, it was likely a nice and livable little piece of real estate.

"Livable?" Stephanie questioned in her mind, "Where had that idea come from?"

Up until a few moments earlier she never would have considered entertaining the idea of actually moving north and living in Schuylkill County. But now for the first time, Stephanie was seriously thinking about the possibility. She, of course, understood such an idea was extremely premature as they hadn't even seen the property.

"Mrs. Wright? Stephanie?" Armstrong called through the cell phone, "Are you still there?"

Startled back to reality, Stephanie said "Um, yes. Sorry. I'm just a bit distracted. And as I said earlier this is all so much for me to absorb."

"Not to worry, Stephanie. I promise I'll do everything I can to help you and your family deal with this. I'd suggest you forget about it for now and get a good night's sleep. Then we can take care of everything tomorrow."

Jason walked back into the kitchen giving her the OK. Stephanie nodded back at him in unspoken understanding.

"Ok. You're probably right," she said into the phone. "We'll see you tomorrow morning. Thank you again and goodbye."

When Stephanie pressed the call end button, Jason could see she seemed to have a distant, slightly confused expression.

"What did he say?" Jason asked with some urgency "What did he tell you?"

After a moment she replied. "Well, he wouldn't tell me much. He wants to save it until we meet with him tomorrow in person. But he did tell me something I didn't know. There is at least some substantial property in the estate, a forty-acre farmette with a remodeled farmhouse as well as several outbuildings, which also have been fixed up."

"Wow!" Jason said, "Ca-ching! That's great to hear. Land always maintains its value, so it has to be worth a substantial amount of money; especially with a farmhouse and other buildings all in great shape. This is almost too good to be true."

She interrupted, "That's pretty much all he'd tell me over the phone. He said anything else would have to wait until tomorrow morning."

"Um, well . . ." Jason said coming back from his distant thoughts having not actually heard everything his wife had said, "I guess, we'd better say something to the kids since they'll be coming along with us tomorrow."

"Maybe we should just explain we have to travel north for some business tomorrow."

"You're probably right. It's going to be hard enough for the both of us to sleep tonight just imagining what might be in store for us tomorrow. But one thing's for sure if we don't sleep well it could be a long, miserable trip up there tomorrow. Then if the kids didn't sleep either and were cranky it would be even worse. I think it's best we make sure they get a good night's sleep."

Stephanie finished cleaning up the kitchen while Jason went in to further monitor the kids' activities while getting some work done on his computer. Every few minutes she could hear him saying something like "No, Sammy. Don't touch that, Sammy. Here's your favorite toy Sammy." She was grateful he had gone in to take over watching the herd so she could start to relax her mind.

About 8:30 Stephanie entered the living room and told the two older kids they were all going away on a day trip the next day and they had to get showers so they would be clean and presentable in the morning. Trying to stall, Cindy asked, "Where are we going tomorrow and what are we doing?"

"We have to go up to the coal region which is about an hour away to take care of some important business." As she said this, Stephanie noticed Jason was busy at his desk doing something on his laptop.

"What the heck is the coal region?" Jeremy inquired. "It sounds like a dirty place. Coal's dirty right?"

"What kind of business?" Cindy chimed in. "Why do we have to go? We're big enough to stay home."

Stephanie had anticipated this sort of response. Lately, both kids were insisting they were too old for baby sitters. But despite the fact they were both quite mature and responsible for their ages Stephanie wasn't ready to cross that particular line just yet. Whenever she and Jason wanted to go out together for special occasions and they didn't want to take the kids along they'd hire one of two seventeen-year-old neighborhood girls to watch them.

Stephanie sighed. "Come on kids. Don't give me a hard time about this. We don't have a choice. We have to go see someone tomorrow morning and I promise I will tell you all about it on the way up there."

"But it's Saturday!" Jeremy complained. "I was going to play some multi-player online games with my friends tomorrow."

"Well, you'll just have to postpone that until we get home. So Cindy, get your butt upstairs right now and get that shower!" Stephanie said more sternly.

Cindy turned reluctantly obeying her mother as she trudged out of the room dragging her feet all along the way. Stephanie figured in a few years the eye rolling, foot stomping, and door slamming would start recalling her own frustrating teen years.

"Cindy? Wait a minute," Jason said from across the room. "I have a great idea for tomorrow. If we can finish up our business in time, how would you both like to do something different? There's an honest-to-goodness authentic coal mine in the town where we're going, and they take you down into the mine like a mile under the earth in real mine cars."

Both children's eyes got as wide as saucers.

Jeremy said boldly, "I'm not afraid. I can do it. So can Cindy. Right, Cindy?"

"Uh, yes. I guess," Cindy said a bit more reluctantly and with a noticeable edge of uncertainty in her voice. She wasn't exactly sure what a coal mine tour was or what the uncertain and mystifying experience might be like, but she knew neither Jason nor her mom would take them anywhere that would be potentially dangerous.

"Alright then," Jason said. "It's a deal. We'll make sure we finish up our work in time to take the mine tour. Now Cindy, get upstairs and get your shower. We have an early start tomorrow and won't have a lot of time to get ready."

Cindy left the room quickly now thoroughly motivated to finish and get ready for bed. Stephanie picked up the baby and started up the stairs after Cindy. Jason said to Jeremy, "Mom and I are going up to give Sammy a bath in our bathroom a while. So as soon as Cindy's finished, I want you to shut off the TV and get your shower."

"Can't I stay up a little later? I'm twelve!" Jeremy complained.

"Nope. Shower then bed," Jason insisted, "And if it's any consolation Mom and I are heading to bed right away as well."

Then after a moment's thought, he said, "And don't think of trying to pull a fast one on us either. As soon as Cindy is done, I'll be checking to make sure you've gotten into the shower. Understand?"

Jeremy said reluctantly, "Yeah, ok. I'll watch TV until Cindy's done. I can't wait to see what the inside of a coal mine looks like."

7

H. **MASON ARMSTRONG** lowered the telephone receiver gently back into its cradle atop his large mahogany desk. He sat with his hands folded in front of him hunched over with the elbows of his suit jacket resting on his unblemished desk blotter. He was deep in the throes of contemplation. He was burdened by troubles which had plagued him during the past month starting shortly after the suicide of Emerson Washburn.

Armstrong was, by nature an extremely neat and orderly man with a desk organized to a level most people might consider obsessive. His soul, on the other hand, was in utter chaos, overwhelmed by the uncertain series of events he suspected he had just set into motion. As instructed Armstrong had sent the certified letter to Stephanie Wright notifying her of her inheritance which was also his legal responsibility as executor of Emerson Washburn's estate. However, he had neglected to tell her everything.

He hadn't warned her about the tragic history surrounding the property. He should have told her about the numerous catastrophes which plagued the homestead starting with her great grandparents and ending with her Uncle Emerson's suicide just a month earlier. Despite the heavy weight of despair on his conscience, he knew he'd remain silent because alive, dead, or otherwise Emerson Washburn would never allow such an infraction to occur.

Then dreadfully on cue, Armstrong heard an odd yet frighteningly familiar noise coming from the darkened rear of his office. It sounded like a thousand worm-like insects squirming madly atop a crinkled sheet of aluminum foil, their writhing bodies sliding in their own slimy secretions creating a sickening wet yet hauntingly metallic sound. Armstrong looked at his desk clock and saw it was about ten o'clock.

He felt he had just hung up the phone from speaking with the Wright woman but that would mean it would have only been six thirty or so. However according to his desk clock and the fact his office was draped in darkness he must have fallen asleep or perhaps fallen into some type of trance for several hours.

In the meager light from his brass banker's light with its translucent green glass shade, Armstrong could see a slight reflection of the semi-dark room around him in a long mirror mounted on a door leading to his private bathroom in the back of the office.

Staring intently at his barely visible reflection in the glass, Armstrong noticed the surface begin to ripple in the shadows, as a voice called out from deep inside the mirror itself. He wasn't shocked by the voice as he had been on the very first occasion he had heard it, but he was disquieted by what it represented.

As the ripples increased Armstrong saw an all too familiar thin, bony translucent bare foot extending from the mirror hovering an inch or so above the luxurious oriental carpet adorning his office floor.

As his eyes reluctantly followed up along the length of the limb Armstrong caught glimpses of the skeletal legs as the hideous creature stepped naked from the mirror into the shadows of the back office. The wretched being was gaunt and hunched, barely recognizable as his recently deceased client Emerson Washburn.

Over the course of the previous year, Armstrong was shocked to witness Washburn's declining health and physical appearance which worsened on a daily basis. That same shadow of a man now over a month in his grave stood across the room.

Flesh hung from its shadowed naked form like deflated balloons. Between glimpses in the darkness, Armstrong saw the dark empty spot where the man's genitalia should have been. He recalled the self-mutilation which Washburn had so gruesomely carried out, the slashing of his wrist, the V-shaped furrows carved in his chest, the severing of his ear and finally the removal of his own genitals. Armstrong would never be able to forget that repugnant sight.

He had been the person called to the scene by Ashton police Chief Max Seiler Jr. to officially identify and claim the body. He recalled how as he stared down into the crimson, blood-soaked bath water, Armstrong had no idea how the man could have inflicted such incredible damage upon himself. Mason had almost passed out when he saw Washburn's severed penis bobbing like a rubber ducky along the top of the bloody pool.

Armstrong looked at the horrifying creature now standing far across the office from him. The thing's shrunken chest still bore the marred V-shaped gashes occasionally visible in partial shadowy glimpses. The creature's mottled flesh had folded down from the savagely ripped incisions in flaps loose and shredded, and from deep inside each of the ghastly slits worms and larvae crawled freely.

He was quite certain they were not creatures of this world as they only slightly resembled any insects he had ever seen, barely enough of a likeness so he was able to think of them as insectile in nature. Perhaps on the other side, in that unimaginable hellish world where Washburn now resided his spiritual body must be susceptible to such an infestation.

Armstrong could see the creature's face was a mask of slashes and its left ear was missing. From within the gaping hole where once Washburn's ear had hung, a long worm-like thing emerged sniffing the air. Then the disgusting creature retreated, squirming back inside of the specter's head.

This was the sixth time Armstrong had been confronted by the specter of his deceased client, but its inexplicable sight still nonetheless revolted him, not to mention the disgusting odor which accompanied its countenance.

Armstrong recalled how on the night of the man's suicide Washburn had called him to the house feigning some sort of emergency. He had always assumed the man had made the call just moments before he decided to begin butchering himself, but now after many post mortem encounters with the fiend, he realized he likely had made the call after he was dead.

A month earlier Armstrong would have never believed such a thing possible; now he only wished it wasn't. It had taken a good deal of acting for the lawyer to convince police chief Max Seiler that his call to Armstrong had been the first time Armstrong had heard of Washburn's death. In reality, after receiving Washburn's call he had hurried to the house and seen the carnage in the tub but had fled the scene without taking any action.

Then he had made an anonymous call from a local pay phone to the police department. This had resulted in Chief Seiler hastening to the scene and eventually calling Armstrong knowing the lawyer was handling Washburn's affairs. He had a feeling Chief Seiler had suspected him of being the person who had made the call, but the chief continued his pretext of ignorance during the entire investigation. Eventually, Seiler had no alternative but to declare the gruesome scene a suicide.

The creature took one unsteady floating air-step after another like a newborn calf unsure of its footing. As it did some of the maggot-like creatures dropped to the carpet and disappeared in a puff of disintegration. Armstrong was certain he could hear the thing's bones rattling against one another. Then before it came into the light of the desk lamp it stopped.

It raised its right bony hand pointing a long skeletal finger directly at Armstrong. Something moved on its finger and Armstrong's stomach turned with revolution when he realized some sort of worm or maggot-like creature.

Speaking in what sounded like multiple voices the creature said, "I've been monitoring your progress Armstrong and I see you've done exactly as I instructed. Very good.

Very good indeed. They're coming. She's coming. And so it can once again be as it was. Good work my minion. Congratulations, you've earned yourself some additional time on this planet. Death will not claim you this day."

Armstrong sat silently not wanting to even acknowledge the presence of the hideous specter. As the Washburn-thing hovered in and out of clarity in the dark shadows Mason could see glimpses of its sagging flesh shining with some sort of thick slimy gelatinous fluid reminding him of translucent coagulated snot as it gave the creature a slick, wet appearance.

"Don't bother trying to ignore me, Mason," Washburn said to the lawyer's downcast head. "You're wasting both your time and mine. Since I have an eternity of damnation ahead of me my time is meaningless. However, your time is still precious perhaps more so than you realize. Now, did you take care of that little problem from last evening?"

The ghost was referring to the fiery death of Jack Moran. "Um, yes," Armstrong said reluctantly. "I spoke with chief of police Seiler and he has decided to rule the death a suicide. For now, Moran's remains have been listed as a John Doe. The car had been reported stolen and even if they somehow were able to identify Moran's blackened corpse they'd simply find he was an ex-con and they'd never be able to tie him or his death to your property. I told Seiler since your estate was my responsibility; I would take care of cleaning up the site of the incident.

"Chief Seiler had a local towing company remove the car from the scene and today I had a landscaper out to the property, trimming the trees by the side of the road, smoothing the gravel and erasing all signs of trouble. As I'm sure you're already aware I went back into the house and cleaned up the mess Moran made in your former bedroom putting everything back in order. I replaced the broken jewelry box with a new one and I returned of its contents to their proper place. That is to say all except for Moran's severed finger. That will never be found. So rest assured. When the Wright family arrives at the farm tomorrow for their tour, they won't notice a single thing out of place."

"They had better not," the specter moaned. "I'm relying on you to make sure they fall in love with the property. You must also be sure to explain the contingencies of the will so they understand they have little choice but to move into the estate as soon as possible."

Armstrong replied with a somewhat haughty tone, "I'd make certain of that whether or not you were involved in the process. I'm a lawyer after all; it's my legal and professional responsibility to make sure the Wrights have a thorough understanding of all the stipulations of your last will and testament. My integrity should never come under question."

The specter ignored the comment and said from the shadows, "Just make sure you do, Armstrong because I'll be watching and more importantly, they'll be watching as well. And the only reason you're still alive and walking the earth is that they still need you and your services. The day that particular need ceases to exist so too, might you. And the fate they'd have in store for you would make my agonizing death seem like a pleasurable experience. However, if you keep them satisfied then great wealth and power could be yours for the rest of your miserable earth-bound life and I know how very important that is to you."

The ghost began to float back toward the mirror and soon dissolved into the glass. Just before the rippling, shimmering surface became still and the foul sulfurous stench began to slowly dissipate, Mason heard Washburn say one last thing, "Understand this, Armstrong. You don't ever want to let us down."

The lawyer sat at his desk with his head downcast, his hands trembling, his lower lip quivering trying desperately not to burst into tears. He wished he had never met Emerson Washburn. He cursed himself for his greed. He may have made a great deal of money from Washburn while the man was alive, but now he was an unwilling servant to the accursed spirit.

Armstrong thought back to how he had falsified records, skimming money from the gangster. He recalled how the sicker Washburn became the more he stole from the man. Now Armstrong realized he wasn't as clever as he thought and was paying the ultimate price for his treachery. He was the dead Washburn's slave in the world of the living.

And he knew Washburn wasn't the only creature involved in this unholy alliance. The specter often spoke of "we" and "us" when discussing Armstrong's requirements. He was certain Emerson was simply another servant in some twisted unholy pecking order of the undead. This thought did little to ease his internal anguish since he suspected when his time came to cross over he'd be at the bottom of that same hellish food chain. It was far too late to consider any other fate; too much damage had already been done. His only chance for at least a temporary reprieve was to say alive with the hopes of finding some way out of his predicament.

8

WHEN JASON WALKED into the bedroom, he could hear water running in the master bath as Sammy giggled and splashed merrily. Before Sammy was born, Jason had all but forgotten how much fun it was bathing little ones and how much they enjoyed the splashing and playing.

"Bubbles, bubbles, bubbles!" Sammy shouted as he slapped the surface of the tub. Jason could smell the sweet, fresh scent of whatever bubble soap Stephanie had added to the water. It seemed no matter how many years passed by, every time he smelled bubble soap; it always seemed to bring back memories of his own childhood.

Stephanie quickly shampooed and rinsed Sammy's dark brown hair then let him sit for a while in the shallow water while she stood and stretched out a kink in her back.

Jason held out his hand with the sleeping pill, and Stephanie winced.

"I know I was the one who suggested it and those things do knock me out, but you know, sometimes they give me nightmares and occasionally I even wake up feeling foggy."

"Well," he suggested, "you can take your chances naturally but for the record, I took mine earlier downstairs so I should be getting sleepy very soon."

"I suppose you're right," she agreed taking the pill from him knowing within about forty-five minutes she'd be out like a light. She swallowed the pill and then fished Sammy from the bath drying him with his favorite bath towel the one with the rubber ducky pattern. She loved how the oversized towel surrounded him and it was clear Sammy did as well.

"Ducky towel!" Sammy exclaimed as he did every time Stephanie dried him with it.

As she snuggled Sammy in the towel she said to Jason, "Did you overhear what Mr. Armstrong and I were talking about just before I ended the call."

"No," Jason replied, "I was in with the kids and couldn't hear what you were saying."

"Well, it's really kind of strange." Stephanie said, "Mason had just suggested tomorrow we should take the kids on that mine tour. He even said he'd reserve a set of complimentary tickets for us. Then just a few minutes later you brought up the tour to the kids. I don't know. It's just a strange coincidence."

Jason said, "Probably not. After all, the tunnel is the main tourist attraction Ashton has to offer. So I'd think it'd only be natural that he suggested it. Plus, I'll bet he probably gets those tickets free to hand out to new clients."

"Yeah. I'm sure you're right. It just seemed a bit weird is all. I suppose I'm just a little on edge from all of this stuff going on today."

"I'm not surprised. But just give that magic pill a few minutes to take effect and by the time you finish getting ready for bed you'll be out like a light."

Once Sammy was dried and dressed in his pajamas Stephanie carried him to his bed to tuck him in. She stood over him singing his favorite lullaby as he drifted off to sleep. She could feel herself getting sleepy as well.

A few minutes earlier Jason heard Cindy finish up in the shower and then go to her room. He was surprised to find Jeremy had listened to him and was already in the bathroom. Jason went downstairs to do a final check to assure all the lights and appliances were turned off and all doors were locked.

As he walked past the large mirror in the foyer, he thought for a moment he saw something out of the corner of his eye some sort of strange image briefly reflected in the glass. When he looked again the vision was gone. But for a second he had been certain he had seen something. He recalled the similar sensation he had experienced that same morning at work in his boss's office.

He couldn't have said exactly what it was he'd seen that time, but he had a feeling it might have been the image of a man, one who had been looking out at him from within the glass like it was a creature existing in some strange other world within the mirror itself.

"Wow! Maybe I shouldn't have taken that pill until I was in bed. It's really screwing with my head already." Then he shook off the strange incident, turned off the remaining lights and went up to bed.

By the time he reached the kids' bathroom, he saw the door was open and apparently Jeremy was already finished and in his room. Jason wondered just how clean the boy could have gotten with such a quick shower, but he decided to give him a pass this time. Tomorrow was going to be a very busy day for all of them and right now sleep was what they needed more than anything else.

He walked into his and Stephanie's bedroom and heard the familiar sounds of Stephanie washing her face and brushing her teeth. He changed into his pajamas and lay on the bed propped up on his pillow, his hands intertwined behind his head as he waited for his turn in the bathroom.

After a few moments she was done, and Jason went into the bathroom to complete his own nightly ritual. Strangely he found himself avoiding his reflection in the mirror as he brushed his teeth. He felt if he was to look directly into the reflective glass it might return the hideous image he had imagined seeing downstairs. He knew the idea was ridiculous but still, he couldn't bring himself to look directly into the mirror.

He finished in the bathroom and realized his wife was already fast asleep. She was barely visible in the light from the lamp on the end table as she was snuggled deep under her covers. He knew he too would be joining her in the world of restful dreams.

But unknown to Jason, Stephanie's dreams would be haunted with horrible and terrifying images. In the morning she would blame the nightmares on the pill she had taken. In reality, they had their roots someplace much more sinister than simple over-the-counter pharmaceuticals.

In her dreams, she first encountered a young woman dressed in an early twentieth century evening gown who looked a lot like she did. The woman in the dream, however, appeared to be mad with rage and was in the process of pulling two young boys across a meadow. The day was cold and overcast. The ground was frozen under an inch or two of snow. The two boys kicked, screamed and cried as she tugged them across the snowy field.

The woman's eyes glowed insanely as she dragged the two boys toward a place at the back of the snowy meadow. Stephanie immediately understood as is often the way of dreams, the woman was pulling the boys toward a well.

Upon reaching the well the woman lifted the smallest of the boys by one arm and hurled him into the well. Then using her two hands she picked up the second boy and likewise hurled him to his death at the bottom of the well. Stephanie could hear their echoing screams for help as they thrashed about in the frigid well water below. She sensed the terror they felt like it was her own. Stephanie wanted to scream "no!" at the top of her lungs but couldn't form the word.

Suddenly the scene changed, and Stephanie was standing in a bedroom of an old house awash with light from candles and oil lamps. She seemed to recognize the house even though she was certain she had never seen it before. She looked down at her hands covered with bleeding scratches. She looked up into a full-length dressing mirror but instead of seeing her own reflection she saw the face of that same madwoman who had just murdered the two boys. The front of the woman's gown was streaked with blood. The eyes staring out from the reflection we're awash with wild insanity.

After a moment a man burst through the bedroom door. Splinters from the shattered doorframe flew in all directions. The man was tall, wore an old-fashioned business suit, and carried a walking stick with an ivory handle carved in the shape of a wolf's head. He bore a startling resemblance to Jason with dark brown hair and wire-framed glasses.

His eyes streamed with tears and blazed with rage as he stormed across the room. He seemed to be shouting angrily at Stephanie. She couldn't hear what he said but sensed her calm was fueling the man's fury.

Then Stephanie felt something in her right hand and saw a large kitchen knife reflecting in the mirror. The woman whose body she now occupied shouted something at the man then thrust the knife out in his direction. The man countered the attack with a cross blow from his walking stick.

Then with his breath hitching heavily in his chest the man raised the cane high above his head and slammed its ivory handle into the side of her skull. Stephanie felt an incredible stabbing of pain as she collapsed to the floor in front of the mirror. Glancing up at the looking glass Stephanie saw the look of madness had left her eyes replaced now by one of complete terror. The man reached down, wrapped his hands firmly around her throat and began to squeeze tightly.

In an instant, Stephanie found herself outside of the woman's body watching the scene from high above floating up near the ceiling. The angry man continued to squeeze the woman's throat ever tighter as her eyes bugged wildly out of her skull. Blood trickled down the woman's neck where the man's fingernails bit into her flesh. He throttled her making her head snap back and forth. Then surprisingly the woman looked up at Stephanie and as their eyes met the woman smiled aware of Stephanie's presence. A moment later Stephanie heard a sharp crack and the woman collapsed to the floor in a dead heap.

Stephanie tried to absorb everything she had just seen with the futile hope of understanding what it all meant. She was sure she was dreaming yet she couldn't wake herself up from the murderous horrors unfolding around her.

The man now sat weeping on the floor cradling the dead woman in his arms. Then he raised his head and looked up at Stephanie offering a smile shockingly similar to Jason's smile that small crooked grin she had fallen in love with. Their eyes locked and Stephanie realized he had become Jason and the dead woman had become her. He stared more intently, almost pleadingly as Stephanie's dead doppelganger's arm dropped to the floor with a thud.

As Stephanie watched in terrorized silence never allowing her eyes to leave the man's/Jason's strange gaze he reached slowly into his suit jacket pocket and withdrew a long ivory handled straight razor. He calmly lifted the razor to his left arm and made a deep horizontal cut across his wrist. Blood pumped from the wound and flooded onto the body of his dead wife. Then he brought the razor up to his throat and while still staring into Stephanie's eyes and still smiling he slit his own throat from ear to ear. The incision opened like a huge crimson mouth, exposing musculature and allowing blood to pour down his arms and the front of his suit, drenching his dead wife's face and torso.

Stephanie mercifully awoke with a start, hovering in that strange state somewhere between asleep and awake. She looked around the bedroom surprised to find her blinds open and their room awash with moonlight. She was certain she had closed the blinds before going to bed. Stephanie heard a scratching, clawing sound coming from the foot of her bed. A cold chill started at the back of her skull and squirmed like a slithering snake down to the base of her spine. She immediately understood something was very wrong. A foul stench had begun to permeate the room. The odor was like that of a dead putrefying animal.

At the bottom of her bed, she saw two skeletal hands creeping up from the floor below. They were covered with withered gray flesh and were gripping the covers as they pulled themselves ever closer. She couldn't move. Nor could she release the scream of terror building deep within her tightening chest.

Stephanie sat bolt upright in her bed awakening from the horrible nightmare, sweat beading on her brow. She thanked God it had all just been a terrible dream. She looked toward the bottom of her bed and experienced a rush of relief seeing the covers lying smooth at her feet. Then she began to feel foolish. What had she seriously expected to see except for her covered feet?

She turned to look at the glowing ghostly blue display of her digital alarm clock and saw it was only 2:22 AM. She was surprised at how bright the clock display was. She wondered why she had never noticed the way it washed the entire room with its eerie cobalt aura before.

She couldn't recall what had actually awoken her but realized she suddenly needed to use the bathroom. She placed her feet on the floor sitting on the edge of the mattress for a moment trying to get her bearings before standing up. The surface of the floor felt unexpectedly chilly on her bare feet as if the temperature along the floor had suddenly dropped thirty degrees.

As she was about to stand up she felt something strange in the chill air surrounding her feet. Icy cold tendrils seemed to slowly wrap themselves around her pale white ankles like some strange invasive plant or vine. She cautiously looked down at the floor seeing her feet take on a bluish-gray appearance from the cerulean glow. Then she realized with horror, long bony fingers from beneath her bed were gripping her legs, pulling her down into some unseen portal below the now liquid floor, into the world of the dead. Stephanie's heart leaped into her throat.

"Mommy! Wake up!" Stephanie heard a distant voice calling from some faraway place. She groggily opened her eyes as the voice became louder and clearer and saw Cindy's pretty face next to her bed as she shook her mother her vigorously, attempting to awaken her.

Stephanie was a bit confused trying desperately to find her way back from the world of nightmares. As she sat up and shook off the sleep and the effects of the sleeping pill she had taken, she saw Cindy was dressed and ready to go.

"Honey?" Stephanie asked. "What, I mean who, I mean, how did you get ready to go already?"

She heard Jason entering the room with Sammy in his arms. The steady computerized tones of a video game in the distance told her Jeremy was downstairs. Surprisingly, Jason was showered, dressed, and ready as well. She must have had a strange expression on her face because Jason said, "Don't worry, Steph. I took care of them. You were sleeping so deeply I figured you needed to rest so I let you sleep a bit longer while we all got ready. Then I sent Cindy in to wake you."

"Oh, my Lord! I must have been sleeping the sleep of the dead." Then a cold chill appeared on the back of her neck upon hearing herself uttering the expression, but she didn't understand why as the memories of her nightmares faded.

Jason said, "I'll take the kids downstairs and make them breakfast while you're getting ready. I'll put a pot of boiling water on for tea for us as well. By the time you're finished breakfast will be ready. Take your time. It's only about 7:15. We don't have to leave until around 9:30. The kids and I were so excited about today we all woke up early."

"Ok, see you in a bit," Stephanie said as she stumbled into the bathroom. Soaking under the hot shower feeling herself come back to reality out from the fog of sleep she had a strange apprehensive sensation growing deep inside her like an intuition of some impending danger.

9

THE FOUR-YEAR-OLD Nissan Quest followed the silver Cadillac along the winding two-lane country road. Jason and Stephanie Wright sat noticeably silent and unsure of what to say. They were trying to come to grips with everything they had just learned allowing the gravity of what they were told that morning in the Ashton lawyer's office to somehow sink in.

Slowly Jason turned his head toward the passenger's seat while simultaneously Stephanie turned to look at him. It was like a type of telepathy, the kind that often seems to exist between older married couples, had suddenly found its way into their still relatively new marriage. They also seemed to share similar facial expressions. Stephanie's eyes were wide with a combination of shock, disbelief and an almost mad giddiness, while Jason's face resembled that of a small child with an all-you-can-eat pass for his favorite candy store.

He glanced back at the road for a moment then looking once again at Stephanie he silently mouthed a question which he was certain had to be on her mind as well. It was not so much a question as a statement the very utterance of which was somehow more incomprehensible than an answer to any question might be. This was something he simply had to get out of his system but which he didn't intend to allow the children to overhear.

"Three million!" his lips silently said as his eyes widened with ever dawning comprehension.

Stephanie slowly nodded her head in agreement trying to somehow; wrap her head around the concept. She didn't reply because she truly had no idea what to say. Instead, she continued to stare at Jason with a small dream-like grin on her face a look she feared might become permanent.

In the back of the van, Jeremy and Cindy were animatedly discussing what they imagined the farm might look like or more importantly what adventures they would discover when they toured the coal mine later in the afternoon. Little Sammy was spouting out a combination of both semi-recognizable words as well as garbled gibberish.

H. Mason Armstrong had read them the last will and testament of Emerson C. Washburn, in its entirety. Then he proceeded to translate the legalese into plain understandable English. Stephanie's Uncle Emerson had accrued an estate worth over three million dollars, and he had left everything to Stephanie. They learned the name of the property was Fallen Stones.

"Fallen Stones?" Stephanie had inquired, "What a strange name! Do you know why he called the property Fallen Stones?"

The lawyer hesitated for just a moment then replied, "No. Not really. Mr. Washburn never explained that to me. Sometimes it was difficult to get answers from your uncle especially toward the end. I assumed if he didn't wish to discuss it then it was none of my business."

During the reading of the will, the children were out in the main office watching television while Jason, Stephanie, and Armstrong met in a side conference room. There were a few very important contingencies pertaining to the estate each of which had the potential to affect their family more than the incredible value of the settlement itself. One was the fact that most of the three million dollars value was in the property itself. Washburn had purchased the land with the farmhouse and all the outbuildings relatively inexpensively because of its run-down condition. He had then proceeded to dump a mountain of money into outrageously expensive renovations and additions.

The lawyer explained how he believed Washburn had begun to lose his mind somewhat toward the end of his life and had spent money with reckless abandon. Armstrong was quick to point out how he did his best to control Washburn's excesses but there was only so much he could do. As a result, the Washburn estate had only about three-quarters of a million dollars available in liquid assets.

Although such a sum was still quite substantial, they quickly learned how a good chunk of those supposedly liquid assets wasn't accessible either. Washburn had insisted as part of the acceptance of the terms of the will that as his heir, Stephanie was not permitted to sell the property at any time during her lifetime. He also stipulated she could only leave the estate to her decedents when she, in turn, passed away. Also, she must draw up her own will and specify whoever inherited the property from her could likewise not sell it. She had a property worth over two million dollars which she couldn't sell.

Armstrong had assured her Washburn had taken care of the tax and property maintenance issues by creating an account that would automatically pay the taxes as well as homeowner's insurance annually and would earn enough through interest to cover those expenditures during her lifetime. Based on some quick calculations the lawyer figured they would be able to have access to about two hundred and fifty thousand dollars cash for their own personal use.

At first, they were disappointed until they realized they'd still be better off financially than their current situation having a quarter of a million dollars to do with as they pleased. If they decided they didn't like the property, they could stay in Berks County and perhaps try to find some legal means to potentially circumvent the will and get permission to sell it later.

However, if the property was half as gorgeous as Armstrong had described they'd have a home and land they would never have previously been able to afford. With Jason being offered a promotion with a substantial raise it was starting to sound like a simple decision, a no-brainer at least at first glance.

If only Stephanie didn't have the bizarre feeling that someone else was controlling her future. Everything was happening so quickly. In a matter of just twenty-four hours so many important life-changing decisions had been thrust upon them. Everything was starting to take on a surrealistic feel.

"When will we get to the farm?" Jeremy asked from the back of the van startling Stephanie from her thoughts.

"We should be there in a few minutes," Jason called back. "Mr. Armstrong said it was just a few miles outside of town. In the meantime, you should look out the window and check out the scenery. Enjoy the ride." Jason tried to sound convincing, but he understood when it came to anxious and excited kids there was no such thing as a short or enjoyable ride.

"All I can see outside is trees and woods," Jeremy replied.

Jason suggested, "Well, woods can be very interesting places to play Jeremy. All sorts of animals live in the woods like squirrels, raccoons, chipmunks, deer, and the like."

"Yeah!" Jeremy replied. "And bears, and cougars, and mountain lions."

Cindy said fearfully, "I don't want to see any bears or mountain lions."

"You don't have to worry about them, honey," Jason explained. "Jeremy's just being goofy. There are too many people living in the area for that."

"What will our farm be like?" Cindy asked.

Jason said, "Our farm will probably be a house maybe a barn or two and lots of land to play on." Jason suddenly realized he had begun referring to the farm as their farm for the first time. This realization of his willingness to accept the idea of them owning the property felt strange to him. They hadn't even seen the property yet, but he was already start-ing to think of it as their own and not just their possession but quite possibly their new home.

Jeremy exclaimed, "Wouldn't it be cool if there was a coal mine under our land? That would be even cooler than a cave or something like that. It would make a really cool place to hang out."

Jason said, "First of all a coal mine is no place to hang out or play. It would be way too dangerous. Besides, this is a farm, which means it's nowhere near any coal mines. The only hole you might find on a farm is may be an old fashioned well and chances are pretty good there won't be any open wells on the property either."

Stephanie suddenly shuddered at Jason's mention of a well. What was it about a well that made her feel so apprehensive? She couldn't recall what it might be but she suddenly experienced a weird sort of momentary flashback where she conjured a mental image of a woman dragging two young boys toward a well off in the distance. Before the image could solidify, it vanished.

"Steph? Steph? Earth to Steph!" Jason was calling from the driver's seat.

"Oh, dear," she replied startled. "I'm sorry, honey. I guess my mind went somewhere else for a moment."

Jason replied, "Not surprising after the day we have had so far."

Up ahead at a break in the trees the Cadillac turned left onto a long driveway which seemed to snake upward through the woods. Jason put on his turn signal to follow the lawyer. "Looks like we're here," Jason announced.

The two older children started shouting, "We're here! We're here."

However, little Sammy said nothing. He was sitting hunched in his car seat staring out the side window toward a clearing along the side of the road which neither Jason, Stephanie, nor the other children had noticed. Sammy was too young to comprehend exactly what was wrong or what he was seeing but whatever it was didn't seem to be something good. Sammy knew how good things looked and how good things made him feel. He also knew about bad things and about sad things. At his young age, Sammy could never hope to put it into words what he saw. It looked like a cartoon or maybe a TV show, but it was playing outside along the road and he could see right through it like it was on a window. The show was of a man in a car on fire.

Sammy knew about fire and knew fire was hot and fire was bad. Sammy knew to never touch hot things and especially to never touch fire. The man looked like he was hurting and like he was screaming but Sammy couldn't hear him. It was like somebody turned off the TV sound. He felt sad and scared and had a strange feeling deep in his tummy. He didn't know why nobody one else in the car could see the bad thing. He didn't know what to do so he just looked away and became very quiet.

As the minivan followed up the long driveway, which seemed more like a road than a driveway, they noticed how dense the woods were along the way. When Stephanie had first heard the property referred to as a forty-acre farmette she supposed it would all be open farmland but there were thick forests on both sides of the access road. Before she could finish the thought their van emerged from the shade of the trees and out into an incredibly bright and open expanse of meadow and farmland. It was as if they had entered another dimension, a special oasis of sorts removed from the rest of the world around them. A large boulder about the size of a Volkswagen Beetle was positioned on the left side of the driveway. Its polished face engraved with the name Fallen Stones.

At the end of the driveway, she saw the Cadillac circle around to the left following the curve of the roadway as it approached the front of an incredible three-story farmhouse. Farmhouse barely described the amazing spectacle before them. Jason hit the brakes, and they sat staring, mouths agape, gawking at the structure looming in the distance. It was truly one of the most beautiful buildings either of them had ever seen.

This truly was an estate. The center of the structure appeared to be the original three-story brick building, but the windows had been replaced and the original brick had been sandblasted and re-pointed to look like new. A large roof capped with copper reflecting like a jewel in the afternoon sunlight extended out over the driveway.

Where the roadway curved around to the front of the house Stephanie could see the blacktop road ended giving way to an enormous circular-shaped pattern concrete driveway which wrapped around a large multi-tiered concrete fountain standing at least ten feet high. Water flowed from the small topmost bowls, down into lower bowls, each one getting larger with each tier until it finally ended in a large circular concrete pool perhaps twenty feet in diameter.

At the largest part of the circle, the driveway continued until it fanned out to allow access to a massive four-bay, two-story garage attached to the left side of the original structure. The garage angled forward so it sat at a forty-five-degree angle to the main structure.

Between the house and the garage, a two-story glass-enclosed atrium served to connect the two. The sight was breathtaking.

The windows of the two-story garage matched those of the original structure and Stephanie could imagine the potential the second floor of the garage had to offer. She immediately had a vision of a combination writing/art studio for the creation of her children's books. This thought caught her by surprise. She somehow knew the space would be perfect, even without seeing it.

Attached to the right side of the main house was a two-story addition. Stephanie could only imagine how many square feet of living space the structure offered but she had to assume it must be in the three to four thousand square feet range. Near the front of the house, she could see Armstrong exiting his Cadillac and waving them to come forward.

"Holy crap!" Jason said.

Stephanie replied, "You can say that again."

Cindy and Jeremy were looking wide-eyed out at the incredible structure and were shouting simultaneously, "Is that our house, Mom? That can't be our house, can it? We're rich. Holy cow, Mom, we're rich! Just look at that house!"

Sammy had gotten over his earlier unhappy feelings and was now eagerly joining in with his excited siblings. "We wich! We wich!" he shouted, mimicking his brother and sister.

Trying to calm the kids down Stephanie said, "No, kids, we aren't rich by any means. But this certainly is a nice house, and yes, it's ours. Now we have to check it out and see what it's like so it's very important you all calm down and relax. Ok?"

"Well, we'd better get up there. Armstrong is waiting," Jason said as he slowly parked the van. He and Stephanie got out and walked around to retrieve Sammy from his car seat. Cindy and Jeremy had already opened the sliding door and were staring up at the house. Both of them resembled first-time tourists in New York City gawking up into the air looking at skyscrapers.

Stephanie walked over holding Sammy on her hip. Jason was by her side holding her free hand. Armstrong waved his arm in a somewhat theatrical semi-circular gesture indicating the property and said, "So what do you think so far?"

"I, I honestly don't know what to say," Stephanie said sincerely.

Jason interjected, "It makes one heck of a first impression."

"Truer words were never spoken," the lawyer agreed, "but you haven't seen anything yet. If you think it looks amazing from the outside just wait until you see the inside. It is quite spectacular."

"Oh, my goodness!" Stephanie said, suddenly overwhelmed. "I just can't believe this is actually ours. It's just so, so beautiful." Then she began to cry. She didn't want to but simply couldn't stop herself.

"No cwy, Mommy. No cwy," Sammy said gently brushing his mother's cheek fearing something might be wrong with her.

She smiled, let out a loving chuckle and kissed little Sammy on the top of his head. "Don't worry, baby boy. Mommy's fine. It's just I'm so very happy."

"Well," the lawyer said to Stephanie and Jason, "time's a' wasting, as they say. Let's check out your new home!" He said this to make a specific point. He planned to continue deliberately making similar statements all during the tour to reinforce the idea the property was theirs and to make them feel comfortable with ownership. He needed them to move into the house as soon as possible because that was what Washburn had ordered.

Armstrong walked to the front door, inserted the key, and prepared to escort the family inside.

10

JASON HEARD STEPHANIE'S breath catch as soon as she walked through the door. Still holding her hand, he followed. The front door opened to a modestly sized entry foyer at the base of a long wide set of stairs leading up to the second floor. Once he stepped through the door, he understood why Stephanie had been caught by surprise.

The woodwork of the stairway leading upward was immaculate. An expensive looking carpet ran through the center of the stairway leaving the restored wood stair treads exposed on the sides. Likewise, the entryway had an equally luxurious carpet surrounded on two sides by the refinished oak flooring. As Jason stepped inside and turned to look at his wife, he noticed how the carpet continued down a long elegant hallway to the right of the stairs.

Stephanie had turned to face Jason and her back was to a wide entryway to what appeared to be an enormous living room.

"Wow!" Jason said surprised, "Look at the size of that living room!"

Stephanie turned as the group headed toward the room with Jason passing her to lead the way when suddenly Jason stopped in his tracks. "What the Hell?" Jason said in a confused and slightly angry tone.

"Oh, oh!" Cindy said from behind them.

"Dad said a swear word," Jeremy chuckled.

Little Sammy, unfortunately, mimicked Jason's surprised expression as he often did in such situations, "Wat a heaw, wat a heaw!"

"Quiet now," Stephanie said to the baby as she tried to divert his attention.

Jason was unable to offer his customary apology for his unplanned outburst and since Stephanie had just seen what had shocked Jason, she was speechless; seeing what they both saw across the room hanging over the hearth of a huge stone fireplace.

"Hey, look," Jeremy said. "It's Mom and Dad in old peoples' clothes."

Cindy stood with her mouth agape staring speechless.

What hung on the wall before them was an oil painting of a man and a woman in early nineteenth century formal attire. The woman was dressed in a long white gown while the man wore a suit complete with a top hat. The woman looked very much like Stephanie, enough to pass for her sister and the man had dark brown hair and wire-frame glasses similar to Jason's. He sported a substantial mustache while Jason was clean-shaven. Nonetheless, he looked quite a lot like Jason, again close enough to be a sibling. The man held a walking stick in his hands an ivory handle sculpted in the shape of a wolf's head.

Stephanie continued to stare in astonishment. The eyes in the portrait seemed to stare out directly at them. The illusion gave Stephanie the creeps. A strange feeling welled deep in the pit of her stomach and for a moment she actually felt she might become faint.

"Who, who are those people?" Stephanie asked with a trembling voice never taking her eyes from the portrait.

The lawyer replied looking somewhat confused, "Why, Stephanie, those are your great grandparents, Dwight and Marie Livingston. I'm terribly sorry. I just assumed you might have seen pictures of them sometime before."

"No. No, I haven't," Stephanie said. "I never even knew their names. Livingston? That was their last name?"

"Yes, Dwight Charles Livingston and Marie Louise O'Hara Livingston. This portrait was created in honor of their wedding day. They were the ones who built the original farmhouse as well as the outbuildings."

Jason asked appearing perplexed, "I can understand why the woman, Marie might bear a family resemblance to Stephanie since she's her great-grandmother but why in the world does Dwight look so much like me? I mean he looks enough like me to be my own great-grandfather. That makes no sense at all."

"It's most likely purely coincidental," the lawyer suggested. "That is unless your ancestors also came from this area, Jason. Then anything might be possible. You see when you start tracing back your family lineage strange connections often pop up. For example, I've learned I'm related to the legendary chocolate manufacturer Milton Hershey seven different ways. Yet before researching my family tree, I had no idea of the connection.

"I wouldn't bother concerning myself with that if I were you two. As I said it's probably just a coincidence. In fact, I'll be more than happy to have the portrait taken down and replaced with something more decorative and more in line with your personal tastes. Just say the word. Maybe you could tuck it away in the attic until you get settled in and then decide later what you want to do with it."

Attempting to draw their attention away from the living room and the upsetting painting he directed them across the hall at the bottom of the stairway to an area of the house he knew was sure to win them over. "This way now; there's more to see."

Jason turned and looked behind him seeing a short hall leading off to the left of the staircase. It opened to what he perceived must have been the enclosed breezeway connecting the house to the large two-story garage. Even from a distance, Jason could see it was not so much a breezeway as it was an incredibly spacious atrium of some sort. Pulling Stephanie by the hand he led her away from the living room with Jeremy and Cindy following behind them.

What they saw was an unbelievable twenty-foot high peaked glass-enclosed living area. The marble floor of the room was bright with afternoon sunshine.

The room was at least thirty or more feet wide and expanded outward about another thirty feet to where it met the door to the garage. It was a masterpiece of modern glass and metal design with large trees, some of them exotic or tropical growing from enormous planters scattered about the room. Several large rock and water features were visible providing the soothing sounds of water falling over stones. They saw several large coy splashing in ponds. Strategically placed track lights high above them provided additional accents to the tops of the tall trees. There were several small modern-looking sofas and comfortable chairs as well as tables with lamps tastefully spread around the space as well. It was a veritable oasis.

"Holy cow! Look at the swimming pool!" Jeremy shouted from behind them.

Jason chuckled and corrected the boy, "No, Jeremy. It's not a swimming pool. It's an indoor fish pond."

"Not that, Dad. I know what a fish pond is," Jeremy said. "I mean out there." He pointed to an area outside the back of the atrium.

Stephanie and Jeremy turned and could indeed see a huge in-ground swimming pool adjacent to a spacious stone patio surrounded by a decorative wall. Jason was certain he also saw what appeared to be a grand outdoor kitchen and grilling area. It was almost too much to imagine.

"We'll show you that later on when we go out back. Like everything else on your property, I promise you it's quite impressive," the lawyer said. "For now let's go see the garage and its second floor."

As they approached an exquisite set of wooden doors leading to the garage Stephanie looked up and saw an expansive deck area jutting out into the space from the second floor. The doors to the garage were located in the shadows beneath the deck. Off to the right of the doors, Stephanie could see a set of curved iron stairs leading up to the second floor.

Armstrong noticed her admiring the stairs and said, "We'll take a quick look in the garage first and then we'll come back through and head up to the loft."

"The loft," Stephanie repeated silently in her mind. That term matched perfectly with the original concept that had popped into her mind outside in the driveway.

"The loft," she mentally repeated yet again. It sounded so right to her. It sounded perfect to her. She recalled various interpretations of artists' lofts she had seen depicted in movies. The sound of the word in her mind brought an even larger smile to her face.

"Yes, I think you'll love it," the lawyer interjected as if reading her thoughts. "It has its own bathroom and kitchen as well. You'll see shortly."

Before becoming sidetracked by the mysteries awaiting them on the second floor of the garage Armstrong opened one of the garage entry doors and reached in to flip on a light switch. The area beyond the doorway was immediately flooded with bright lights recessed in the ceiling. The space was immaculate. The floor of the garage was made of some type of Epoxy-based membrane material like the types of floors Jason had seen used in high-end NASCAR racing garages. It was mostly white but had silver, blue and dark gray specks.

The garage was about one and a half times the depth of a traditional garage. The floor of each of the four bays of the garage tapered slightly downward on all four sides and at the intersection of the sloping floors, Jason could see four separate drains.

As if he were reading Jason's thoughts Armstrong said, "The garage is heated and completed insulated. So between that and those floor drains, you'll be able to wash your cars inside all year round."

A stainless-steel workbench lined the back wall of the garage along with a full selection of both wall and floor-mounted cabinets. Jason loved to tinker and work on cars but could scarcely afford even the cheapest tools or tool chests. It had always been his dream to be able to afford real top-quality tools and have a shop of his own.

The lawyer explained, "Those drawers and cabinets along the back of the garage are stocked full with virtually every top-of-the-line mechanic's tool you can imagine in both English and metric varieties."

At the far end of the garage by the last bay, Jason noticed the room made a sharp right turn. Armstrong led the procession to the far end of the garage and as they turned Jason's breath caught in his throat when he saw something he had never expected. Behind the fourth bay of the garage was a complete woodworking shop with walls of hand tools, cabinets and virtually every power tool he could have imagined. In the center was a thick oak workbench complete with old-style woodworking vises.

"There is an intercom system for communicating with the loft upstairs as well as the main house," the lawyer said pointing toward an area along the right wall.

He reached into a space along the wall at the back of the garage from which the woodworking shop extended and pulled out a hidden pocket style door. "You can close these interconnected doors to separate the shop from the garage to keep the dust from getting on your cars. This area back here is designated for woodworking while the tool cabinets and workbenches out in the main garage area are designed for doing work on your cars. That is if you like to tinker."

"Oh, boy! Do I ever!" Jason said genuinely flabbergasted. "This is beyond amazing. This shop has everything!"

The lawyer replied, "By the way, there's a door on the back right side of the woodworking shop which leads to an enclosed entryway. From there you can go out to the backyard or you can take a set of back stairs up to the loft. Oh yes, I forgot to mention; the larger power tools are on wheels for easy mobility. And one more thing; if you didn't notice the back of the woodworking shop has its own automatic garage door if you want to open it to enjoy the air or have a larger project to move out of the workshop.

"Unbelievable! This Washburn guy must have been a genius! He thought of everything!" Jason said.

The lawyer grimaced slightly at this then said. "Well, these weren't exactly Mr. Washburn's ideas. You see he wanted the best garage and shop money could buy and he put me in charge of the project. I hired a team of designers who specialize in innovate ideas."

"It's so sad he passed away before he even had a chance to enjoy his house," Stephanie lamented.

He chose to ignore Stephanie's comment to avoid any further discussion where Washburn was concerned. He hadn't told the couple Washburn had committed suicide. Armstrong recalled the man's bloody death immediately turning his stomach with revulsion and transforming his face into a grimace.

"Are you all right Mason?" Stephanie asked.

He replied, "Oh um, yes. I'm fine. Sorry. I just have a lot on my mind. There's always so much work to do and so little time. So let's all go back out into the atrium and check out the loft upstairs."

"Here Honey," Jason offered, "let me take Sammy off your hands before we head up those stairs. I have a feeling you're going to want to look around." Stephanie couldn't help but notice how even Jason somehow seemed to know the loft was meant for her. Perhaps it was simply another coincidence. But she knew by the look in her husband's eyes, he was having many of the exact same thoughts.

The group exited the garage and walked up the stairs to the elevated deck. When they reached the top Stephanie discovered a large spacious area tastefully decorated with potted plants and a variety of thick-cushioned patio chairs. The outside wall of the loft was lined with three large double-French door units with lacy curtains displayed behind the glass multi-paneled panes.

"These three doors can all be opened fully to allow for a spectacular view of the atrium," Armstrong said.

Stephanie turned and looked out toward the railing of the deck and for a moment felt a minor attack of vertigo. The view of the atrium area truly was amazing and when she looked out into the expanse of the backyard the feeling was overwhelming. She teetered slightly and Armstrong grabbed her right arm helping her regain her footing.

"Easy there," Armstrong said, "It might take a while to get used to the view. You just have to be a little careful at first. After all, we can't have anything bad happen to our new homeowner, now can we?" Then he chuckled strangely, and Stephanie got an odd and unsettling feeling. If she didn't know better, she would have thought there might be a trace of madness in that laugh. Again, she forced herself to ignore the bizarre feeling and followed Jason and her kids into the loft area.

Like everything they had seen of the house so far, the loft space was phenomenal. The room was well lit by a wall of large windows across the back. The ceiling was awash with illumination from skylights and the area was decorated with scattered sofas and chairs in a style exactly suited to Stephanie's taste.

"Wow, Steph!" Jason said. "It looks like you decorated this place yourself."

The entire loft occupied an equal amount of square footage of the main part of the garage but the area of the loft above what would be the forth bay of the garage was dedicated to a small kitchen area as well as an additional room of some sort.

Armstrong said, "The kitchenette is state of the art has everything you need."

Stephanie held back a laugh since the so-called kitchenette was actually larger than her present kitchen in their townhouse. If Armstrong considered this small she couldn't wait to see the real kitchen in the main house.

The lawyer continued, "That room next to the kitchenette is a small bedroom and has a full bath and shower as well. I don't know if Mr. Washburn planned on ever renting out the space at some time in the future but it certainly would make a nice apartment or guest area someday."

Stephanie knew she'd never use the area for an apartment. It would most definitely become her writing and art studio. The bathroom and bedroom would be handy for Sammy's afternoon naptime while she was doing her creative work and the kitchen would be perfect for preparing his snacks. She suspected she'd be spending most of her days in the space. It was then she realized she had made the decision if it could actually be considered a decision at all. They'd be moving into the home as soon as possible.

The group left the loft and headed back into the main farmhouse. The lawyer suggested they see the upstairs bedroom area first before touring the rest of the house. When they reached the top of the stairway, they could see a long hall leading back toward a closed door. On both the left and right sides of the hallway, there were three doors. Armstrong explained there were two bedrooms and a bathroom. The door at the far end of the hall led to a master bedroom suite, which occupied the entire length of the back of the house over the expanded kitchen area downstairs. He explained how Washburn had added living space to the back of the original farmhouse as well.

Pointing behind them Armstrong indicated a door at the front right side of the house which led to a space above the stairway. "That's the door to the third floor of the farmhouse. It's the only area of the house besides the basement which hasn't been renovated. Mr. Washburn only used it as an attic for storing some of his personal items which never found a place in the new home. I suspect with all the square footage available in this place you probably won't have much use for it either.

"As for the basement, we dug down further in order to have ten feet of head clearance and added a cement slab floor. In addition, we sealed the walls so there's little chance of water seepage down there.

"Other than to gain access to things like the water heater, gas furnace, and air conditioning units, I doubt you'll have any need to use the basement either. Now let's head down the hall and peek in each of the bedrooms."

The first bedroom at the top right of the stairway appeared to be designed as a guest room with very little personality whatsoever but it was clean, very neat, and orderly.

The real surprises came when they looked into the other three bedrooms. It was as if each of them had been designed specifically for each one of their children. On the left side of the hall, the bedroom was obviously decorated with Jeremy in mind. In fact, it looked oddly similar to his current bedroom but with a lot more living space as well as furniture, including a television, desk, and desktop computer with a large flat-screen monitor.

"Whoa!" Jeremy said. "I claim this room. This has got to be my room." There was no need, however; as everyone knew instantly it was meant for him.

The same was true of the bedroom on the right located just outside of the master bedroom. It looked ready for Cindy to move in immediately with many of the same decorations and styles she already had in her own bedroom.

"Mommy, this looks just like my room back home only a lot cooler!" the girl said through a huge smile.

Even more unusual was the bedroom, directly across the hall from the room they already thought of as Cindy's room. It was the perfect room for a toddler, and as it was right next to the master bedroom, it made the location excellent as well. In addition, it shared a bathroom with the room Jeremy had claimed which would be perfect for when Sammy got older.

"This is all so very strange," Stephanie said with a noticeable tremor in her voice. "This place was renovated like it was designed just for us. We never met Emerson Washburn so how could he possibly know so much about us? And even if he did why would he design his own personal living space with us in mind?" She was suddenly beginning to feel a bit uncomfortable about how the tour was progressing.

Once again she had the bizarre sensation she was losing control of her own destiny. She felt their privacy had somehow been compromised. She started to wonder what type of man this Emerson Washburn might actually have been. Then she began to speculate about the integrity of his lawyer, Armstrong as well.

How far did Washburn have gone to learn about Stephanie and her family?

11

HE LAWYER IMMEDIATELY recognized the discomfort not only apparent with Stephanie, but he could see it spreading to the rest of her family as well. He hadn't anticipated this sort of negative reaction. Now considering things in hindsight he realized he should have. Regardless of his miscalculation, he had to quickly take what was rapidly deteriorating into a potentially bad situation and find a way to turn it around; to make it right.

He said to the perplexed couple, "Look, I can see why it might seem a little strange at first. But as I mentioned earlier your uncle Emerson was never married, had no children of his own, and had a bit of an unsavory past. Suffice to say Emerson was probably searching for something missing in his life; the family he never had.

"When he left his former life, he decided to settle down and do his best to lead a normal life. He also wanted to learn more about his own relatives. He once told me this interest was sparked a decade ago when his brother and sister-in-law, your mother and father Stephanie, were killed in a car accident. He apparently had been estranged from them for many years. He felt learning of their deaths was more than simple happenstance. He believed everything in life happened for a reason."

The lawyer continued, "As I mentioned briefly in our meeting this morning, Emerson hired a private investigator to track down family members current and past, but he took a shine to you and your family Stephanie. I think he wanted in his own way to know what it was like to be part of a family again." After a pause, Armstrong added for emphasis, "Part of *your* family."

Then Armstrong further explained, "Although he never told me so directly, I suspect before he became ill Mr. Washburn hoped at some point in time he might have been able to introduce himself to you and perhaps even invite you up for a visit. I believe he may have wanted to make the house look as much like home as he possibly could for you both."

Not a single word of his last statement had been true. It was all a pack of lies the lawyer had dreamed up on the fly to win over the Wrights. Armstrong was operating in full damage-control mode and was making things up as he went along based on either the positive or negative reactions of the couple.

"Since he had no intention of the property ever being sold, I suppose it didn't matter to him how much money he sank into it. Just so you're aware no one has ever used any of these bedrooms, and he kept their doors closed. His room, his personal space, was the room behind the door at the end of the hall.

"So does that seem to make a bit more sense to you now?" Armstrong asked. He could tell by their expressions he had been successful in his persuasive monologue.

Jason cautiously replied, "Well, um, yes. I suppose it does."

Looking a bit sad and perhaps even somewhat guilty Stephanie said, "Yes. I think it makes perfect sense now. I actually feel bad for my Uncle Emerson. We were only fifty or so miles away and yet we had no idea he was here. It's so tragic he had to die alone."

Armstrong liked how she had referred to the man as "Uncle Emerson." She was starting to accept the man as part of her family. He also found it all a bit amusing. The phrase conjured up an image of a kindly old uncle rather than a notorious gangster and thug who ended up sick, rail thin and lying dead in a blood-spewed bathtub reeking with the stench of his own self-mutilation.

This image made the lawyer wince as he suddenly recalled not only how Washburn had died but also the horrid undead creature the man had since become. And here Armstrong was, lying through his teeth to convince these people to move into the house when he suspected no was certain something bad awaited them. He didn't know exactly what Washburn and the other unseen entities inhabiting the house had in store for these people, but he knew his own soul would likely rot in Hell for the part he now played in convincing the Wrights to move into the house. Regardless, he had no choice but to continue with an assuring and convincing air.

"Well. As I've often heard said, 'No matter how many people are with us at the end we all truly die alone.' Perhaps that's an accurate statement." The lawyer was now completely satisfied to see he had smoothed things over at least for the time being. So before Stephanie could offer a reply he directed them into the master bedroom suite.

If either Stephanie or Jason was still feeling any residual apprehension at the oddly familiar decor throughout the rest of the house, they quickly forgot their anxiety when they saw the interior of Washburn's private space.

The room was about as far from their decorative tastes as it could possibly be. The space occupied the entire width of the home and was at least twenty feet deep. However, there was very little light in the room due to a wall of heavy dark drapes which covered every window in the room. There was a dank and musty sort of smell to the room from the old furniture and draperies. The funky almost foul scent reminded Stephanie of the odor often found in old libraries with shelves lined with ancient tomes.

Seeing the unpleasant and surprised expression on the couple's faces Armstrong explained, "It's a bit odd, to say the least but you'll be happy to know money has already been set aside for you to redecorate this room. Mr. Washburn wanted the space to resemble your great-grandparents' era as much as possible. Although their actual bedroom was never as grand or as large as this, the location, furniture, and carpet are all original. Anyway, I believe Mr. Washburn felt living as they did might help him to understand them better. I realize how eccentric it may seem but again that was Mr. Washburn's way.

"I'd recommend redecorating this space in lighter shades to take advantage of the windows Mr. Washburn had installed along the back wall." The lawyer walked over and pulled back the drapes to flood the room with afternoon sunlight. The room looked even more dismal if such a thing was possible. Every single beam of sunlight flooding across the room was awash with billions of moving dust particles.

As the outside light continued to flood through the room Stephanie saw her original impression was correct. Antique furniture filled the room and old, tattered carpeting covered the floors. It looked like the room of an elderly pauper rather than a multi-millionaire. She realized this was likely what the entire house had looked like when Washburn had taken ownership. It served to help her appreciate what an enormous feat the renovation had been.

Then the lawyer showed them the incredible view of the rear of the property through a panoramic wall of glass. In the center were two tall glass doors opening to a massive second-story deck.

Stephanie walked toward the windows and looked over the vast expanse of land. She saw several outbuildings all of which appeared to be new and pristine. One of the buildings, in particular, caught her attention. It was far off to the right in the distance and strangely hexagonal in shape. She felt a similar strong attraction to the building as she had with the loft area. Somehow she knew it as a building constructed for her to enjoy.

Directly below the deck, she caught a glimpse of the enormous in-ground swimming pool surrounded by concrete, patterned and colored to resemble stone. She also saw a large area next to the pool with a roof shading it. Inside she only saw an outdoor grill and she suspected a complete outdoor kitchen accompanied it. Still somewhat overwhelmed she turned to re-examine the master bedroom.

Despite Armstrong's explanation, Stephanie couldn't comprehend how or why someone would choose to sleep in the same room with such musty-smelling furnishings. She wasn't a lover of antiques and found the ancient, nauseating smells of the room almost overpowering. She suspected it would take a great deal of work to remove the foul stench from the room forever. She imagined opening the windows to let in the fresh spring air, tearing off the wallpaper, and ripping up the carpeting. She then would have to scrub the walls and floors, but she was determined to make this room as different from how it now appeared as possible.

In the far corner of the room, she noticed a large full-length mirror surrounded by a heavy wooden frame and for some reason, she felt drawn to it.

"That mirror looks very old," she said. "Is that one of the original pieces from the house as well?"

"Oh, yes," Armstrong replied, "that mirror, as well as all of the other pieces you will find in this room, are original to the home. Your great-grandparents purchased it when they built the farmhouse. It was handmade by a local craftsman at that time. It's almost one hundred years old. I think there's something very special about knowing when you look into it, you're looking into the very same glass your ancestors looked into so many years ago."

Stephanie too found herself awestruck. Such an idea had never occurred to her before. This mirror was a part of history and not just history but her family's history. Her great-grandmother and great-grandfather, the two people from the portrait in the living room had actually stood in front of that same mirror almost a century earlier and looked into it just as she was doing now. Once again, she felt a slight pang of recognition.

Just then Stephanie heard a high-pitched keening sound coming from behind her, a sound she immediately recognized as coming from little Sammy. He always made that particular sound when he was about to cry. But this time the noise was much stranger in tone than she had ever heard him utter before. She turned and saw Jason holding

Sammy looking at the boy confused and uncertain. The child was staring intently at the mirror with his mouth agape his eyes rimmed with tears and a look of utter horror on his tiny face. Reacting quickly, Stephanie hurried to Jason, grabbed Sammy from his perplexed father and held him tightly against her chest as she carried him from the room.

Jason followed quickly as did the other children and the lawyer. "Is the boy all right?" Armstrong asked.

"Yes. I'm sure he's ok at least I think so," Jason said a bit overwhelmed by the incident. "I think he might have been weirded out by the room, by the dark colors, and by the funky smells. He's very perceptive. He always seems to notice things older kids or adults seem to pay little attention to."

Armstrong suddenly realized he might have a problem with the little boy. He pretended to be unfazed by the child's outburst, however, and said with a tone of understanding, "Yes, I know exactly what you mean. I have several grand-children and a few of them have quite vivid imaginations and tend to interpret things somewhat differently than we adults do. Things we tend to ignore or take for granted can suddenly appear quite frightening to a young, sensitive mind."

Sammy buried his head in his mother's shoulder whim-pering and stayed in that position until he heard the door to the bedroom close behind them. Then he slowly began to look about the brightly lit hallway and the terror faded from his young face.

Although he was too young to comprehend exactly what he had seen in the mirror Sammy knew it was not a good thing. At first, he had seen his mommy looking out at him. Then he knew the lady in the glass wasn't his mommy but a lady who looked like his mommy. She was wearing an old lady dress as he saw in the big picture downstairs. But the lady was not an old lady; she was a young lady like his mommy, and she was very pretty like his mommy.

Then she stopped being pretty. The lady's eyes got big and scary like she was mad at Sammy. Sammy didn't know why she was mad at him. He wasn't being a bad boy. He was being a good boy. The big scary eyes looked right at Sammy. It made Sammy think the lady wanted him to know she could see him. Then she started to get all yucky and her skin changed to a bad color and her face got really skinny. Sammy thought of the bony faces he sometimes saw on kids' t-shirts. Sammy knew his brother had a shirt with a bony face on it. He called it a skulk or something.

The lady's face had changed to a bony skulk face and her teeth got black and some of them even fell out. At first, it didn't scare Sammy too much, but then her big eyes got bigger and blew up like a balloon. Sammy liked balloons, but he didn't like the mirror lady's balloon eyes. He felt like crying when they got big because he knew what happened when balloons got too big. Balloons that got too big popped. When balloons popped, they scared him. He didn't want to see the balloon eyes get too big and pop.

Then he started to think about something else. He thought of what bad things might come out if the ugly balloon eyes popped. He thought for some reason maybe yucky bugs might live in those ugly balloon eyes. Sammy thought he could see all kinds of yucky wormy bugs moving inside of the big balloon eyes. He didn't want to see any yucky bugs or maybe even worms come out of the scary balloon eyes. He started to cry so Mommy would take him away from the stinky room and the big glass and the bad lady with the bony skulk face and balloon-popping-buggy-eyes.

When Sammy heard the door close, he looked around and saw he was back in the nice hall and there was no more scary glass or a bony skulk-face lady with buggy balloon eyes. He saw his daddy and brother and sister and that fat man they called "Armsong." The bad things were gone, and he started feeling much better right away.

"Are you all right now, baby?" Stephanie asked Sammy. "All that bad stuff is gone now. Don't worry Honey. Mommy won't let anything happen to you."

Sammy was always ok when his Mommy hugged him. He seemed to lose all of his sad and scary feelings and smiled saying, "I ok Mommy." But he still held more tightly than normal to his mother's neck as she moved aside to let the fat man called "Armsong" pass. Sammy didn't like the fat man. He didn't know why but the fat man made him not feel so good in his tummy.

"Well, then," the lawyer began, "now that everything appears to be all back to normal let's go downstairs and look at the rest of the house."

12

THE REMAINDER OF the tour of the farmhouse was, for the most part, uneventful although the couple did find themselves giving another furtive glance at the strange painting of Stephanie's two great-grandparents as they passed by the formal living room. And each time they looked at the portrait those strange eyes seemed to follow their every move.

Even though they hadn't discussed it yet, both Stephanie and Jason had made up their minds the spooky painting would quickly find its way along with the mirror up into the attic where they'd remain covered with tarps until the couple could determine what best to do with them. They also assumed when the remodeled the master bedroom all of the ugly old furnishings would wind up either in the trash or would be sold to an antique dealer. Although Washburn's will had specified the house or land couldn't be sold Stephanie figured she'd be able to get rid of those furnishings she didn't want. She supposed she should clarify that with the lawyer but decided a little bit of ignorance, in this case, would be to her benefit.

Stephanie knew exactly which painting she would use to replace the horrible portrait in the living room. Shortly after she and Jason were married, they had attended a charity art auction and had purchased an original oil painting by a world-renowned Italian artist named Guido Borelli. It was a bit of an extravagance for them as they really didn't have the spare cash for such a purchase. But Stephanie had fallen in love with the work and the proceeds from the sale went to help the charity as well.

Although not really an art enthusiast Jason agreed with the purchase not only because he was impressed with the painting, but also because he wanted to make Stephanie happy. He was quite fascinated with the various Italian scenes Borelli rendered in his paintings. Since that time the couple had become great fans of the artist's work and had acquired several of Borelli's signed prints. They had also gotten to know him personally through email correspondence. They had attended several of his art shows and met with him whenever possible when he toured the United States.

Stephanie had never felt there had been an appropriate location for her favorite Borelli piece in their small townhouse. The painting was actually the only original work of art she had ever owned and now she believed she could proudly display it in a place of honor. Satisfied with her decision she followed the group as they progressed through the rest of the house.

They were all once again pleasantly surprised by both the size and modern design of the eat-in kitchen not to mention the adjacent formal dining room. Every appliance was state-of-the-art and although the space was quite large it was designed with functionality and efficiency in mind. The dining room was equally large and would do a good job of accommodating their needs.

Stephanie was happy when Armstrong mentioned the door next to the hall entrance of the kitchen which he said led to a first-floor laundry. When she opened the door and saw the size of the area, she was even more pleasantly surprised. In addition to having a large capacity washer and dryer it also had plenty of cabinet space and shelves as well as a countertop and double-bowl utility sink. On the left side of the room near the ceiling, she also noticed a laundry shoot which would permit her kids to drop down their clothing saving her the trouble of having to carry everything in baskets down the stairs.

"The laundry shoot is in the hall just outside the master bedroom," the lawyer said. "I'm sorry. I forgot to point that out when we were upstairs. You may have already noticed it. And directly inside the master bedroom off to the left is a small powered dumbwaiter in a closet. This will come in handy so you don't have to carry all the clean laundry up the stairs when it is finished. You can use it for pretty much anything you can think of, but it does have something of a weight limit so it's not safe for human transport. I wouldn't recommend letting the children ride in it. It is equipped with an electronic safety locking device and a code."

They walked toward the back of the kitchen as Armstrong opened the rear door of the house revealing a second expansive deck leading out and terracing down to the pattern concrete patio surrounding the luxurious in-ground pool. Stephanie realized it was likely the pool had only been recently opened probably in preparation for their visit as the water glistened with crystal-like clarity in the afternoon sunlight.

"Can we go in the pool? Can we, Mom?" Cindy asked, knowing they hadn't come prepared for swimming. In addition, May in Schuylkill County wasn't quite as warm as it was fifty miles further south and most of the time only the most daring swimmers chose to hit the water before the end of May or early June.

"Not today, honey," Stephanie said. "We have a lot of business to take care of first and don't forget about our trip to the coal mine later today."

Cindy replied with disappointment, "Yeah. You're right. I guess we can't do everything in one day. But boy, oh boy does that pool look good." Stephanie knew Cindy would want to use the pool as much as possible.

"Don't worry, Cindy," Jason said. "We own this house now so soon we'll be able to swim in this pool anytime we want to." Jason looked over at Stephanie and they knew even without her saying they were both in agreement about the direction their future would be taking.

"What's that over there?" Jeremy asked pointing off to a feature located in the shadows just below a part of the upper deck. It circled out around the far left side of the pool.

"Oh my gosh!" Jason exclaimed in surprise. "It's a . . . I believe it's called a grotto."

A twelve-foot high man-made stone feature resembling a mountain stood before them. Because it was positioned under the master bedroom deck, they hadn't been able to see it from upstairs. From the top, a continuous waterfall flowed down along its surface ending in a large pool at its base. The pool was surrounded with assorted sizes of artificial stones with a small opening at the front to allow access.

Jason walked over to the opening in the rocks and look down into the water in amazement. Although it was disguised to create the image of a natural setting by the man-made stone the pool itself was actually an enormous Jacuzzi hot tub with built-in lights and what looked like dozens of jets. Looking closer Jason saw there were also speakers present in some of the simulated rocks for enjoying music while relaxing.

It was unbelievable. Jason stood looking at the feature in amazement. "Wow. Now I'm the one who wants to get in the pool." He was already trying to figure out how he and Stephanie could find time to sneak away and be alone in the grotto. He knew it would be tough if not impossible with three kids, but he was determined to take full advantage of the pool for personal romantic purposes sometime.

"And look at this," Stephanie said pointing. Off to the right of the deck, down along the side of the pool, was a complete stainless steel outdoor kitchen under a gable-style roof.

"This outdoor kitchen looks like it has more features than our indoor kitchen back home has." She walked over toward it. "And look. Besides the gas grill and the refrigerator, there's a regular oven, a convection oven, a microwave and . . . Holy cow! Look at the brick pizza oven, for God's sake. This is amazing!"

Jason walked over to check out the area not really wanting to leave the grotto or the fantasy he was imagining. But as he approached the area, he was glad he had. "And look at that!" he said. "It's a full wet-bar and it's stocked with all kinds of goodies as well. Wow!" Along the decorative brick wall behind the bar hung a long, tall mirror with several shelves each of which was lined with many of the couple's favorite brands of liquor.

"I'm just speechless," Jason explained. Stephanie just stood shaking her head in amazement. He said, "This is all so unreal. It's almost too good to be true."

The lawyer replied, "But true it is. And it's all yours; along with the forty acres and the outbuildings."

"Right," Jason said, the realization hitting him. "We haven't seen the outbuildings yet. What are they like?"

"Let's go take a look," Armstrong replied. "There are four of them spread around the property. Two are simply storage sheds or places to keep things you may need when you are working out away from the house. But the other two of them are a bit more special. Let's all head over to the large barn over there in the distance beyond the pool. That barn is one of the buildings I need to show you. I think you'll like what you see there."

The barn was a two-story structure. When they walked through the small man-sized access door within the double barn door Armstrong flipped on a light switch illuminating the massive two-story structure with a flood of bright overhead lighting.

Where there was probably once a dirt floor there was now a concrete slab covered with a similar Epoxy membrane to the one they had seen in the garage. And sitting on the floor in the distance was a top-of-the-line John Deere garden tractor with a large mowing deck as well as both a front loader and backhoe attachment sitting off to the side.

But the truly amazing thing, which completely flabbergasted Jason, was the sight of a brand-new cherry-red Ford F-150 pickup truck. It was the most gorgeous vehicle Jason had ever seen. Then Jason saw a large chrome snowplow sitting against the sidewall. The device could easily be mounted to the front of the truck as necessary.

Armstrong said, "I see you noticed your new toys, Jason. Mr. Washburn wanted to make sure he had everything he would need to keep the driveway clean and he also wanted to have a powerful enough vehicle to get around in the winter weather. You will, of course, have the option of doing your own snow plowing if you would like or I can recommend the name of a local handyman who formerly did some snow removal for Mr. Washburn. He also maintained the landscaping and other yard work as well. His rate is cheap but as you can see you have everything to do the work yourself if you want."

Then the apprehension struck Jason of exactly how much work might be involved in maintaining a property of this size. He wasn't one to avoid hard work and he was young and strong. But when he thought about it the maintenance of such a large estate did seem a bit overwhelming. He recalled how during the past six months or so things had been so stressful and hectic at work he scarcely had time to think when he got home at night. His present townhouse was essentially maintenance free and for that, he had been grateful.

He also assumed once he accepted his promotion with its many new responsibilities, things would get even busier for him. He decided it might be a good idea to have someone standing by to help if needed. With the money they got from the estate as well as his pay raise, he was certain he could afford the occasional use of the handyman's services.

He wasn't the only one whose responsibilities would increase with ownership of the property. Stephanie's would as well, perhaps even more so than his own. His goal had been for Stephanie to be able to have the time and energy to devote to her book writing. However, he knew if she were bogged down with the tasks of taking care of the kids as well as cleaning and maintaining such an enormous house that goal might never be realized.

"Yes," Jason replied without any further thought, "I think I might want to have that gentleman's name." Then he surprised himself by asking, "Also, do you know of anyone you can recommend who is available maybe one or two days a week or so to help Stephanie take care of the house?"

He looked over and winked at Stephanie who was staring at him like he had completely lost his mind. She had never considered the idea of hiring a cleaning lady before. It wasn't that she was opposed to such an idea, but it was simply not something they could have ever considered being able to afford before. The awareness of their newfound financial status hit home with her as well and she too understood they actually could afford what was once considered an unimaginable luxury.

"Well, yes, in fact, I do," the lawyer replied. "The handyman is a gentleman named Wilbur Franks. He is in his midfifties but still in very good shape and quite skilled, not only with yard work but also with plumbing, electrical and general contracting needs. His wife Constance cleans houses for a number of prominent local folks and I'm certain she'd be happy to help you both out as well. I'll email their contact information to this you evening. And if you'd like I can take the liberty of contacting them ahead of time on your behalf."

"Excellent," Jason replied suddenly catching himself off guard. He was oddly surprised at how quickly he was adapting to their new lifestyle. He almost had to laugh to himself for the way he had just said "excellent," as if hiring domestic help was common to him something he had done all of his life. He stifled a chuckle.

As the group walked from the barn Jason felt a pang of uncertainty for the first time wondering what potentially negative effects this new lifestyle might have on him and Stephanie not to mention on their kids. Both Jeremy and Cindy were old enough to still remember what it was like to grow up in a household with constant financial struggles and might not be affected to any great degree, but Sammy was young. He would only remember this new life. He'd grow up knowing nothing but affluence.

He made a mental note to be sure to speak to Stephanie about the subject and to try to do their best not only to keep themselves grounded but also to not let their newfound prosperity affect their children negatively. He didn't want Sammy to become some snobby, obnoxious, heartless teenager someday. Jason had no idea if they could be successful at handling such a responsibility, but he was determined to do his best.

Stephanie interrupted Jason's train of thought as he heard her ask the lawyer, "What's that strangely-shaped building over there?" She pointed to the hexagonal outbuilding which she had originally spotted from the master bedroom window. Again, she felt strangely drawn to the structure.

"Oh. That building is the spa," the lawyer said nonchalantly.

"The spa?" Stephanie questioned looking over at Jason quizzically.

Jason said, "Why would this place need a spa? It has an atrium, several decks, a pool, a hot tub, and a bar. It has plenty of places to chill. I'd think the last thing it would need was a spa."

"You're probably right, Jason," Armstrong replied, "but Mr. Washburn liked his privacy and even though he lived here alone and could find plenty of places to unwind he still wanted to have a place far from the house where he could go and be totally isolated. As it turned out, the building in its original hexagonal shape suited his needs perfectly. No one has any clue why it was built this way. And even more unusual as far as we could determine from its structure and from historical records the original purpose for the building may have been very similar to its current purpose."

Stephanie asked, "Do you mean to say it was originally built as a spa by my great-grandparents?"

"Well yes, sort of," the lawyer tried to explain. "I'm not sure, but I don't believe they referred to such places as spas back in the early 1900s. It wasn't uncommon for people of great financial means to have places where they could go during the cold months to relax in large tubs of hot water basking in the steam next to a hot fireplace. Also, keep in mind back when these outbuildings were originally constructed there was only a farmhouse. There was no atrium or swimming pool, deck or outdoor hot tub. That building would have been the only place the master of the house had to get away to relax in private."

"Wow," Jason said, "I never thought about that."

The lawyer replied, "Well, then let's head over to the spa. As it turns out that was the other outbuilding, I wanted to make sure you had the opportunity to see during our short visit today."

Then Armstrong suddenly recalled how the little boy Sammy had reacted to the mirror in Washburn's bedroom. What if he was truly as sensitive as Stephanie had suggested? Taking the young child into the building where such unspeakable horror had occurred would likely have severely negative results for Washburn's plans. The last thing Armstrong needed was for the little brat to get all weird on him again and start bawling. He suspected whatever so-called sensitivity the kid possessed would likely go off the charts in the spa.

So he offered an alternative suggestion. "Why don't you let the kids run around outside for a while? You know let them get some fresh air while I show you and Jason the spa."

"I don't know," Stephanie said uncertainly. "What about the swimming pool? I don't want them going near the pool." The group was far from the pool practically near the back of the property, but Stephanie was still concerned.

Jason believed Stephanie was always a bit overprotective of the kids and especially of Sammy perhaps because he was the baby or perhaps because he was likely the last baby she'd ever have. He also thought the lawyer was right and it might be good for the three kids to walk around a bit and have a little freedom. He asked the kids, "Jeremy? Cindy? If we let you take Sammy and play over there in the field for a while will you promise to stay over there and not go back near the house? Stay away from the pool. Do you understand?"

He had already determined before they moved into the house he'd have a fence installed around the pool and grotto area to make sure Sammy couldn't accidentally wander too close. So today would be the only time they'd have to be concerned about it.

Stephanie looked at Jason uncertainly. He winked at her again and she reluctantly set Sammy down and told him. "Sammy, you take Jeremy's hand and don't let go of it and do whatever he tells you to do, all right?"

"Germie hand," Sammy said incorrectly pronouncing Jeremy's name as he always did.

"And Jeremy, you're the big brother so you're in charge. We'll keep the door to that building over there open so we can hear you," Stephanie instructed. "If Sammy gets away from you or if you see something you don't like even for a second just yell to us and we will come right out. Ok?"

"Ok, Mom," Jeremy replied. He was visibly proud of having big brother responsibility. "Don't worry, we'll be fine."

Cindy said, "Yeah, Mom. Don't worry. I'll help watch the little stinker too."

"All right then," Stephanie said as the three headed off into the meadow a short distance from the spa each holding one of Sammy's hands. Whether she liked it or not her kids were growing up.

"Well then let's go inside," the lawyer suggested as he took them in to show them the very place where Emerson Washburn and butchered himself. However, he was quite confident no specters would appear until the time was right. The ghosts had a specific future in store for the Wright family and Armstrong was certain things were not likely to end well for them.

13

"**I KNOW I MUST** sound like a broken record," Jason insisted as he looked about the interior of the spa, "but this place is simply amazing. Just when I think I've seen everything we walk through another door and discover something even more incredible."

"Yes, it truly is," Armstrong replied.

They were walking around the interior of the gorgeous hexagonal-shaped building admiring the craftsmanship of the unique structure. At the center of the space, the large cast iron claw-foot bathtub stood like a porcelain-encased sentry, its lustrous white finish glimmering in the sunlight streaming through the small windows up high near the ceiling.

"You might be interested to know that tub is original to this room," the lawyer said. "In its day, it was considered the latest thing in bathing comfort. However back then it was just a solid piece of molded cast iron with no faucet or handles. During the renovation, we sent it out to a company specializing in tub restorations and not only had it refinished but also added the appropriate modern plumbing fixtures. Back in the old days any water to be used for bathing had to be carried in buckets from a nearby well and then heated in the fireplace over there."

Stephanie startled at the mention of a well. 'The well," she thought to herself. "What is it about a well that has me so off balance?" She didn't know why the mere mention of a well on the property should make her feel so uncomfortable, but it did. She asked the lawyer, "You mentioned a well Mason. Do you know is there still a well somewhere on the property?"

"Yes, as a matter of fact, there is," Armstrong replied, "but not the type of well I was talking about. You see, the farmhouse is supplied with water via an underground well and a pump typically found in almost all rural homes."

"I'm aware of that type of well," she explained. "What I was referring to was the old style wells you know, the open top wells like you often see in books where you have to put in a bucket on a rope and pull up your water."

"Oh, I see," the lawyer said. "Yes, such a well did exist on this property at one time."

Stephanie suddenly had a mental image of the well a circular stone structure perhaps four feet tall made of random sized fieldstones held roughly together with a type of cement or mortar. The appearance of the wall was very rough and almost primitive in nature. There was no tall wooden structure or roof constructed overtop of the well like those she had seen depicted in pictures. There was no cylindrical cross member with a rope, crank handle or bucket to function as a pulley for retrieving water either. This was simply a stone wall, surrounding a hole in the ground.

She was suddenly filled with the understanding that the well had existed on the property long before her grandparents had every purchased it and built their home. She had visions of many other homes over many other centuries built on the land then falling to ruin or being destroyed by fire or other natural calamities only to be replaced by yet another building. And all during that time, since the beginning, whenever that happened to be the well had been here.

The unexpected awareness of the well caused Stephanie extreme uneasiness. At first, she assumed it was because as a concerned mother she worried her young child falling to his death. But there was more to her concern than just safety. She didn't understand why she seemed to know about the age of the well and had no idea why the fact the well had existed for so many centuries bothered her. After all, it was just an old well. Of course, it was built to last and if constructed properly might it not be expected to last for many hundreds of years?

What Stephanie didn't know was the reason the picture of the well was so clear in her mind and the reason for her sudden awareness was that she had actually seen the well before. The well was the same image she had seen in her dreams the previous night.

"You said the well did exist at one time. Is it still here?" Stephanie asked the lawyer with obvious concern. "I mean is it still on the property somewhere? I wouldn't want such a potentially dangerous thing around—you know—not with my young children."

Armstrong assured her, "Not to worry, Stephanie. County records show the well was filled in with dirt and stone more than fifty years ago. In fact, I'd be hard-pressed to even begin to try to find the location of where it originally stood. Apparently, the well had been on the property for several centuries. You see your great-grandparents were not the first to build on this land."

"Yes, I know," Stephanie said without thinking.

The lawyer got a startled look and asked with surprise, "You know? I don't understand. What do you mean you know?"

Stephanie realized her mistake and saw Armstrong looking at her with concern. Jason too was looking at her strangely. The truth was she honestly didn't know anything about the property. She thought at first she had just experienced some type of epiphany but it was likely more imagination that revelation.

"No. I don't mean I actually know," she corrected. "What I meant is I surmised how such a thing could be possible."

Feeling more at ease the lawyer said. "Well, you won't have to worry about your kids. I assure you this place is about as safe as you can get."

Stephanie said changing the subject, "That fireplace certainly is quite beautiful."

The lawyer continued, "Yes, I must agree. During the restoration we had it equipped to handle either wood or natural gas. However, the fireplace is simply here for the ambiance. The entire building is well-insulated, and the heat is controlled by a thermostat mounted over there along that wall." He pointed to the device.

As Stephanie and Jason's attention was diverted to the thermostat Armstrong found himself involuntarily looking over at the sparkling bathtub. Prior to the Wright family's visit, Armstrong had made sure to remove any evidence of Washburn's suicide. He doubted even a team of forensic investigators could find any trace evidence of the horror which had occurred there. Armstrong had actually hired both the aforementioned handyman Wilbur Franks and his wife Constance to do the cleanup.

Armstrong was quite certain Franks and his wife could be trusted to keep their mouths shut about the messy situation for as long as he needed them to. That was one of the reasons he had recommended the couple. He was formulating a plan for the Franks to be his eyes and ears on the property so he could stay informed on their daily lives.

The lawyer and Wilbur Franks had a history a very convenient history. In addition to being people he occasionally hired for odd jobs, the Franks were also Armstrong's clients. Several years earlier Wilbur Franks had been charged with a minor drunk and disorderly infraction after an evening of too much revelry and found himself spending the night in one of the two cells in the Ashton jail. Armstrong had smoothed things over with Chief of Police Max Seiler and had managed to get Franks off with just a slap on the wrist. Although extremely grateful, Franks didn't have the money to pay Armstrong for his services, so the lawyer made sure he took advantage of this unpaid debt whenever he found it convenient. Yes, Armstrong knew the Franks would both stay quiet and would be sure to keep him informed as necessary.

He prided himself on how as a lawyer he had been able to outwit virtually every opponent he encountered by anticipating the next several moves they would most likely make. Now, although unsure he was praying his abilities wouldn't fail him when trying to outmaneuver the dead. He could only hope his skills were good enough to get himself out from under the thumb of the vile specter.

As Stephanie looked about the inside of the spa, she observed the various wall-size mirrors. Several times she felt as if someone was watching her, but when she turned in that particular direction, she'd see only her reflection and sometimes that of Armstrong or Jason. It was creepy. She wasn't exactly sure what she might do to the interior decor of the building, but she was certain the mirrors would have to go.

Jason noticed Stephanie looking strangely at the mirrors and asked her, "What do you think of all these mirrors, Steph? Kind of kinky don't you think?" He gave her a knowing wink. She knew as always Jason was thinking with the wrong head. Unfortunately, Jason was going to have to give up this particular fantasy because as far as she was concerned the mirrors were history.

"If I'm ever going to come out here for a bath, I'm going to have to lose a few pounds and tone up a bit," Stephanie joked hoping to discourage her husband as she looked around at the bothersome mirrors.

The lawyer interjected, "Nonsense, Stephanie. Don't be so hard on yourself. Just imagine what an old fat fossil like me would look like standing here in my altogether." Then he hesitated for a moment, feigned embarrassment, chuckled and said, "On second thought, you might not want to do that." They all laughed at Armstrong's self-deprecating comment and whatever tension Stephanie was feeling began to disappear.

Stephanie genuinely liked Armstrong. The lawyer seemed so friendly and easygoing. She noticed how Jason even seemed to be warming up somewhat to the man which was unusual for her husband as he was not a fan of lawyers in general.

However, H. Mason Armstrong was a skilled manipulator and was equally proficient at hiding his treachery. Neither Stephanie nor even Jason had been able to see the truth. However, Sammy had seen it. The little boy with his special intuition had sensed something wasn't right with the lawyer. But he, of course, was too young to understand or to explain.

As they continued to walk around and study the room, they suddenly heard a frantic cry coming from outside in the meadow. It was Jeremy shouting. "Mom! Dad! Come out here. Hurry!"

The couple raced immediately from the spa. Stephanie looked instinctively in the direction of the meadow while Jason looked back toward the swimming pool. They were expecting to find one of the kids injured or worse but were surprised to see the three children standing in front of a cluster of low bushes along a wooded area near the back of the property hand in hand their backs to the couple resembling three cutout dolls joined in a line.

By the time Jason and Stephanie reached their children, they were both out of breath. Being overweight and dangerously out-of-shape, Armstrong had chosen to stay behind and was standing on the walkway outside of the spa. He shielded his eyes from the sun trying to see what was happening.

The three kids were staring out into a small area of underbrush just outside of the woods. None of them appeared to be injured or in any danger. Jeremy and Cindy stood as if transfixed a mixture of fear and disgust visible on their faces. Sammy, however, wore a completely different expression than the other two children. Although he too was staring into space, he didn't look frightened or upset. He looked at peace. It was as if he was seeing something completely different than they were.

Jason looked at Sammy and saw the boy's slightly smiling lips moving slowly. Although he couldn't hear what if anything the boy might be saying, he could almost read his lips. Sammy seemed to be repeating something; a word starting with the letter "b." Jason raced through a list of b-words that he recalled Sammy knew. "Big," "boy," "bad," and a few others came to mind, but he couldn't be sure. Regardless, Jason couldn't comprehend why Sammy looked so happy while Jeremy and Cindy looked so horrified.

"Jeremy! What's wrong?" Stephanie demanded, breaking Jason's concentration. He realized he had temporarily been in a bit of a trance himself trying to understand what was going on with Sammy. He was usually great in emergencies but this time he had dropped the ball.

"Ball?" he thought for a moment. "Was Sammy saying ball?" Jason was thankful Stephanie was too preoccupied with the kids to notice his misstep or he might have found himself in hot water with his normally understanding wife.

Stephanie scolded, "We said to call us if you had trouble."

Jeremy just lifted his trembling free hand still holding Sammy's with the other and shakily pointed toward the woods not taking his eyes off the grassy area. "There's something horrible out there, Dad. It's ugly and all bones like a skeleton. And there are flies, millions of flies around it."

Cindy stood stock-still holding Sammy's other hand her eyes pleading for Jason to do something. Sammy remained smiling wearing his beatific expression, his lips repeating the unknown b-word. "Bones?" Jason wondered silently. "Could Sammy be saying bones? Did he know the word bones? And, if so, why the hell would he look so happy?"

Putting the thought aside Jason climbed up into the tall grass and pushed aside some of the bushes not certain what he might find hiding behind them.

14

AS JASON MADE his way into the area, he feared he might find some sick or injured woodland creature frothing and snarling in the underbrush, mad with disease and just waiting to bite him. This thought slowed him down somewhat making him more careful than he originally had planned.

"What do you see?" Stephanie called impatiently wondering how the kids had been able to see whatever it was from where they stood, yet Jason had to move aside tall grass to try to find it. Then she realized from the children's low vantage point they were likely to be able to see beneath the same clumps of tall grass which blocked Jason's view and forced him to move them aside.

"Just give me a second!" Jason said with growing frustration. He knew he was being overly cautious and perhaps a bit short with Stephanie, but he couldn't get the mental picture of the salivating rabid creature from his mind.

Much to his relief what he found were the skeletal remains of what was once a deer, perhaps only a young fawn. The carcass was no bigger than a large dog and for a moment Jason thought it might actually be a dog. But when he saw its hooves and the white spots present on what little fur remained on its decaying form, he confirmed it was a fawn. The poor creature had been practically picked clean by scavengers and was rapidly being transformed into a maggot condominium.

The stink from the rotting animal was appalling. And the continuous buzzing sounds from the swarm of insects surrounding the remains was hypnotic. So much so Jason found himself involuntarily losing touch with reality. Within the space of less than a few seconds while Stephanie waited to see what Jason had found something unimaginable happened to him.

It was as if he was mentally transported to another plane of existence where reality seemed to move at a rate thousands of time faster than in his own world. He was aware of Stephanie and the kids standing still, unmoving as if frozen in place. He could see the hundreds of flies hanging virtually motionless in the air about him. He felt as if he was inside of a bubble in an inconceivable reality. Seconds seemed to crawl by in this place while hundreds of thoughts simultaneously raced through Jason's mind.

The carcass of the dead deer appeared to be staring up directly at Jason through its blackened hollow eye sockets the tasty morsels long gone, obviously the meal of some creature. Staring back into the hideous empty openings, Jason thought, "The eyes. Why do they always take the eyes first?"

He began to feel the world around him spinning sensing an uncomfortable tightening in his chest. He feared he might pass out and drop face first into the putrid carnage or maybe he'd simply drop dead on the spot. For the briefest of moments, Jason thought death might have come for him and was mocking him through the eye sockets.

Ants and other bugs were stopped in their tracks where they had formerly been busy cleaning what residual skin there was off the bones as well. Through his mental haze, Jason could see a pinkish collection of organs inside the torso of the creature. He wondered why those particular organs were still there. He would have suspected they too, might have been the first to go.

The stench of death and decay was thick and soupy in the air around the skeleton. Just when he thought he could take no more Jason felt the fog which had enshrouded his mind begin to lift and he sensed as if time was once again returning to normal. Through the renewed buzzing of insects, he heard Stephanie call to him.

"Jason? Honey, are you all right?"

Jason had no understanding of what had just happened to him. It seemed to as if several hours had passed but only a few seconds and gone by. Slowly coming back to reality, he turned and looked over his shoulders and said to his wife, "Yeah, um, yes, yes, I'm fine. This is just a bit upsetting, that's all."

He noticed Sammy was still staring off into the distance and wearing that strange smile. Jason wanted to have the boy taken as far away from this area as possible. He said with great effort, "Honey, why don't you take the kids to the house. I'll be there in a minute or so."

"What is it?" she asked with noticeable concern.

"Nothing. Nothing really," he said. "Just a small deer; a fawn I think. It looks like it's been lying here for quite a while." He was making a disgusted face. "Just take them back by the house. I want to look around here a bit first."

Jason didn't turn again to look at his family because he suspected if he did, he'd see Jeremy and Cindy still wearing their looks of horror while Sammy smiled and stared off into space repeating the mysterious and illusive b-word.

Stephanie could tell what he had found had greatly upset him and she assumed he needed the minute to regain his composure. Jason liked animals and probably felt terrible about the dead fawn. She bent down and picked up Sammy and took Cindy's hand leading them both back toward the spa. Jeremy stood for a moment looking at Jason as if unsure of what he should do.

Jason sensed his son behind him and said, "Go ahead, Jeremy. Go on back with them too. I need you to take care of your sister and brother."

The boy hesitated for a moment not wanting to leave his father with the horrible dead thing. He also didn't like the strange look in his father's eyes. Nevertheless, he obediently turned and followed behind his stepmother and siblings. Yet as he walked away he ventured a look back at this father still uncomfortable with the strange way Jason stared down into the grass.

Jason was looking at the rotting carcass realizing an important aspect of their new rural lifestyle and that was dealing with nature on a daily basis up close and personal. He had been accustomed to either living in a town or in a subdivision. His daily routine took him from his house to his job then back to his house in the climate-controlled comfort of his car. The couple didn't go on camping trips or any other sort of outdoor activity. On those rare occasions when they did vacation, they stayed in the best hotels they could afford. Jason often joked how his idea of "roughing it" was staying in a hotel without in-room movies or a wireless internet connection. He turned slightly and looked out across the property, their property, and saw nothing but meadows, fields, and woods for as far as he could see. This vast amount of land was something else entirely.

"Oh, my Lord," he said aloud. "What have we gotten ourselves into? This place is huge!"

He was starting to doubt if he could take care of such a place even with the help of Armstrong's handyman. What was his name? Franks? William Franks or was it Wilbur? How much could one man help him? They might own a multi-million dollar property, but they weren't rich, not by any means. Two hundred and fifty thousand dollars cash wouldn't last very long if he tried to live the type of lifestyle such a lavish property suggested. And they couldn't sell the place even if they wanted to. He began to question if he was cut out for the daunting task ahead of him.

He also thought about other potential problems nature might send his way; rain, flooding, lightning, snow, ice and maybe high winds. He was certain any trees, downed in storms or any broken branches hanging limply would bother his sense of organization every bit as much as the dead animal did. How could he possibly hope to keep his land orderly when nature was free to wreak havoc on it at any time? Even if all of his waking hours could be dedicated to the property, he doubted he could hope to keep up with the problems nature could send his way. He could never possibly maintain his idea of order in such an environment.

He understood if he was going to survive and stay sane, he'd have to learn to deal with the chaos of nature. Then he questioned how property so vast could possibly be considered a just a farmette and not a full-fledged farm. He didn't want to attempt to imagine what a farm with several hundred acres or more might look like if their property had only forty.

Jason turned slowly, once more looking back toward the woods. He was going to have to ask the lawyer just how far their property extended beyond the meadow, how far into the woods was his responsibility. He was hoping it ended just behind where he stood so this clump of bushes and that the woods beyond were someone else's problem. But regardless of where his land ended dealing with it was going to be a major adjustment for him and his family to make.

15

JASON LOOKED DOWN into the weeds just a few feet ahead and noticed sunlight reflecting off something dull and gray jutting out of a clump of wild grass in front of the dead fawn. He hunkered down and pushed the grass aside trying to stay as far away from the repulsive remains as possible and was surprised to discover something he never expected to see. What had caught his eye in the reflective light were actually two small rectangular-shaped stone signs of some sort.

Then he realized they weren't signs but were small grave markers about eighteen inches tall, a foot wide and a few inches thick. The stones were lying flat on their backs having fallen over at some point.

Jason studied the tombstones more carefully. Near the center of the slightly arched tops of the stones, he saw two identical images carved inside a circle. They were angels or cherubs of some type, typically seen on grave markers of small children.

As he pushed aside more of the grass, he could see an inscription, barely legible just below the image on the weathered face of the first stone. It read, *Matthew James Livingston, June 12, 1916–December 19, 1922.* The second one said *Charles Edward Livingston July 2, 1918–December 19, 1922.*

"Livingston?" he said aloud and recalled the portrait of Stephanie's ancestors in the main house. "That was the name of Stephanie's great-grandparents."

Jason calculated the ages of the boys as he read the inscription once again. Since the boys had been so young at the time of their passing, Matthew six and Charles four, they must have had some terminal childhood disease. He knew the mortality rate for young children was high in the early part of the twentieth century. He thought about his own children especially Sammy and how lucky he was to have been born at a time when such deaths were few in this country. Then he reread the inscriptions and saw something he missed the first time. Both boys had died on the same day. He wondered what sort of tragedy could have occurred, perhaps a fire or some other similar disaster.

He looked down at the first stone once again and noticed another inscription just below the date. He hunkered down closer to get a better look at the writing, dusting the dirt from the front of the stone. The message was carved in a different font than the previous notation, one more calligraphic in nature. When he read the inscription, it bore the cryptic phrase, "Taken From Us Too Soon, By The Hand Of Evil." He looked closer at the second stone and saw it too bore the exact same inscription, "Taken From Us Too Soon, By The Hand Of Evil."

"What the Hell!" Jason exclaimed. He felt the need to put some space between himself and the ominous grave markers. He tried to shuffle backward away from the stones but because of his awkward position he stumbled and fell flat on his backside, catching himself with his hands. As he did so he felt something soft and cold beneath his right hand. Then he sensed something crawling between his fingers.

He looked down and saw his hand had sunken deep into the open cavity of the fawn's torso and into the pink gelatinous cluster of organs. He saw hundreds of white worm-like maggots crawling between his splayed fingers, their shiny flesh glistening in the afternoon sunlight.

"Oh, Jesus!" he cried out, struggling to his feet. He shook off as much of the vile gooey matter as was possible while trying desperately not to vomit. Stirring up the mass of entrails had caused a new wave of stench to rise up from the remains creating an invisible cloud of foul odor Jason swore he could taste. A swarm of insects flew up from the rotting carcass and encircled Jason's face as if he too, were a dead thing. He swatted at them with his clean hand careful to keep his filthy hand as far away as possible.

Not wanting to wipe the disgusting substance on his clothing he looked around for some large leaves or perhaps a clump of grass, anything he could use to clean himself. As he struggled to wipe himself clean in the tall grass, he inadvertently uncovered a few other headstones. He could see they were quite old as well, much older than the first two he had found but he didn't take the time to examine them or read their inscriptions. He realized this wasn't just some random cluster of weeds, but he was in a family plot, a small private cemetery.

When his right hand appeared to be as clean as he could get it, he walked out of the grassy area and headed back toward the spa where Stephanie, Armstrong, and the kids waited. He held his right hand away from his body not wanting to get it any closer to him than necessary. As he walked, he forced himself to regain his composure for the sake of the kids. He already knew he was going to have to do something about that graveyard situation before they moved in.

Jason recalled when he and the family would take week-end drives in rural Berks and Lancaster counties; they would see Amish and Mennonite farms with small fenced in family cemeteries. Stephanie had often commented on how it "grossed her out" to think about living a normal life while "all those dead people" were buried nearby. It didn't seem to matter if the people were deceased loved ones; to Stephanie, they were simply dead bodies. It wasn't that she was superstitious or would believe the property could be haunted by the souls of the departed. She just didn't like the idea of knowingly sharing her property with the dead. Jason decided he wouldn't mention his discovery to Stephanie unless he absolutely had to.

As he walked back toward his family he began to wonder. "What if there were no actual bodies buried in the cemetery? What if it was just a shrine?"

He was rationalizing. He was trying to convince himself there were no bodies buried in the tiny cemetery so it would make it easier for him to do what he realized he needed to do. He wondered if he would be able to sleep at night once he was finished.

Jason would make sure he visited the house alone during the move-in process and remove every one of the headstones. He had made up his mind he didn't want to deal with what he assumed would be the bureaucratic hassle of relocating any graves to a different location.

This wasn't just because of the red tape or the potential cost involved. He simply had no desire for Stephanie to even know the bodies had been there at all. Relocated or not, that mere fact might not sit well with her.

If he simply removed each of the headstones and destroyed them by smashing them into small pieces, he could easily dig a hole out along the back of the property and bury them. All he'd need was a shovel and a sledgehammer. He could even use the lawn tractor with its cart to help him. And when he was finished no one would be the wiser. He could even use the site as a dumping ground for yard waste thereby covering it with more layers of soil and debris. He especially liked that idea. The property was incredible, and he wanted his family to start this next chapter of their lives enjoying it as soon as possible. Jason was certain he had made the right decision.

"Are you ok?" Stephanie asked as Jason approached them near the spa building. "You look upset."

Jason replied as casually as he possibly could, "Uh, yeah, I'm fine. It's just, you know me. I'm not used to dealing with dead stuff and nature."

"Yes. I know how you are about stuff like that." Then she gave an involuntary shudder. "Me too I suppose." She wouldn't have liked to even stand on the same grassy area as the dead thing.

Then Sammy raised his hand and pointed back to toward the place where Jason had found the graves and stunned Jason by asking "Daddy see boys?"

Jason stood staring at his son uncomprehending. "Boys?" He wondered what boys Sammy was talking about; there were no boys back there. Did he really mean the two boys whose graves Jason had seen? Beads of sweat began to form on the back of Jason's neck and trickle down his back.

Stephanie said, "I have no idea what he's talking about. He's been smiling and talking about boys since we left that clearing. The only thing I can think of is being back there must have reminded him of some boys he must have seen somewhere some other time, maybe at the playground. I really don't know."

"Surely he couldn't have seen them," Jason thought to himself. "Surely, he couldn't have seen those long-dead boys."

The instant he had the thought Jason realized just how ridiculous it sounded. He was obviously on edge because of his discovery of the cemetery. No, Sammy hadn't seen any dead boys. In fact, he had most likely seen nothing. He simply had a very active imagination and often fantasized things that made sense to no one but him. Jason thought back to the day Sammy was looking into space and saying "doggie." There was no dog present; it was all his imagination, but to Sammy, it was as real as if the dog had actually been there.

Sammy, on the other hand, felt confused. He didn't know why his mommy or daddy or Germie or Dindy didn't see his new friends. Why didn't they ask the little boys to come and play? Sammy wanted the boys to come down from the grass to play but they wouldn't. They just stood smiling at him. So Sammy smiled back. He tried to call to them, but he didn't know their names. He kept saying "boys, boys, boys," but the boys just stood looking at him and smiling.

At first, they scared Sammy like that lady in the big glass in the house because they looked like they might be sad and looked a little sick. Their faces were white, their lips were blue and their eyes had dark rings around them. But then they smiled Sammy felt much better. The boys seemed nice. That lady in the big glass wasn't nice.

Sammy also didn't think the fat man "Armsong," was nice either. He looked back to see if the boys were still in the grass, but they were gone. Maybe some other time they'd come back and play with him.

Stephanie noticed Jason holding his right hand away from his body. "What's wrong with your hand? You seem to be holding it out weirdly. Did you get hurt?"

"No," Jason said feeling a bit weak and perplexed. "I, um, lost my footing back there and had to catch myself with my right hand. I figured with the dead deer and all the bugs and stuff I'd better keep it far away until I get a chance to wash it off."

Armstrong interjected, "Inside the spa near the tub, is a cabinet with all sorts of cleaning supplies and towels. In fact, I believe I saw an unused bar of soap on a stand near the tub when we were inside."

"That sounds good to me," Jason said glancing at the wristwatch. "Steph, why don't you, Mason, and the kids work your way back to the house? I'll be there in a minute and we can wrap this up for today. Mason has other business to attend to and we did promise the kids that coal mine tour."

The lawyer replied, "Yes that's probably a good idea. As soon as you're done, we can go out front and finish up."

Jason washed and dried his hands thoroughly using water as hot as he could stand. Steam billowed into the air surrounding him. Suddenly Jason felt like someone was watching him. He looked around the room seeing nothing but his own reflection in large mirrors as well as the rising cloud of steam. Perhaps the steam reflecting in the mirrors had created the illusion.

He finished his business and left the building, stopping once to look behind him as if expecting to see someone but he remained alone. Jason closed the door tightly behind him and headed to meet his family back at the main farmhouse. Back inside the spa, the surfaces of several of the mirrors rippled wildly as maniacal laughter echoed from deep within the glass walls.

16

"**IT'S OFFICIAL**," **STEPHANIE** said, her face beaming with an ear-to-ear smile as Jason walked into the kitchen where she, Armstrong, and the kids stood waiting. "Look. Mason gave me the keys to the house. It's all ours now." She held out her hand palm up to display the two sets of keys. Jason noticed each set was attached to a key ring with a gold fob emblazoned with a stylish "W" like the monogrammed towel he had used in the spa building.

Stephanie said, "He suggested we take a few days to let everything sink in and then start planning our next course of action. This is all so exciting. I feel a bit scatterbrained."

"That's to be expected," the lawyer said. "And remember, during the time you're away if there's absolutely anything you folks need from me don't hesitate to call me. That also goes for any time in the future as well. As I mentioned earlier, I hope you're satisfied with the job I've done so far and will consider using my services for all of your future legal needs."

"Um, yes," Jason responded a bit distantly. He was preoccupied still unable to get the distracting image of the family graveyard out of his mind. "I think we need some time to absorb everything that's happened in the past two days. I'm also sure there'll be many things I'll need to take care of at work as well. I think after the next week or so we should have a good plan in place."

He looked again at the keys in his wife's hands and inquired, "Are these the keys for the house as well as the rest of the outbuildings?"

"Actually," the lawyer explained. "All of the doors on the property, front back, side as well as all of the outbuildings are keyed exactly the same, so you only need a single key to get inside any of the buildings. The other keys on the rings are for the Ford pickup and the tractor in the barn. The four remote openers for the garage doors are in the top drawer of that cabinet over there." He pointed to one of the base cabinets along the wall. Jason walked over, opened the top drawer and saw the four garage openers.

The lawyer continued, "That reminds me. I should have pointed out each of the garage doors also has a keypad mounted to the side of the doorframe with which all use the same four-digit number combination, 1-2-3-4 to open them, but I recommend you change the combination."

"Thanks, Mason," Jason responded. "That's a good idea." As he looked at the lawyer, he thought he saw a momentary dark expression pass across the man's face. He couldn't put into words what it was about the look that didn't sit well with him. It might have been the way it had appeared and then disappeared so quickly as if the lawyer had inadvertently let down his guard. For a moment Jason thought he might have misinterpreted the look, but the expression had been so intense and gave him such an uneasy feeling deep down in the pit of his stomach, he was certain there was something to his suspicions.

And then Jason began to wonder if the set of keys Stephanie held were in fact, the only set. What if he'd made a copy? If the man did make his own set of keys then he wouldn't care one bit if the garage door opener combinations were changed.

Jason usually wasn't so mistrustful of people, but he would be the first to admit he didn't particularly care for lawyers. Armstrong hadn't really given Jason any reason to distrust him but when he combined the gut feeling he was experiencing with the strange look he thought he had seen pass over the lawyer's face he began to wonder if he might actually be correct.

Jason's thoughts drifted to wondering if Armstrong had stolen paintings or jewelry or other such items from the property and had already sold them. Jason had seen some paintings on the walls which even to his untrained eyes seemed to be quite valuable. He and Stephanie knew nothing about her uncle prior to his death so they had no idea about the extent of his possessions. It would make any thievery early on simple to hide.

And how could they ever know the true value of the estate or the extent of the lawyer's thievery? Since Washburn had apparently been a solitary type of man with no relatives, no friends and who had led a shady former life; it was unlikely even the best forensic accountant could accurately inventory his holdings and determine if anything was missing.

Jason didn't want to appear ungrateful to the lawyer and even felt a bit guilty about his suspicions especially since the man had been so helpful, but Jason now felt certain about his distrust. He made up his mind to find an area locksmith and have all the door locks changed. Maybe he was paranoid, but he needed to protect his family.

He had also noticed the property didn't have an alarm system. He had seen smoke alarms at strategic places around the house, but he didn't see any burglar alarm type system or control panel of any kind. He decided to broach the subject with the lawyer and see how he handled the question.

"Mason?" Jason asked pretending not to sound suspicious. "I couldn't help but notice there's no alarm system. Seems strange, especially when you consider the value of this property . . . and you mentioned Mr. Washburn had a bit of an unsavory past. I would suspect such a man might want some type of early warning system in place to protect himself."

"You're absolutely correct, Jason. And quite observant I might add," the lawyer replied. "Mr. Washburn didn't believe in security systems of any kind, especially those with cameras. He felt he had taken care of himself his entire life. He even hated the smoke and carbon dioxide alarms as well, but local building codes required them and there was nothing he could do to get around that."

"But even we have a security system in our little townhouse," Stephanie suggested, "and our entire house isn't worth as much as just the garage in this place."

The lawyer explained "Perhaps so, Stephanie. But you live in a much more highly populated area than here and with that also comes a higher crime rate."

"But still," Jason interrupted, "no security system? I just don't get it."

"Well, I guess you just had to know Mr. Washburn. He was set in his ways."

What Armstrong did know, however, was there was no need for a security system of any kind. The beings inhabiting the property kept the home safe from any unwanted intruders as was evident by the recent fiery demise of Mr. John "Jack" Moran.

The lawyer suggested, "I know of a local security firm I'm certain would be happy to install such a system for you. That is if you truly feel one's necessary."

Jason replied, "Thanks, but that won't be necessary. When we're ready, I'm sure we can take care of it ourselves." Jason decided he needed to cut the cord with the attorney as soon as possible and this was as good a place to start as any.

"As you wish," the lawyer said. Then he held out an arm directing the family toward the front hallway. "I have another appointment shortly, so I must be on my way. I know you folks will want to be heading into town for your mine tour as well."

"Thanks, Mason," Jason said, sounding as sincere as possible. "You've been a great help and we appreciate it. And thanks for the tickets too. But I think we want to wait here for a little bit longer and talk in private about a few things before we lock up and head out. If there's anything we need in the future, we'll contact you."

The lawyer could tell by the tone of Jason's voice he would likely never be hearing from the man again. It was apparent

Jason didn't trust him. Armstrong had done his legal duty and had carried out the demands of his evil tormentor as well. Although he feared for the Wright family, he now feared more for himself. He was concerned he might have exceeded his usefulness to the specter. He prayed Washburn would leave him in peace. But somehow, he didn't think that particular prayer would be answered.

17

H. **MASON ARMSTRONG** sat behind his massive oak desk as the sun began its slow descent over the western silt-covered mountainous horizon on that Sunday evening. The glorious spectacle was visible in all of its majestic amber and crimson splendor as he watched through his large office window.

He hadn't yet switched on any of the lights inside his office. The glow from his computer monitor reflected in his reading glasses as darkness began to engulf the room. He had been intently scouring the Internet nonstop since the afternoon of the previous day following his meeting with the Wright family. He had been searching for any shred of information to help him out of his unholy predicament. However, so far his search had proven to be fruitless as he simply couldn't find the answer he so desperately needed.

Throughout his entire career, Armstrong had lived by the philosophy that knowledge was power; the more he understood his enemy the easier it would be to defeat him. That way of thinking had never failed him in the courtroom, and he was certain it could only benefit him now.

The lawyer had been researching various occult and spiritual sites looking for information on ghosts, spirits, poltergeists, demons, zombies, and even other such evil mythical entities as vampires and werewolves but couldn't quite find a category in which to place Washburn.

Armstrong wondered if Washburn had actually become a ghost, a demon, or some strange hybrid. He had read simple ghosts or specters could do nothing to bring physical harm to living beings. Poltergeists on the other hand, when angered might be able to cause inanimate objects to move or maybe make things fly off shelves. He supposed if he found himself in the path of a flying plate or book he could possibly be harmed.

The lawyer noted how Washburn hadn't appeared to be corporal but ethereal. He began to wonder if there were such things as demon-ghost hybrids. It did make sense that Washburn might fit into such a category. The lawyer recounted how at first Washburn had appeared to Armstrong only in mirrors, but at their latest several encounters the creature had left those confines and had floated across the room, never making contact with things of this world.

Then he recalled how when the maggot-like insects had fallen to the floor they had shriveled up and disintegrated in a puff of vapor. He wondered if he somehow were able to get Washburn to touch something physical during one of his manifestations, the horrible specter might disappear? And what would happen if Armstrong reached out and tried to touch the creature himself?

If Washburn was in fact, some type of demonic ghost it might have powers Armstrong couldn't even imagine. Perhaps these specters might have the ability to temporarily inhabit others, take over their wills and cause them to harm themselves. He thought of both Washburn's suicide as well as that other man's death by fire. What if they had not actually killed themselves of their own accord?

If only he could learn how to drive these creatures back into their world of the damned. That was the very crux of his dilemma. He simply didn't know what the full extent of their power might be.

As he stared at the computer monitor, searching over another seemingly endless list of supernatural websites something caught his eye. He saw a link to a site which claimed to have knowledge about something called demonic ghosts.

"Demonic ghosts!" he said aloud. This was exactly what he had been thinking about only a few moments earlier. Perhaps that was the website he needed. After a bit of wary hesitation, he clicked the link.

Then Armstrong saw that this site, like virtually every other website he had investigated previously, was designed to look as creepy and sinister as possible with dark gray and black backgrounds and plenty of Gothic style fonts. And of course, the lettering was not only blood red in color, but it also was a font appearing to drip blood down the screen.

"Oh, boy," the lawyer said sarcastically, "that certainly is original."

He was ready to give up and back out of the site when he noticed a small icon located off to the left and toward the bottom of the screen. It seemed somehow familiar to him. It appeared to represent some type of picture like a portrait of a couple. He immediately reminded of the painting "American Gothic" but it was too small to see for certain.

When he placed his cursor overtop of the icon. A screen hint appeared with the caption "Click this icon. You don't want to miss this." He figured he didn't have anything to lose. He had already spent a sleepless night and all day trying to find his answers; maybe his solution was only a click away. So, he selected the icon and the screen filled with an image that shocked the lawyer to the very core of his being, making the pit of his stomach feel as heavy as a lead weight.

On the computer monitor, just inches from his face, was the image of Dwight and Marie Livingston, the very same scene depicted in the painting from the living room of the Washburn farmhouse.

"What the hell?" the lawyer shouted. It was impossible. He looked up at the top of the screen to read the URL, but the bar was missing as was his back arrow and other navigational tools. The image took up the entire monitor screen.

"Wonderful," he thought with disappointment, "must be some kind of virus." As he was about to press the power button to shut down his computer, he saw the picture begin to change.

The first thing he noticed was the eyes of Dwight Livingston's wolf-head cane began to glow a bright red, increasing in intensity until they became an iridescent almost blinding white. He lifted his hand to shield his eyes from the luminescence, but the light disappeared as quickly as it had appeared. Then he noticed Livingston's fingers move ever so slightly on the head of the walking stick.

This was obviously some sort of computer animation technique geared to make the viewer feel uncomfortable and perhaps even frightened. But he couldn't understand why the site owner had chosen this particular portrait and where he might have gotten a digital image of the painting.

Then the faces of both Dwight and Marie Livingston began to change. The normal pallor of their skin turned from a healthy pink to a dusky gray. Their flesh began to shrink back on their skulls, wrinkling and gaining a leathery appearance as if the couple were withering into mummified corpses right before his eyes. Large dark circles surrounded their sunken eye sockets from which their red-rimmed orbs stared directly at Armstrong as if boring a fissure into his very soul.

The corners of their shriveled mouths slowly curled up in sinister smiles. The image of the woman began to fade and drift backward out of the screen while Dwight began to grow and become much clearer and three-dimensional in appearance.

The lawyer backed away from the screen sinking deep into the leather upholstery of his desk chair as the likeness of Dwight Livingston continued to grow until its cracked and blackened lips filled the entire computer screen. As the lips slowly began to part, they revealed blackened, cavity-riddled teeth. A thick blackish-red liquid the consistency of melted tar began to flow slowly from the spaces between the rotten teeth.

Then dozens, if not hundreds of glistening yellow-white maggots drizzled from inside the hideous thing's cavernous mouth, spilling over its lips and falling out of the computer monitor and onto Armstrong's computer keyboard where the wretched insects writhed in pain before eventually disappearing vaporized in gray-green puffs of foul-smelling smoke. The air around Armstrong was thick with the vile, sickening, sweet stench of death.

Terrified with fear, Armstrong reached down and pressed the power button on his computer, but the image didn't disappear. Instead, the maggot-infested mouth on the screen opened wider and the lawyer could see even more blackened and yellowed rotted teeth, many missing in places looking like randomly scattered and skewed grave markers, fallen stones from an abandoned cemetery.

The man's withered blackened tongue, serpentine in appearance and still covered with squirming larvae snaked itself along the tops of the rotting teeth, occasionally snagging the paper-thin flesh on a jagged edge of decayed enamel. Instead of blood trickling down from the cuts, a thick, sickening, dark green, puss-like sludge oozed hideously from the wounds. The disgusting stench emanating from the screen had gone beyond anything Armstrong had ever previously encountered.

Then the gaping mouth began to slowly close as the face of Dwight Livingston backed away until his entire visage once again filled the screen. Marie likewise began to slowly emerge back into the foreground and eventually took her place by her husband's side. Armstrong noticed for the first time, deep handprints on Marie's neck and a long open slit across Dwight's throat extending practically from one ear to the other and hanging open like a second, much larger mouth.

Within a few moments, the flesh began to reappear on both corpses and the image gradually returned to reflect the original painting. The lawyer felt a momentary bit of relief assuming what he had just witnessed was nothing more than a sophisticated computer simulation dreamed up perhaps by some local teenager as a prank. The kid must have gotten a picture of the painting somehow, perhaps months earlier when Washburn was still alive. He suspected if he clicked the icon again it would replay. He realized the smells and the burning maggots were probably the result of his imagination caused by his exhaustion.

He breathed a sigh of relief. Then, incredibly, the eyes of Dwight Livingston began to focus and stare insanely at Armstrong as it moved its lips then unbelievably spoke directly to him, "Hello, Mr. Armstrong. Do you know who I am; who we are?"

The lawyer could only stare in paralyzed horror at the sinister specter addressing him from within the monitor. His mouth hung slack-jawed as he was certain he had either completely lost his mind or was well on his way to doing so.

Then the image spoke again, "Yes, I can tell you know exactly who we are. And I suppose you're wondering why we're here and what we might want from you." The lawyer stared silently, realizing he was paralyzed and incapable of even the slightest movement as a steady stream of drool dribbled from his slack lips. Then the thing spoke again.

"Marie and I have come here via this mechanical box of yours to thank you for the outstanding work you have done in getting our descendants to agree to come and live with us in our home."

Then the repugnant face on the computer screen spoke again, "And in addition to offering you our eternal gratitude, we've also come here to kill you."

Before the lawyer had a chance to react, Livingston's two translucent hands shot out from the screen, one on each side, pulling the surface of the screen along with them as if it had been transformed into some type of protective elastic ethereal condom. The hands quickly reached across the space on the Lawyer's desk and then effortlessly passed through him sinking deep into the lawyer's chest.

Armstrong felt a sharp pain in the center of his chest as his left arm became numb and he broke out in an icy cold sweat. He sensed an incredible pressure building inside as if an elephant was straddling him, crushing him. He was unable to breathe and Armstrong looked down wide-eyed at the arms jutting from his upper body with the rubber-like monitor screen trailing behind them. Soon the image faded from his vision as his world sunk into a vale of blackness.

His lifeless body slumped in a heap on his chair stone cold dead. His head lolled backward as his tongue dangled from the side of his slack-jawed mouth resembling a recently killed deer. The ghostly arms slowly retreated back into the monitor.

Then, displayed on the screen, three people could be seen walking away in the distance: a man in a turn of the century finely tailored but worn suit, using a walking stick on one side and a woman dressed in a white wedding gown yellowed with age on the other.

Between the couple walking with his head down as if cowed and beaten was a heavy-set man dressed in a rumpled business suit. The man in the center turned and Armstrong took one final look out at his earthly remains lying dead in his leather desk chair before he took his place with the others for eternity.

18

THE FOLLOWING WEDNESDAY morning Jason walked alone slowly from the back of the house toward the large barn off in the distance. He was in no hurry for the task awaiting him, a responsibility he had been both anticipating and dreading since his discovery of the family plot the previous Saturday.

Moments earlier Jason gave final instructions to a crew of workers regarding the installation of a security system and rekeying of all the locks. Keeping the gravesite a secret from Stephanie might be the hardest thing he would ever to do because the idea of deceiving her went against everything he believed in. She was unaware he was even at the property. She believed he was at the Ashton manufacturing facility at an important meeting concerning his promotion. It simply worked out that the day of that meeting he was able to kill two birds with one stone.

Jason had looked up a security company in the southern Schuylkill County city of Yuengsville on the web the Saturday evening they had arrived home. Jason left a voice message and was surprised when the owner of the company called him Sunday afternoon. Jason was eager to get the property secured so he was happy they had been prompt in returning his call. Luckily Stephanie hadn't been home at the time so he could make his plans without her knowledge.

After Jason had spoken with the security company owner, he had arranged to meet a team of their technicians at the Ashton house first thing Wednesday morning. The owner of the security company assured him they seldom worked in the Ashton area and were unfamiliar with the lawyer, Armstrong.

Jason had instructed the owner to have his crew come prepared to do a complete wireless security system installation. Jason also planned to add motion sensor lights around the property, but that could come later. His main concern for the immediate future was getting the farmhouse secured. Because he had agreed to pay a premium for the service everything would be completed before 3:00 P.M. that day.

As he walked back through the grass which was moist with morning dew, he thought not only about the unpleasant task awaiting him, but he also thought about the previous Saturday. Although the day had been extremely hectic, they had managed to find time to take in some local sights and take the kids on to the local mine tour.

The children had loved the steam locomotive ride which the tour guide referred to as the "Lokie." The train took its passengers about a mile out around a mountain where they got an amazing scenic panoramic view of the town of Ashton and its surrounding area. Jason was also surprised at how much the kids enjoyed the Pennsylvania Coal Museum. He was afraid they might become bored, but they seemed fascinated by the various displays of coal mining photographs as well as the displays of various tools of the mining trade dating back over a hundred years.

Then Jason recalled how unusual their tour of the Miner's Tunnel coal mine attraction had been, and how he had been truly amazed at seeing the inside of a real coal mine. He thought about how he enjoyed studying the rough-hewn timbers, which held up the low ceilings of the main gangway as the mine-car tracks sloped steeply downward into blackness leading over a mile into the very bowels of the earth. Everyone enjoyed riding in the special mine cars and since they arrived at the mine close to closing time there weren't many people on their tour, which gave Jason the opportunity to ask many questions. His tour guide was extremely knowledgeable of the mining industry and his authentic coal region accent made his comments even more interesting.

Jason was surprised when he found they could leave the mine cars when they reached the bottom of the tunnel and they were able to walk around inside the mine. Bright electric lights illuminated the area allowing for a detailed examination of the various tunnels. The walls and the ground seemed to be covered with a film of moisture from water seeping through the soil surrounding them. Coal glittered like black diamonds where the water slid along its surface sparkling in the lights. Each of the tourists had been given jackets to wear on the tour, and when Jason felt how cold and damp it was, he was grateful for the extra layer of warmth.

The kids especially enjoyed the last leg of the tour. While their mine car traveled about halfway up the slope the guide stopped the cars to give the tour a demonstration of just how dark it could be inside a mine when there were no lights. Unfortunately for Jason, that part of the tour turned unexpectedly into a very bad experience, one he had not anticipated and one he would likely never forget.

Jason had been in what he considered very dark places before and wrongly assumed one dark place was the same as another. But he had never imagined darkness as inky black as what he experienced that day in the mine. With the flick of a switch mounted on a heavy wooden timber, the group was plunged instantly into a state of darkness the likes of which Jason had never imagined; the complete absence of light.

The tour guide explained through the blackness in his thick coal region accent, "Dis is wat dey mean wen day say 'pitch daarrk.' Wen ya can't ev'n see yer hend in fronta yer face." Jason was astonished by just how dark it was so far below the earth and was unexpectedly surprised to find himself thinking about the small graveyard he had found on their property earlier that day.

He couldn't prevent an image from forming inside his mind as clearly as if he were watching it take place right before his eyes. He imagined himself being one of the decaying bodies of the young boys confined inside of their rotting wooden coffins far below the surface of his land unable to speak, unable to move, yet somehow completely aware. He had realized the darkness he was experiencing in the mine was likely the same level of darkness in the grave and he began to feel as if he had been buried alive. His pulse began to quicken as did his breathing which started to come in short, uncomfortable gasps. Then his heart began to race as he broke out in a cold sweat. He could feel an uncontrollable, claustrophobic sensation engulf him from head to toe and feared if he had to stay in the blackness of the mine much longer his heart would explode inside his chest.

Just then he felt something small and cold crawl across the top of his hand and Jason was certain a rat had made its way onto the car and was just seconds away from biting him with its disease-ridden teeth. He knew rats often could be found in dark, damp places such as mines. Then he heard a tiny voice whisper, "Hold my hand, Daddy, I'm scared." With relief and feeling a bit foolish, Jason realized what he had felt was Cindy's tiny hand. She needed him which meant he had no time for his own ridiculous imaginings. He held her hand gently in his and felt his own irrational fears slowly fade away.

Nevertheless, he was thankful when the lights returned, and the tour concluded. Jason was certain the entire time the lights were out until they came back on again was no more than twenty or thirty seconds, but it felt like an eternity to him.

"Eternity," he thought to himself and once again imagined the bodies buried in the ground on their property. Those decaying remains would be confined to earth forever. Once he destroyed their grave markers there would be no more record of their existence. They would spend time without end trapped beneath the cold damp ground until they became one with the earth.

"Are you ok?" Stephanie asked as they exited the mine car into the fading afternoon light. "You look a little pale."

Jason replied, "Ah, um, yeah. I'm fine. Things just got a bit weird down there when the lights went out. Cindy got a little scared, but she was ok when I held her hand."

"You're a good dad," Stephanie said as she reached over and kissed Jason on the cheek.

But what truly bothered Jason was the fact he was not normally claustrophobic, nor was he prone to wild imaginings like those he had experienced in the mine. He had never experienced the strange out-of-body sensations as he had felt back in the graveyard either.

Jason returned to the present as he opened the door to the barn, switched on the light, and entered. He saw the shiny John Deer tractor right where they had left it Saturday. In addition to the backhoe attachment, Jason saw the trailer cart. He hooked the trailer up to the tractor assuming it would make the job of transporting the small headstones a bit easier. He also planned to hook up the backhoe attachment if necessary after he found a suitable location to dig the hole where he would bury the soon-to-be-broken-up grave markers.

If he couldn't figure out how to use it, he'd simply have to dig a hole by hand. As a precaution, Jason found a shovel and a large sledgehammer near the back of the barn. He also found a canvas tarpaulin, which he felt would work well to prevent his cargo from scratching the paint on the bed of the trailer. He wanted to keep any evidence of his activities at a minimum. Jason started up the tractor and eased it slowly out of the barn.

19

AS HE SAT ATOP the tractor acclimating himself with its operation Jason thought about their upcoming moving plans. He and Stephanie decided they could spend the next two days packing some of their lesser-needed items into boxes to get a head start. They would also have to contact moving companies for estimates as well as get in touch with a realtor about selling their Berks County townhouse.

Stephanie suggested they buy paint and spend the weekend gutting and repainting the master bedroom. She already had an idea of what her color scheme would be. "We can take out all that old junk and tear up the old, worn out carpeting. Then we can strip the walls and give the whole room a fresh coat of paint. We will worry about getting new flooring later, but I think we could accomplish quite a bit in two days. I wish the kids were finished with school. If they were, we could head up Thursday and have four days to work. But they're not done until next Wednesday."

"There's no hurry," Jason said. "We still have to sell this place."

"I know, but I simply can't wait to see the house again," Stephanie replied excitedly. "I'm ready to move in tomorrow."

Then Jason asked, "If we're gutting and painting the master bedroom where are we supposed to sleep Saturday night?"

"Well, there is no way I'd sleep in that musty dark bedroom. I'll share a bed with Cindy, and you can sleep with Jeremy."

"Ugh!" Jason replied. "Jeremy snores and kicks his feet in his sleep. That's why I haven't slept in the same bed with him since he was small."

Stephanie said, "Well if that doesn't work out there are plenty of sofas and large chairs around the place. You could always sleep in one of those."

"Well, I guess you're right," Jason conceded. "Thursday morning after Sammy wakes up and is ready, we can head into the home center and pick out what supplies we will need. But to be honest with you, I think you may be a bit ambitious with your plans for the weekend. We'll be lucky to get the bedroom cleaned out, let alone prepared and painted."

"Yeah, you're probably right but I'd still like to have the paint and stuff ready. Just in case."

"No problem. We can do that on Thursday. Right now, I have to think about getting everything ready for my visit to the Ashton plant on Wednesday."

Then Stephanie asked, "I don't suppose there is any way Sammy and I could come up with you on Wednesday morning is there?"

Jason knew at some point Stephanie was going to ask to come along, and as such, he already had his reply prepared.

"No, that won't work. You know I'd love to take you both with me, but I have to be at the plant early, which means I'll be out the door before any of you even wake up. Plus, you have to get the two older kids off to school, and someone has to be here when they come home. I won't get back until dinner time if I'm lucky."

"Won't it drive you crazy being so close to the house but not able to stop by?"

"No. Not really. I'll have so much to do to get ready not only for the job transfer but also learning about my new responsibilities in Ashton that by the end of the day my brain will be so fried the house will be the last thing on my mind."

Stephanie suggested, "Well then why don't you stay overnight at the house Wednesday night and head back first thing Thursday morning? You're off from work anyway."

"That might be a good idea," Jason said with very little enthusiasm, "but no. I don't think I will. I want my first night in the house to be with all of you. That'll make it much more special."

The fact was Jason was certain that after dealing with his unpleasant graveyard task the last thing he'd want would be to be alone in the unfamiliar environment. He felt a cold chill race down his spine and did his best to ignore it. He didn't believe in ghosts or spirits but the idea of desecrating a gravesite and then staying alone in the house on the same night just seemed a bit too creepy even for him.

"Sometimes you are so sweet," Stephanie said and then kissed him.

The memory of their discussion faded as Jason's tractor passed the spa building. Jason recalled the strange feeling of someone watching he had experienced the previous Saturday. He experienced so many strange feelings that day he had pushed the sensation aside. Yet now as his tractor passed the odd structure, the hair on the back of his neck began to tingle. He pressed down on the gas pedal, eager to get down to business.

As he bounded along the meadow getting closer, Jason recalled a conversation he had with his boss earlier that week. On Monday as planned, Jason went to work and told Walter he would accept the promotion. As promised, his boss agreed to Jason taking off Wednesday through Friday to get moving plans in order.

"By all means," Walter had said. "As I mentioned, if you can just help me while the folks from Ashton are here today and tomorrow that won't be a problem."

Jason said, "Thanks, Walt. I appreciate that. By the way, who is coming down from Ashton today anyway?"

"Well," Walt replied thinking, "as far as I know the man you're replacing, Jim Dodson, as well as two of his engineers who, now that I think about it, I suppose will very shortly be your engineers. One guy by the name of Brian Josephs and another named Ken Jackson. Do you know them?"

Jason felt a strange sensation in the pit of his stomach. For the first time, he realized the two engineers who would be arriving shortly were going to be his subordinates within a matter of a few weeks. He had met all of the Ashton engineers at one time or another. He had gone out for drinks and pizza with most of them at some point in time but that was as their equals. Now things would be different. It would be strange to meet them again knowing he was going to be their boss, especially since Walt had told him they had no knowledge of his upcoming promotion.

Jason knew Brian Josephs to be a good, hard working type of manufacturing engineer concerned only with doing the best job possible. Ken Jackson, however, would be a different situation entirely. He was the senior manufacturing engineer and was likely the one Jim Dodson had been grooming to take his place. He wouldn't be happy to learn Jason had gotten the job. Ken was a local boy, born and raised in Schuylkill County with many friends in the area. He knew how the system at Ashton worked and how to get what he needed. If any of the Ashton engineers would be a problem for him, it would likely be Ken.

Jason managed to keep himself busy Monday and was able to avoid the Ashton group entirely.

On Tuesday however, Jason was required to sit in on a meeting with Walt and the Ashton contingent to discuss various technical aspects of the many pieces of equipment on their list for transfer. It was a bit awkward for Jason so he avoided eye contact as much as possible. Jason did notice Jim Dodson look at him several times in an appraising fashion. He assumed Jim was aware of Jason's acceptance of the job and Dodson might be comparing Jason to his own choice for his replacement wondering if Jason measured up to his expectations.

Jason left that image drift from his mind as the tractor pulled alongside the copse of tall grass and weeds where he had discovered the burial site. He positioned the tractor so the cart was directly in front of the thicket and the tractor itself was blocking any view of the area from the house. With great trepidation, Jason stepped from the tractor up over into the family graveyard.

20

AS JASON'S FEET touch ground on the burial site, he felt a strange sensation he hadn't experienced the previous Saturday. His entire body felt as if it were straining to move against some force, which seemed to turn the very air around him into gelatin.

Jason forced his gaze downward, not wanting to trip and fall during what had become a painstakingly slow progression. He saw the remains of the dead fawn, now all but completely gone save for blanched bones and a few random tufts of hair. He hoped if he could just keep moving forward the strange hypnotic spell might pass. Then the temperature seemed to drop thirty degrees and the light faded all around him to a dull gray, sending icy chills throughout his body. He noticed a foul stench, perhaps that of decomposition. He sensed it was coming up from deep within the soil of this strange place. The feeling caused him terror deep in the pit of his stomach.

Then as he had hoped, after a few seconds and a few more challenging steps forward he was able to once again move normally as the light returned and the temperature rose. Likewise, the rancid stench had disappeared almost completely. Jason felt as though he had made it past some strange sort of barrier. Now safely on the other side, he was unsure of what he had just encountered.

He turned slowly and looked behind him. Jason began to wonder if the barrier had really been there. If it had been and it still was, would he ever be able to return through it or might he never again be able to penetrate the blockade? Had he passed into some sort of alternate dimension? Was he no longer in his own world?

He had a momentary attack of anxiety, imagining himself trapped behind the barrier unable to get back. And if he were trapped would he ever be found? He wondered what someone on the opposite side of the transparent wall would see if anything. He could still see the tractor and trailer right where he had left them. He began to panic.

He couldn't wait any longer. He had to find out immediately. Jason reached out his hand expecting his fingers to sink deep into what he thought of as the "gelatmosphere" and feel the icy cold encompass his hand. However, he was surprised to find nothing. Whatever that previous sensation had been, real or imagined, it was now gone.

Jason shook his head as if trying to clear away the residual cobwebs of some strange disorienting dream. He felt he had just experienced a bizarre hallucination, one so detailed, so authentic it seemed to be real. But he knew such things could never actually occur. It was obviously some sort of spell or perhaps a type of seizure. He'd have to be careful and watch for any other similar signs as it might mean the onset of some serious medical condition.

He walked cautiously forward and knelt to examine the two small gravestones once again. He reread the identical cryptic addendum carved into each small stone, "Taken From Us Too Soon, By The Hand Of Evil."

"Boy one and boy two," Jason spoke aloud. Then he said, "I suppose if you had lived you two would have been great uncles to my wife, Stephanie. I wonder why it was you both died so young and on the same day . . . and what this strange inscription might mean."

He looked about and found a few other gravestones, six of them altogether. They were so thin, old and worn; none of the inscriptions could be read. It seemed to Jason perhaps several hundred years had passed between the time the last of that family was buried in the plot and the time when the two boys had been laid to rest in the graveyard. He realized it was more than likely the occupants of the other graves weren't even related to Stephanie's family but were put there by previous owners of the land.

He bent down and picked up one of the unreadable head-stones finding it to not be as heavy as he might have expected and easily carried it over to the tractor, placing it gently down on the tarp he had laid across the bed of the truck. Each time he passed by the grassy edge of the cemetery he expected to encounter the strange barrier, but for whatever reason, it never returned. In several trips, Jason had picked up the remaining illegible stones as well as the Livingston boys' markers and placed them in the trailer. Once he was confident he had all the stones, he looked around and discovered something he hadn't seen earlier.

The remnants of what appeared to be a low stone wall surrounded the gravesite. After a closer examination, he decided it was hardly a wall although at one time it might have been. It was actually just a rectangular border of a few carefully placed stones now spaced far apart. Jason decided it would be best to remove these stones as well. He had no desire for the area to even slightly resemble its original purpose.

Then he wondered why had the two boys been the only members of the Livingston family to be buried in the cemetery alongside the graves of strangers? Where were their parents laid to rest? Shouldn't they also have been buried here in the family graveyard? It seemed strange. Then, with a pain in the pit of his stomach, Jason realized he was going to have to look around the rest of the property to make sure this was the only burial site. The thought of a second or even third site was something he didn't want to consider.

After placing the last of the stones in the back of the trailer and covering them with the tarpaulin Jason decided he'd drive along the back perimeter of the property to see if he could find a suitable place to break up and discard the headstones and to locate any other burial plots. He could only hope he'd find no more. He climbed into the seat of the tractor and looked across the expanse of the field preparing to head left. Then he would eventually make a complete circle of the property and finally returned to this point of origin.

With any luck, by that time he would have successfully disposed of the tombstones in a safe and unidentifiable location.

He drove slowly along the periphery of the field looking over toward the woods surrounding the property on his right. After a few hundred feet he stopped the tractor, seeing someone in the distance he hoped he was only imagining.

"What the hell is *he* doing here?" Jason said angrily to himself.

Far off in the distance from where the tractor sat idling Jason saw the shape of a man in a business suit, standing near the back of the property upon a slight rise similar to the one where he had found the grave markers. He was certain even from this distance it was that lawyer, H. Mason Armstrong. His rotund shape was unmistakable. Jason was furious at the sight of the man. Armstrong had no right to be roaming around their property yet there he was just as Jason had feared might happen.

Oddly, the lawyer didn't wave to him or acknowledge him in any way; he only stood stock still staring at Jason as if in some strange trance-like state.

"Well, I suppose now I'll have to go over there and set this guy straight about a few things. I was hoping to avoid a confrontation with the guy, but I guess he's left me little choice. Pushy damned lawyers. It looks like its time for a 'come to Jesus' meeting my fat little friend."

Not wanting the lawyer to see the cargo he carried in the back of the trailer, Jason got down from the tractor and strode purposefully toward the site where the lawyer stood.

"Armstrong!" Jason shouted as he walked. "What the hell are you doing here? I didn't ask you to come out here!"

The closer he got to the man the angrier he became. Not paying attention to where he was walking, Jason stumbled over a hole in the field and fell face first. Luckily, as the ground came flying up to meet him, he was able to twist and roll to deflect most of the impact. The result was just a bit of personal embarrassment and perhaps a bruised ego. Jason imagined the lawyer chuckling to himself over his clumsiness. This only served to further fuel his rage.

As Jason slowly got back to his feet he looked over to the place where the lawyer had stood and was surprised to see he was no longer there.

"What the hell! Where did he go?"

Jason could see a large expanse of the field to the left of the lawyer as well as a substantial distance before it ended at the adjoining woodlands. He doubted Armstrong with his unhealthy bulk, could have possibly run or even walked fast enough to reach either the house or the woods so quickly . . . so where had the man gone?

Jason walked back toward the spot where he had seen Armstrong standing. It appeared to be as good a place as any to bury the stones. It wasn't visible from the house since its view was blocked by one of the outbuildings. His temper had begun to subside, and he was once again able to think more clearly. Fortunately, he had changed from his office clothing into work clothing before the security team had arrived. He'd have been hard-pressed to explain to Stephanie how he had gotten field dirt and grass stains on his good pants. He looked down at the ground and was surprised to not find a single trace the man had ever been there; no grass was trampled or disturbed in any way. Jason thought surely a man of Armstrong's weight and size would have had to make shoe impressions in the dew-moist morning grass, yet not a single blade of grass was disturbed.

Looking about for any trace of the attorney Jason saw something dark reflecting in the morning sunlight. As he approached, he discovered two objects. He could tell immediately by their shapes they were more gravestones. Both of the markers had fallen down and were lying on their backs in the moist soil.

"Damn!" Jason said aloud in frustration. "Not another graveyard!" For the second time, he was reminded of the property's name, *Fallen Stones*.

Then he realized he hadn't actually found another graveyard but had only found two additional grave markers. These two appeared to be alone out in this isolated area of the yard far removed from what one might think of as the official family burial location. This seemed like a purposeful shunning of the inhabitants of these graves; as if someone had deliberately segregated them from the others. He recalled hearing stories of how many years ago suicide victims were often buried away from church cemeteries so they wouldn't be permitted to lie in hallowed ground. Perhaps this was the case for these people buried below this soil.

Jason also continued to speculate about the lawyer. What had Armstrong been doing hanging around his property not to mention that particular area? It would really put a kink in his plan to keep the graves secret if Armstrong knew about them. There was always the risk he might say something to Stephanie. Maybe the lawyer would try to extort money from Jason in order to keep his secret. Jason decided sometime soon he would have to speak to the lawyer in private and make sure he had no choice but to forget anything he knew about the headstones. He'd likely have to bring up attorney-client privilege and maybe threaten to file a complaint with the bar association or some similar professional ethics board if necessary.

Jason decided he might as well get rid of these stones along with the others. He knelt to read the inscription on the first marker and was shocked to read the name, which although well-worn, was still legible. The caption read *Dwight Charles Livingston July 23, 1890–December 19, 1922. Devoted Husband, Loving Father, Tragically Taken In The Prime Of Life.*

"Dwight Livingston?" Jason said aloud. "That was the name Armstrong used for Stephanie's great-grandfather when he showed us that wedding portrait."

Then he knelt down to study the inscription on the other tombstone sensing it had to be Marie's but not prepared for what he would find carved on it. He read it aloud, *Marie Louise O'Hara Livingston June 6, 1892–December 19, 1922. May Her Wretched Soul Rot in the Bowels of Hell for Eternity.* He stared dumbfounded as an icy chill ran down the middle of his back.

21

JASON NOTICED THAT both Dwight and Marie Livingston died in the same year 1922. "Now wait a second!" He said realizing for the first time not only had they both died in the same year but on the exact same day.

He hurried over to the cart, pulled back the tarp and re-read the inscriptions on the two boys' headstones. One said *Matthew James Livingston, June 12, 1916–December 19, 1922."* And the other said *Charles Edward Livingston July 2, 1918–December 19, 1922."*

Not only had both boys died on the same day, but the parents had died as well. An entire family wiped out in one tragic event. Then he realized that assumption couldn't have been correct. Even if both parents and two children had somehow died in some horrible catastrophe the whole family couldn't have been killed. A brother or sister of the boys must have survived in order to carry on the family lineage. He recalled Stephanie mentioning she had a grandmother named Sarah. The surviving child must have been Sarah. Otherwise, Stephanie never would have been born. Still, the entire situation was quite disturbing.

"Four dead on the same day," he said aloud. "And what's with these strange messages?"

There was a real mystery existing within Stephanie's family, and he definitely was going to have to talk to Armstrong about keeping his big fat lawyer mouth shut. But before that, he was going to make sure the gravestones were all destroyed, buried, and would never be seen again. He walked about ten feet to the left of the place where he found the Livingston parents' stones; not wanting to inadvertently disturb any possible resting place and grabbing a pointed shovel began to dig a hole.

He was surprised by the soft, almost sand-like quality of the soil. His spade cut through it like a knife through butter. Within a few minutes, he had a substantial hole dug, more than adequate to bury the remains of the soon to be smashed headstones.

"Remains?" he thought for a moment and felt the return of the chill he had experienced earlier.

Jason put on a pair of safety glasses then walked over to the cart and retrieved two of the tombstones whose names could not be identified. He placed them on the ground and suspended them between Dwight and Marie's fallen stones. Next, he grabbed the sledgehammer from the back of the cart and raising it high above his head, prepared to bring it down on the stones.

For a moment he seemed to freeze in place, the sledge-hammer hanging motionless in the air above him. Then the sledgehammer came down with a crash shattering the gravestones into several smaller pieces. Jason stopped for a moment looking around certain something bad was about to happen, but nothing did. The sun continued to shine, the air was calm, and he could hear birds chirping in the nearby trees.

He repeated the process for the remainder of the stones including those of the two boys. Then he leaned both Dwight and Marie's tombstones on the accumulated pile of broken markers and proceeded to break them up beyond recognition as well. When they were all shattered to bits he shoveled the broken pieces into the large hole he had dug. Then he covered them with soil.

As he stepped back to check out his work, he couldn't help but notice how the mound of dirt looked uncomfortably like a freshly dug grave. Fortunately, he had kept the upper layer of sod which he had removed in clumps. He tamped down the mound with the back of the shovel then replaced the clumps of weedy sod on top. Jason was pleased with his work. Even from his close proximity, he found it difficult to see where he had buried the stones. He suspected by the time he and his family moved onto the property more weeds and grass would spring up making it completely indiscernible from the rest of the ground.

He wiped the sweat from his brow, brushed the dust from his jeans, and prepared to clean and return all the equipment to the barn. Then he planned to go into the house, shower and change into office clothes in preparation for his return trip home. First, he had to complete the planned circle of the property just to make certain there were no more stones anywhere.

He realized he would have some time to kill so he decided to take a trip to see H. Mason Armstrong might be in order. It was time he and the lawyer set some ground rules about the property. Just thinking about the man made Jason's anger begin to rise once more. He hoped he could control his temper when he spoke to the lawyer face to face.

As he placed the last tool in the cart and was getting ready to start the tractor his cell phone rang. He looked down at the caller ID and saw it was Stephanie. He took a moment to compose himself and to be ready for any questions she might have regarding his supposed business trip. Then he pressed the answer button.

"Hey, Steph. What's up?"

She replied with a troubled tone in her voice, "Oh, Jason. I'm so sorry to bother you at work but I had to call you."

"Is everything alright, you sound worried?"

"Yes, well no, not exactly," Stephanie said. Then she hesitated for a moment and mentioned. "Jason it sounds like you're outside."

Thinking quickly Jason said, surprising himself with how easily he could come up with a lie, "Um, well, yes. I am. I was walking through the plant when I felt my phone vibrate. It was noisy in there so I walked outside so I could hear you better. Plus, I suspect the cell reception is much better out here than inside. Anyway, that's not important. What's the matter?"

"I had an upsetting call this morning from Mason Armstrong's office."

Jason thought silently, "Oh, great. That damned lawyer called to rat me out already before I even had a chance to talk to him." Then with a tone of frustration, Jason asked, "Well, what did he want? I thought everything we had to do with him was taken care of."

"It wasn't Mason who called Jason," Stephanie explained. "It was his secretary, a woman named Mrs. Flannery."

"His secretary? What did she want?"

Stephanie hesitated for a moment then exclaimed, her voice breaking, "He's dead, Jason. Mason's dead."

Struck with shock and disbelief, Jason asked, "Dead? What do you mean he's dead? I just . . ." he almost blurted out that he had just seen the lawyer that very morning. He managed to catch himself. "I just can't believe it. I mean when, how, what happened?"

"Mrs. Flannery said he must have been working late on Sunday evening and he apparently had a massive heart attack. She found him in his office dead in his chair when she reported for work Monday morning. It must have been horrible. His computer was still turned on. She could hardly talk about it."

Jason stood shocked unable to reply at first. He would have sworn under oath he had seen the lawyer standing in his field but now he knew that was impossible. Who had it been? Who had been standing out there staring at him? He was certain it was Armstrong. But then again, he had been certain he had walked through a strange gelatinous transparent barrier earlier. Now that he thought about it, hadn't he been feeling a bit strange and perhaps out of sorts all morning? Maybe he was coming down with some sort of spring flu or something. The more the thought the more he was beginning to believe it must be so.

"Jason? Honey, are you still there?" Stephanie asked. Jason realized he had been standing for a few moments and had not said a word.

"Un, yes. I'm . . . I'm . . . h . . . h . . . here . . ." he stammered. "I'm sorry, Steph. This just all caught me, you know, by surprise."

"I know exactly what you mean. I probably wouldn't have even bothered you and would have waited until you got home, but I guess I just needed to hear your voice and know everything was ok. You know what I mean? It's just all so disturbing for me."

He understood completely. She was fifty miles away and alone with a toddler trying to deal with all of the latest life-changing events. Then to have her stress compounded with the news of the lawyer's death. He knew what she needed. She needed her husband. He looked at his watch and saw it was almost 1:00 pm.

"Look, I'm almost finished here. I can wrap things up and head home a little early. Whatever is left can wait until another day. I should be home by two thirty or so."

"Oh Jason, you're so sweet, but I really didn't mean to mess up your work schedule today. Why don't you just finish your day and I will see you around five. I'll be ok, I'm sure."

"I'm sure you would be fine, but I really want to come home to be with you. Also, to be honest, I haven't been feeling like myself all morning. I feel like I might be coming down with some sort of flu or something. My head is feeling heavy and strange you know, like right before you get sick. I may just be tired or stressed and need to rest. Anyway, I'm going to head home shortly and if I still feel this bad tomorrow, we'll cancel our shopping plans and just take it easy for a day."

"Ok, I suppose. Just please be careful driving home, especially if you're not feeling well."

"Don't worry, Steph. I promise I will, and I'll tell you what. I'll give you a few calls along the way so you'll know I'm fine. Deal?"

"Deal," she said reluctantly. "Love you."

"I love you too, sweetheart. And I'll see you shortly."

Jason quickly completed his circle of the property but didn't find any more graveyards or tombstones. Then he put his yard equipment away in the barn and walked back to the house where he informed the security company workers he had to leave on a family emergency.

He quickly washed up then got changed back into his office clothing. When he was ready to leave Jason saw the security company owner stopped by to check on his workers' progress. He told Jason they were on schedule and would have the system completed by the end of the day. He said someone would stop back on Saturday afternoon to show Jason and Stephanie how the system functioned. Jason had already planned on telling Stephanie he had contacted the firm and gave them access to the house, but he wouldn't say he had been present.

"And Bob?" Jason asked, "Could you or whichever of your workers comes back on Saturday not mention I was here today? I wanted this to be a surprise and if I told my wife I was up here today without her, surprise or not, she'd have a fit. She's dying to come up here to see the house again."

"Not a problem. Mr. Wright," Bob said. "In fact, I'll be sending someone up on Saturday who wasn't even here today."

"That'll be perfect. And for now, just leave the security system inactive. We'll activate it on Saturday when your man arrives."

Jason got in his car and headed home. As he passed the front of the house, he thought he saw someone at the end of the field near the woods but when he stopped the car and looked in that direction, no one was there. The chill returned to creep with icy claws once again down Jason's spine. For the briefest of moments, he thought he had seen the dead lawyer standing and watching him from the place he had buried the broken gravestones, looking on with vacant mournful eyes.

22

ON A BRIGHT sunny morning near the end of June, Stephanie woke up feeling especially contented. The sun was streaming in through the wall of windows in the master bedroom and the day had shown the potential of being a good one. The recently redecorated room was bright and pleasant in direct contrast to the dark conditions which had originally defined the space. Likewise gone were the gloomy antique furnishings, replaced with a brand-new bedroom ensemble.

She looked over at the clock on her nightstand and saw it was still early, only 7:30. Jason had already left for work but by the lack of sound in the house, she could tell the kids were still sleeping. She knew it wouldn't be long until Sammy began to stir and then the rest of the kids would follow.

After lying in bed and basking in the glorious silence for a few heavenly moments longer, Stephanie decided to get up and shower so she would be ready when it came time to corral the kids and get them ready to go. She wanted to make a trip into Ashton to the grocery store. They had made a family shopping trip about two weeks earlier, but it was way past time to make another as the cupboards were getting bare. Jason had kept them in staples by making quick stops periodically on his way home from work. His plant was only about a quarter of a mile from the local supermarket.

And although she did appreciate him stopping and getting whatever they required, he had been working long hours and many weekends trying to get up to speed in his new job and Stephanie hated to ask him. Plus, she really wanted to get out and explore the area. Although there wasn't much in the line of shopping in town there were a few scattered stores and restaurants. She knew Jeremy might complain at first but once she told them they'd be going out for breakfast at Maggie's Restaurant before heading to the supermarket she was sure he'd come around.

She figured she could get everything done and be home by lunch. The day looked promising weather-wise, so she and the kids would likely want to spend the afternoon in the pool.

Stephanie had finally started sporadically working on her children's book again but lately found it difficult to find the time. She did what she could when she was able. The important thing was she was making progress.

An hour or so later the kids were all awake, dressed, and loaded into the van and they were on their way. As they approached the town Stephanie realized Ashton had something of an unusual appearance. It was situated along the side of a continuously climbing hill. The main street in town was known as Centre Street and ran from it eastern end at the "bottom of town" to its far western end at the "top of town" for a distance of about a mile or so. At the crest of the hill was Maggie's Restaurant which occupied a corner building formed from what were once two wood-framed row houses. The town was made up of hundreds of similar two- and three-story structures ranging from eleven to twenty feet wide. They were leftover remnants from the turn of the twentieth century days when coal companies built these "company houses" to accommodate their employees, most of whom were, European immigrants.

As they stood in front of the restaurant, Stephanie noticed for the first time a sign at the intersection of Centre Street and another perpendicular road reading "Cantrania 3 miles." She had heard of that town before, in fact, it had made national news because of a mine fire which had been burning beneath it since the 1960s. She had forgotten it was so close to Ashton. As she recalled, the entire town had to be demolished because of the unsafe conditions the fire had caused. She decided if they had time today maybe she and the kids would take a trip to Cantrania to see what the place looked like now.

On the large pain front window of the building where they stood was a sign whose letters were worn but still legible spelling out "Maggie's Restaurant." Inside the restaurant, a group of apparently regular patrons sat eating breakfast while engaging in boisterous conversations. She saw the restaurant was divided into two rooms, a front and rear dining area. The front space consisted of booths while the back seemed to have tables and chairs. As Stephanie cocked her head to look back in that direction, she noticed there didn't seem to be anyone seated in the back room.

"We haven't opened up the back room yet this morning," a woman said from Stephanie's left apparently seeing her interest. The attractive woman was standing behind a counter surrounded by stools all occupied with patrons. "But it looks like we might have to soon."

She wore a dark tan shirt with the name Mary Ann embroidered over the left pocket. She appeared to be in her late forties. Stephanie assumed assumption Mary Ann was in charge by the air of authority surrounding her.

"Please follow me," the woman said cheerfully. "I think we still have a booth or two available over on this side." Stephanie and her family followed Mary Ann to an empty booth near the back part of the front dining area. "There you go," the woman said. "This should be just fine."

Stephanie and the children sat in the booth with Sammy elevated on a booster seat, which Mary Ann had picked up on their way to the booth. "Your server will be with you in a minute," Mary Ann said. "Her name's Maggie. She's my daughter."

"Maggie?" Stephanie asked, "What a neat idea. You named the restaurant after her?"

"Well, not exactly." Mary Ann replied. "It's sort of a long story but I can give you the two-minute condensed version if you'd like."

Stephanie replied, "Sure, why not?"

Mary Ann took a deep breath and in a series of quick sentences, she told her story in a concise manner, which obviously had evolved into its current format from answering that particular question hundreds of times before.

"The original owner of this restaurant was a woman named Maggie Maloney during the 1940s. My mother, Jeanie Wilkins started working here in 1960 when I was five years old. In 1975, Maggie decided to retire, and my mom scrapped together the money to buy the restaurant from Maggie. I started working here in 1983 and found myself pregnant with my daughter. Then Maggie Maloney passed away before my baby was born, and at my Mom's suggestion, I named my daughter Maggie. My mom got sick in 1995, passed away and left the restaurant to me. Now Maggie is learning the trade and will be taking over the business whenever I get around to retiring. So eventually, Maggie's will be Maggie's once again." Mary Ann took a breath and said, "Wow. That was pretty quick. I should have timed it. I think I may have set a new record."

Stephanie looked at her smiling with amusement. "That certainly was a great story. I can't wait to tell my husband. I'll bet he's never heard it before."

"Well, if he eats here very often, he's bound to hear it sooner or later," Mary Ann replied.

Just then a pretty young waitress about twenty-five years old approached shaking her head and smiling. Even before Stephanie saw the name "Maggie" on her uniform she knew the girl had to be Mary Ann's daughter. She looked like a younger version of the woman, "Mom! Don't tell me you're boring these nice folks with your story."

"That's quite all right," Stephanie said. "We asked to hear it and loved it."

Maggie replied, "Well, maybe the first hundred and fifty times but after a while, it gets a bit old." Then she immediately got down to business. "Can I get you folks something to drink while you decide what you would like for breakfast?"

"Sure," Stephanie said nodding at Cindy and Jeremy. "What'll it be, kids?"

"Coke," they said simultaneously.

"Two Cokes. Got it," Maggie said smiling at the kids.

Stephanie said, "I'll have a cup of hot tea, and can I have a cup of chocolate milk for this one?"

"Choka mook," Sammy said.

"What a little sweetie pie!" Maggie replied. "And what beautiful big eyes! That one is destined to be a big hit with the ladies someday. I'll be back in a jiffy with your drinks."

A few minutes later, Maggie returned with the drinks. "Are you ready to order now?"

After Stephanie and the kids placed their orders, Maggie inquired, "Are you folks just passing through town today? I don't recall seeing you here before. I'm pretty good with faces."

"Actually no," Stephanie replied. "We moved to the area a month or so ago and are still getting settled. Were living outside of town and barely had enough time to look around. In fact, I hope to drive around a bit before heading down to the grocery store."

Maggie said, "Well there ain't too much to see around here. There's a mall down in Yuengsville but other than that, not much around other than the essentials. But I think you'll like it here. The folks around here are nice enough. I'll be back soon with your order." And with that, the busy woman turned and left to get their breakfasts.

Stephanie looked about the restaurant and realized what Maggie had said was true. The people in the room all seemed to know one another and there was a genuine feeling of the relaxed family-like atmosphere which only small-town living could bring. Maggie was right. Stephanie was going to like living in Schuylkill County.

Soon Maggie returned with their order, plates overflowing with pancakes, eggs, sausage, and hash browns. Jeremy and Cindy's eyes grew wide with anticipation.

Maggie looked at Jeremy as if recognizing him and asked. "You look familiar. Were you ever in here before? Remember I said I'm pretty good with faces."

"Once," Jeremy said over a mouth full of pancakes, "With my Dad."

"Jeremy, don't talk with your mouth full," Stephanie scolded.

"Mm-kay," Jeremy said, again with a mouth full of food. Stephanie chose to ignore him, not missing the irony.

"My husband, Jason brought Jeremy in maybe a month ago. He works downtown at Technofacture International."

"Jason. Jason," Maggie said as if trying to recall. "That's right. I do remember now. Your husband comes in here often. Now I see where the little one gets his good looks."

For some reason, this statement suddenly bothered Stephanie. She knew it was offered only as a compliment, but it was troublesome to think of another woman eyeing up her husband in that way. In addition, she had no idea Jason ate at Maggie's so often. It sounded like he was a regular. No wonder he headed out for work so early. It wasn't that she didn't trust Jason, but having been through one divorce from one unfaithful husband she was sensitive to reactions of other women, especially younger and attractive women.

"So," Maggie asked, "where do you folks live? Do you live outside of town somewhere?"

"Um, yes," Stephanie said, recovering from her momentary discomfort. "We live a few miles outside of Ashton. On a property, I inherited from my uncle Emerson Washburn. It's called Fallen Stones."

Maggie's mouth visibly dropped open and she stammered, "Fall . . . you mean the old Livingston place?"

"Why, yes," Stephanie replied. "Are you familiar with our property?"

"Yeah, I mean, no." The girl didn't seem to know what she meant. "You see, that place, not the place as it is now, but how it was before, all run down and abandoned. It sort of had a reputation around here."

"Reputation?" Stephanie asked curiously. "What sort of reputation?"

Maggie hesitated for a moment then said, "Well, it's sort of silly now that I think about it. But back when the place was in ruins, kids used to drive out there and hang out. You know?" She hesitated, looking cautiously over at the two older kids.

"Yes, I think I know exactly what you mean," Stephanie said suppressing a smile assuming the girl was likely talking about whatever sort of mischief teenage kids got up to when left alone in an abandoned property nowadays. Stephanie was thinking in terms of sex and beer but what Maggie was referring to was something much more sinister.

"Well, um. I've got to get back to work now. This place is really busy. Nice meeting you."

Before Stephanie had a chance to reply the girl turned and fled. Stephanie watched her and saw her head directly for her mother. She watched Maggie whisper something to Mary Ann and the woman's face took on an expression similar to the troubled one her daughter had just worn. Stephanie had a strange feeling there might be something about her property these local people knew but she didn't. Maybe they had heard about her Uncle Emerson's unsavory past or maybe it was simply a case of local kids making up stories about a broken-down abandoned farmhouse. She recalled how as kids, she and her friends would take great pleasure in fabricating mysteries about haunted houses and ghost sightings in old barns and such.

She decided that must be it. Obviously, there was very little for young people to do in a small town like Ashton, so an abandoned wreck of a property would be fertile ground for making up stories and legends.

As Stephanie and the kids ate their breakfast, she occasionally watched Maggie going from booth to booth taking and filling orders. She thought she might be imagining things, but it appeared as if in addition to doing her duties, Maggie seemed to be saying something to each of the patrons and occasionally looking over in their direction, almost as if she were talking about Stephanie and her kids. She wasn't normally prone to such feelings of paranoia, but this all seemed a bit peculiar to her. Even if the place had become the subject of some fictitious local legends the property was now completely remodeled and was a palace compared to the types of small row homes where most of these people lived.

Maybe that was part of it, Stephanie realized. It was jealousy, class envy. These locals knew about the money her Uncle Emerson had put into the place and were simply jealous of the amazing property she now owned. Suddenly Stephanie wasn't as comfortable with the small-town atmosphere as she had been a few minutes earlier. It no longer seemed quite as friendly or appealing, but it had taken on an air of animosity.

"Small town, small minds," she thought to herself. It was as if she had peeled open a beautiful piece of fruit only to find the insides teeming with maggots.

The thought nauseated her, and she was no longer hungry. When the kids had finished eating Stephanie stood up and began to slowly walk them up to the main counter to pay their bill. All of the busy chatter in the restaurant abruptly stopped. She felt as if the cash register was miles away.

The two older kids noticed as well. "What the heck are they looking at?" Jeremy whispered to Cindy.

"Beats me," Cindy said. "Mommy, why are they looking at us that way?"

"Shush," Stephanie said. "Let's just get pay for our food and get out of here."

They approached the cash register where Mary Ann waited with their bill in hand. Gone was her pleasant demeanor and in its place was a look of uncertainty. Stephanie resisted turning to look back at the restaurant patrons, certain they'd all be watching her. She handed Mary Ann a twenty-dollar bill and abruptly said, "Keep the change." Then she led her children out of the restaurant and into the morning light, which never looked better to her.

After the unpleasant incident at the restaurant, she no longer had any interest in checking out the rest of the town. In fact, she had no desire to even go to the grocery store, but she knew she had to restock the pantry so they had little choice. Even when they were shopping at the supermarket, Stephanie felt like people were staring at them.

Stephanie decided to put the entire experience behind her as there was nothing she could do about it anyway. They finished their grocery shopping and headed straight home.

23

S TEPHANIE RELAXED ON the sofa out on the atrium deck outside the loft. Sammy was inside taking his afternoon nap in the small bedroom. She looked out across the expanse of the atrium into the backyard.

In the distance, she could see the first signs of autumn approaching in the slightly changing colors of the leaves. She couldn't believe it was the first week in September already. The two older children were already settled into their new school. It seemed like only yesterday they had learned of her inheritance and now she was comfortably relaxing in her luxurious home as if she had lived there her entire life.

Inside the loft, a decorative mirror hung in the center of the back wall. In the silence of the large space, the surface of the decorative mirror began to shimmer and then ripple in concentric circles. Soon an image, faint and faded at first began to take shape. It was the face of Marie Livingston. The image stared at the woman reclining there who resembled Marie enough to be her sister.

For the past several months Marie Livingston and the others had chosen by design to stay quiet and out of sight. They had no desire to make their presence known or to do anything to frighten the Wright family into leaving. They had waited almost a century for this and the time for action would soon be upon them.

Marie had appeared this day to plant the first of many seeds which would eventually put the wheels of fate in motion once again. As Marie looked out at the woman on the deck her hatred and envy toward the woman grew. She cursed Stephanie for being alive and for having all the things the dead could still remember but could no longer experience: the touch of a loved one, the joy in a sunset, or simply the feeling of being alive.

On more than one occasion Marie had been tempted to reach out to take control of Stephanie's mind and force her to slowly kill herself in some incredibly horrible fashion. But that was not in her master's plan. She had forced herself to hold her anger and stick to the timetable as her husband had demanded. Eternity was a very long time to suffer his wrath.

It had also proven to be more of a challenge than antici-pated to remain unseen by that infernal small child Samuel who had been constantly milling about inhibiting their abil-ity to monitor the family. The child had a natural ability to sense their presence and see them whenever they appeared. Marie discovered this the very first day the family had vis-ited the property and the boy had seen her watching them from the large mirror in Washburn's master bedroom.

The young boy was getting older and his vocabulary and understanding were increasing daily. In the beginning he not only couldn't comprehend the meaning of their ap-pearances, but he didn't have the vocabulary necessary to express himself. Marie recalled how the child had almost revealed the presence of the other two, those damnable boys when he had seen them at their gravesite.

The spirit wished she could see the boys herself, wished they were accessible to her. Then she'd fix them so they could never cause her problems again. But they apparently moved on to some other plane of existence, separate from her own and although she could sense their occasional pres-ence she could not see them or get to them. She didn't know if they could see her and Dwight from where they existed either. Even after almost a hundred earth years she was still relatively new to the spirit world and unable to understand everything about her reality.

Marie was in constant turmoil worrying about what would happen if the boys continued to manifest themselves to the small child. Eventually, he would find a way to let his parents know what he was seeing. Marie had wished she had the ability to float a pillow over the boy's head as he lay sleeping in his daybed and smother the very life out of him putting the brat out of their way forever.

But she, unfortunately, didn't possess such power. And even if she had she knew Dwight would never tolerate such an irresponsible act. She knew they required the three of them–Jason, Stephanie, and Samuel–to complete Dwight's plan. If anything should happen to the boy, it might take several more centuries until they once again found the right combination of souls to complete the circle.

Out on the deck, Stephanie was thinking about how it had been another productive day of putting the final touches on her illustrations. Things had been going extremely well with her latest children's book over the past few months. Stephanie believed she might be able to declare the work finished at last.

She had been thinking more about researching her ancestry lately; perhaps she'd begin that project next. It might make for a good change of pace. Although unknown to Stephanie the idea hadn't actually been her own. Since the day she first learned of Emerson Washburn, Stephanie's mind had been receiving occasional subtle suggestions from the creatures of the dead to begin her research. It was critical to their plans. But even more important was for Stephanie to believe the idea was her own.

As she looked out at the cool September afternoon Stephanie shook her head in disbelief trying to come to grips with how the entire summer had passed by so quickly. And so much had happened during those months as well. Jason had taken the new job and they had sold their old home and moved into the Ashton estate. They remodeled the master bedroom and had sold off most of the antiques for a substantial profit which helped to make up most of the cost. They had kept the tall mirror from Emerson's bedroom as well as the portrait of her great grandparents but had stored them in the attic along with a few other items they thought they might want to keep.

Stephanie liked the mirror but decided to hide it away because of the way it had bothered Sammy. That particular incident had been so strange. She wondered what it was about the mirror that had bothered him. Perhaps when Sammy was a little older, she would bring it down from storage and try once again.

However, neither she nor Jason cared for the portrait. The thing disturbed them both to no end.

24

S TEPHANIE HEARD A rattling sound from down below and immediately recognized it as Mrs. Franks, Connie, dusting the furniture in the atrium area. Stephanie was so very grateful to Jason for suggesting they hire Connie to help her with maintaining their new home. Without the woman's assistance, she might never have been able to finish her book.

Connie's husband, Wilbur, had become a great asset to Jason as well, helping him with the yard work and other duties. With his new job and growing responsibilities, Jason often had to go into work very early and stay late into the evening. Although Jason was enjoying his new position it was also a great deal of stress for both he and Stephanie. His came in the form of overworking and hers in the form of loneliness. She found herself spending far too much time by herself especially now that the two older kids were settled in school.

She found the time alone to be something of a double-edged sword. From a writing perspective, it was a blessing because it allowed her time to think, to work, and to illustrate her projects. But from the standpoint of a wife and mother, it simply meant she had far too much time in solitude; too much time to miss her husband and far too much time to imagine.

Being a creative person, her imagination often found itself in high gear particularly during the alone times and not necessarily always in a positive way. She had often found herself imagining things about Jason she knew he would never do, could never do, but still, the ideas came.

Stephanie found this situation to be quite ironic since prior to meeting Jason she would have given her eyeteeth for one-tenth of the time she now had available. Now she would give something equivalent just to have less free time. She silently scolded herself for being so ungrateful.

She also missed being only twenty minutes from the bustling and trendy shopping districts in West Reading and Wyomissing or the cultural opportunities of downtown Reading. All of that was a good hour or more away now. She had considered returning to Berks County for some day trips. However, if Ashton was to be their new home then she had to find ways to make it their home.

Stephanie also worried about the move's impacts on her marriage. There was a time not long ago when Jason couldn't seem to keep his hands off her. Now that had changed, too. By the time he finally got home from work Jason was exhausted and mentally stressed, and it seemed sex was the furthest thing from his mind. Stephanie had done all she could think of to keep herself in shape and to keep Jason interested, but nothing seemed to work.

For the briefest of moments during one of her dreary days of solitude when her mind chose to wander to one of those places it had no business going, she began to feel the slightest stab of concern or perhaps suspicion about Jason. She had even started to imagine Jason might not be working as much as he claimed but might instead be involved with another woman, perhaps someone at work. She didn't believe it was possible for someone as devoted as Jason to become caught up in such a thing. But she also knew it had happened to her before with her first husband, Bill and that time she had also been caught by surprise.

"Once bitten, twice shy," she recalled.

Maybe it could be happening to her again. She hated when she had those thoughts and tried to force them from her mind. She blamed them on too much time to think and to imagine the worst. But hadn't Jason also seemed different lately? Didn't he seem distant, distracted and even short-tempered with the kids? Had she been imagining that, too?

"It's time," a sinister voice said to Marie Livingston as she stared angrily from her world inside the mirror. The voice had not really spoken as it had simply appeared in what Marie still thought of as her mind as the voice always did. It had come from her husband, Dwight.

"Time?" She questioned. She had been so intently staring at her descendant she hadn't sensed his approach.

The "voice" now took on an angrier tone and seemed to reverberate deep within her as it shouted, "Why do you question me, woman?!"

Marie knew she had inadvertently done something she should never have done; she had questioned the Master. "No. No, my husband. I don't question you," she quickly replied. "You only caught me off guard. I'm so sorry."

She knew she was never to question him. In life, he had been her husband, her friend, her lover, but now in death, he had taken on a new roll. Marie was now the submissive servant and Dwight was the heartless and unforgiving master. She only hoped this was an interim step in her journey into the afterlife and not her final destination.

Dwight now did with her as he chose and made her suffer whenever the mood hit him. She understood she likely deserved such a fate after the most heinous acts she had committed while on earth. She had suffered for almost a century and hoped the end was in sight.

"You know what you must do," he commanded. "You must start putting the wheels in motion. But be sure to take it slowly. It must be gradual. They cannot suspect anything. Do everything as I've explained, and all will happen according to my plan. But the final act must take place at the prescribed time."

Not wanting to anger him further, Marie said, "As you wish, my husband." She despised the horrible creature her husband had become. She thought she couldn't possibly hate him more than when he was alive, after his deceit but realized what he had since become was so much worse. And what she had turned into was a nothing more than a pathetic cowering creature.

After a moment Marie sensed her husband's presence moving away, although he was never completely gone from her. Now she had to put a carefully orchestrated series of events in motion which, like a snowball rolling down a hill, would continue to grow and progress until its final climax on the designated date: December 19th, the anniversary of the deaths of their two sons and the day Marie and Dwight themselves had died as well.

From inside the mirror, Marie Livingston began to focus her concentration toward Stephanie Wright and extending her gnarled index finger out of the mirror she sent out the tiniest wisp of sparkling white illumination in the direction of the unsuspecting woman. When the light reached Stephanie, it hung above her head spinning in a circular pattern resembling a small wreath before settling down atop her head like Christ's own crown of thorns. Then the lights slowly began to seep in, tingling working their way deep inside of her mind where they were to become the first seeds of doubt and eventually, the seeds of destruction.

Stephanie's eyes opened wide taking on a new intense look of suspicion. Only a moment earlier she had been criticizing herself for thinking such horrible and distrustful thoughts about Jason. Now she was having those thoughts again and they felt truer to her than ever. She found her mind drifting to someone. There had been a young female accountant in the financial department of the building where Jason now worked. She recalled him mentioning her once at dinner. At the time it had seemed innocent enough, just a coworker.

She recalled how she hadn't wanted to allow her own insecurities to make her feel jealous and suppressed those emotions. But she knew her husband and knew if he was taking the time to mention someone it was for a reason. Perhaps it was simply his way of showing respect for her professional skills or perhaps it was more. God, she hated thinking that way but it seemed lately the less she saw of

Jason on an intimate level the more they seemed to become distant.

"If he's not getting it at home," a voice inside her said, "he's getting it somewhere else."

She had no idea where that had come from, but it planted itself deep in her subconscious. She began to wonder if she might have been wrong about not being more concerned about this woman, this potential interloper.

"What was that woman's name?" she thought to herself. "Jo something. Joan? No that wasn't it. Jolene! Yes, her name was Jolene, Jolene Roberts. That was it."

Stephanie had only met the woman once during a visit to the office and in Stephanie's estimation; she had been a "knockout." In fact, she was drop-dead-gorgeous, divorced, and definitely looking for a pair of male slippers to put under her bed. Now Stephanie began to wonder if the woman might be setting her sights on Jason, biding her time until the moment was right. Stephanie was certain if Jolene Roberts chose to sink her claws into Jason it would take everything he had to resist her advances.

She decided to pay more attention to the way her husband behaved and monitor his comings and goings more carefully. She also would try to find out more about this Jolene Roberts and determine what her intentions might be. She trusted Jason; she believed in him, but she also knew how seductive some women could be. She wouldn't allow some bimbo to ruin her marriage and break up their new family.

From behind Stephanie another small burst of sparkling light flew, encircling her head once again before settling down and her train of thought changed. In fact, she had completely forgotten about Jason, Jolene, and her suspicions.

Stephanie felt an uncontrollable urge to go up into the attic of the main house and find a box. She couldn't recall seeing the box during any of the times they had hauled junk up to the attic, but she could now imagine it as plain as day. It was a brown cardboard box with the initials LFH written on the front and top. And just as she mysteriously knew about the box, she also somehow knew what the initials meant. They stood for Livingston Family History.

The box contained the records of the genealogical research Emerson Washburn had commissioned several years earlier. She had to find the box and had to do so immediately.

"Connie?" Stephanie called to the woman dusting the atrium below. "Can you please come up here for a moment?" She decided she'd ask the Franks woman to wait and listen for Sammy while she went to the main house and found the box. A few minutes ago, she wasn't sure what she would do with all of the idle time suddenly available to her. Now she felt as though there weren't enough hours in the day to do what she needed to do.

Back in the shadows of the loft the rippling mirror returned to its natural state and deep in the world on the other side of the glass could be heard an evil and sinister laugh. "It has begun," the voice said.

25

JASON DROVE THROUGH Ashton heading back home after a late day meeting with the factory manager, Tom Mc-Clellan. Tom had been nothing but complimentary of the way Jason had transitioned into his new position as well as how he was rapidly reorganizing the manufacturing engineering department. He believed Jason was the "breath of fresh air" the company needed to help it continue to grow and prosper long into the future.

Jason loved his new position as well as his new responsibilities. At first everything he attempted seemed to be a monumental task and something to be feared; however, he had risen to meet every challenge head-on. Initially, that meant long hours and an incredible amount of stress but then the pressure gradually began to ease.

He knew the long hours away from home were beginning to take their toll on Stephanie. She had been very understanding and tolerant, but he sensed her patience beginning to wane a bit more each day.

Now, however, he had decided things would be different. Beginning the following week, he was determined to start bringing things back to normal both at work as well as at home. This meant he would be putting in fewer hours on the job and spending more time at home with his family. The kids were all growing like weeds and the past summer had gone by in a blur. He had decided it was time to slow down a bit and make things right with them. He had discussed this with Tom McClellan at their meeting that afternoon, and Tom agreed with Jason wholeheartedly.

Jason stopped on his trip through town and picked up a bouquet of flowers for Stephanie at local florist while trying to think of something interesting his family could do over the weekend.

Maybe it was time to consider taking some of that money and planning a trip to Florida or some other warm location over the Christmas holiday. By that time Jeremy and Cindy would be home from school for their holiday break and he hadn't used much of his vacation yet. He decided to discuss it with Stephanie after dinner while the kids were out of earshot.

Jason drove up their access road as the sun began to set in the distance looking at the breathtaking view of their home in the distance. He recalled how he had joked about him and Stephanie finding a way to be alone in the hot tub grotto or in the spa. But neither had happened. It wasn't like them to go so long without intimacy. The realization of how little attention he had been paying to his wonderful wife suddenly made him ache with guilt. It was like he had just awoken from a coma to realize several months had mysteriously slipped away.

He pulled his car into the garage, and as he walked out into the atrium, he could hear the kids playing in the family room. He and Stephanie had decided there was little need for a formal living room in their lives, so they had immediately converted the first-floor front room of the house into a family room with plenty of comfortable sofas and chairs for reading or watching TV.

"Hey, kids. What's up?" Jason said enthusiastically as he crossed the foyer. Looking to his left he could see Stephanie in the kitchen making dinner. He held the flowers behind his back. She didn't seem to see him or acknowledge his arrival.

"Great!" Jason thought. "I'm in trouble!"

"Hi, Dad," Jeremy said, raising his left hand in a cursory wave not taking his eyes off the movie he and Cindy were watching on the huge flat-screen TV. She too gave a brief wave obviously just as engrossed in the movie as Jeremy was.

Sammy who had been sitting on the floor stacking blocks stopped and ran toward Jason hugging his leg and shouting "Daddy! Daddy! Daddy!"

"Hey, stinker," Jason said picking the toddler up with his free arm and giving him a big kiss on the cheek as Sammy squeezed his neck tightly.

"Aggggh!" Jason said with a comical chocking sound as he stuck his tongue out the side of his mouth. Sammy gave a great belly laugh as he always did when Jason played these games with him.

Then he sat Sammy back down on the floor and said, "Ok, buddy. Go back and play with your blocks now for a bit before supper. I need to go out and talk to Mommy for a little while." Sammy looked a bit disappointed but went back to his playing. The other two were still sitting entranced by the movie and likely didn't hear a word.

Walking down the hallway toward the kitchen being careful to keep the flowers hidden behind his back, Jason could see Stephanie still busy at work. She glanced up at him as she was setting the table for dinner.

When Stephanie's eyes met his Jason saw or perhaps imagined something for the briefest of moments and it caught him off guard. In the matter of a millisecond as if time itself had slowed to a crawl, he saw the look in Stephanie's eyes go through a series of impossible changes.

First, she looked at him as if she had no idea who he was, a total stranger. Next, a glint of recognition entered her eyes. He expected to see the look change to pleasant surprise at his early arrival home but that wasn't what happened. Instead, her look changed to one of anger like she had just encountered someone she detested rather than loved.

Then the hostile glare disappeared just as quickly and was replaced with a calm and aloof look as she returned to setting the table. "I see you're home early for a change," she said coolly. "To what do we owe this honor?"

Jason was still mentally reeling from the many intense emotions he had just witnessed and stammered, "Um . . . ah . . . yes . . . Sorry. I suppose I deserve that. I was able to get out early today. And look what I brought you." He held out the flowers.

Stephanie ignored them and instead said sarcastically, "Well then, I suppose we should all be thanking the heavens above you have chosen to grace us with your wonderful presence."

Jason hesitated for a moment choosing his words carefully. It didn't take a rocket scientist to know Stephanie was in a foul mood and likely looking for an argument. As such he said with extreme caution, "Look Steph. I understand your frustration. And believe me when I say I'm so very grateful for your patience. I honestly couldn't have done this without you and without your help."

Stephanie didn't reply but Jason believed he saw the cloud of anger begin to slowly fade from her troubled face. He said, "Look. Just so you know, I spoke with Tom Mc-Clellan today and told him I needed to get back to a more normal schedule. The extra hours were taking its toll on my family and I was in danger of burning out. I figured the worst that could happen was he might fire me, but I didn't care anymore. I decided I simply couldn't expect you and the kids to put up with this any longer."

Stephanie now looked at Jason as if she was seeing a side of him she had never seen before. The Jason she knew was a hard working dedicated professional and a good corporate soldier who did whatever was necessary to succeed at his job. But the idea of him standing up to the plant manager and essentially demanding to have more time for his family was something she'd never expected.

Now she suddenly felt ashamed at the way she had just spoken to Jason, recognizing she had been out of line and he deserved better. She didn't know what had come over her. It had almost been like someone else had put a bunch of strange ideas into her head. Jason had been working his fingers to the bone for the past several months to make a better life for her and the kids and here she was treating him like dirt.

"Jason, I'm really sorry about . . ." she said as her eyes welled up with tears.

Jason moved the flowers to the countertop and reached out, taking Stephanie in his arms.

"No, Baby. You have nothing to be sorry about. I'm the one who should be sorry. I guess I got all caught up in this promotion thing and temporarily lost sight of what really matters." He looked into her eyes and said, "I'm so very sorry and I promise to do my best to make it up to you and the kids." They embraced again, and as Stephanie rested her head on Jason's chest, she was certain everything was going to be okay.

In the attic of the farmhouse, the surface of the antique full-length mirror began to shimmer and ripple as the residents of the netherworld beyond the glass silently howled with frustration at the turn of events taking place in the kitchen below. They had been trying to drive a wedge between the couple to make it much easier to complete their plan. And although this brief setback was no more than a bump in the proverbial road it was nonetheless aggravating.

As the predetermined time crept closer they were going to have to rethink their strategy. They'd double their efforts if necessary. They'd get their way eventually and there was no force in Heaven or on Earth capable of stopping them.

Downstairs in the kitchen, Stephanie backed away from Jason and dabbed at her eyes with a napkin. Jason decided to change the subject and asked, "So how's the book coming? Is it done?"

"Yes. I just finished it this afternoon," Stephanie replied. "I emailed Sean, my publisher, today and told him I'd send him the rough draft in a month."

"In a month?" Jason asked, "If it's finished why not send it now?"

Stephanie remembered Jason was unfamiliar with her writing methodology. "Well usually, I finish the book then set it aside for a few weeks, maybe a month. During that time, I do something else, something new. Then I come back and look at it one last time and make any improvements before sending it on to the publisher."

"Oh," Jason said contemplating, "that sounds smart. Makes sense to me." Then he thought for a moment and asked, "So what are you going to work on in the meantime? Are you going to start another kids' book or do something different?"

"I was thinking of something really different," Stephanie replied. "Ever since we learned about this house, I've been thinking about doing some research into my family tree. You remember I mentioned that to you a few times?" Jason nodded and Stephanie said, "Mason Armstrong had told us Uncle Emerson hired someone to do a good deal of research for him. I believe it's all in a box I found today in the attic. I didn't take much time to check it out, but I should be able to find all sorts of stuff there. Depending upon how much I learn I was thinking of organizing everything into a nice understandable document. You know into book form. And then maybe using one of those online print-on-demand places, I could make a few copies for us, the kids, and for my brother Chuck and his family. It might make for a nice Christmas gift for them."

Jason replied enthusiastically, "That's a great idea. Wow. I never would have thought of that."

"To be perfectly honest with you I can't believe I thought of it either. I have no idea where the idea came from. It just seemed to pop into my head." She turned and looked at the timer on the oven the told Jason, "Honey, could you go and tell the kids to wash their hands and get ready for dinner?"

"You bet," he replied, happy to find things quickly returning to normal once again.

Upstairs in the attic, a quiet guttural burst of laughter could be heard coming from deep within the old mirror. Dwight Livingston's ghostly voice said, "Well, it looks like some of the suggestions you gave to the woman have taken root after all. Now we simply have to wait for her to read what she needs to read in the documents. Then she'll be ours, once and for all."

26

STEPHANIE SAT WITH her legs crossed on the worn wooden-plank attic floor. A large brown cardboard storage box was next to her. In the meager lighting coming from the single bare bulb suspended from the fixture high above Stephanie's head, the attic was every bit as grimy and disordered as ever. The place always gave her the creeps. She had a natural dislike for attics in general but this one seemed much less hospitable than most. It was filled with some of the unsold antiques from Washburn's bedroom as well as many other mysterious unopened boxes and crates. These containers had been stored there most likely by Washburn prior to her family moving in.

She should have had Jason carry the large box to her loft workspace when she first found it. She'd ask him later when he got home from work. In the meantime, she was briefly looking through some of the photos and notes to see what she might want to take with her immediately.

Fortunately, Sammy had gone down for a nap in the loft bedroom a half hour earlier and Connie Franks had been nice enough to agree to watch him while she dusted the loft area. This gave Stephanie a brief time where she could sit down and go through the box she'd found.

Stephanie noticed Sammy seemed to be sleeping a lot lately during the day. It didn't cause her any concern yet, but she had made a mental note to watch his sleep patterns more closely for possible signs of trouble.

Upon examining the box, Stephanie was surprised by how disorganized everything inside was. Absolutely nothing was in any proper arrangement. She had naturally assumed a highly paid private investigator would have done a more systematic job of keeping things organized. Perhaps the investigator actually had done so but Washburn, unstable in his last month of life, had muddled the files. Stephanie knew she was going to have a big job ahead of her. Rather than becoming frustrated with the potentially daunting task, she found herself excited over the challenge. As she thumbed through the top-most layers of documents, she discovered a large stack of assorted photos bound by a thick rubber band. She decided rather than submerge herself into a stack of textual documentation at this early stage; she'd start with the photos.

She wondered if there would be any dates or identifiers written on the backs of the pictures, something to help her determine when the photos were taken and perhaps who was in them. She recalled how when she was a little girl she'd help her mother put pictures into their photo albums. Her mother would always write the date names of the people in the photos on the backs of each picture. She assumed her mother must have learned that practice from her own mother and hoped the tradition had started even further back in her lineage. Or maybe the private investigator had made personal notations on the back of the pictures. If so, then it might go a long way to help her quickly get things reorganized.

Stephanie turned over the first picture on the top of the stack. It was a photo of two young boys perhaps ages four and two years old. She was amazed at how much the two boys not only looked alike but also bore a striking resemblance to her own little Sammy. She held the card up to the light to see if she could read the caption on the back which was written in an elaborate, flowing cursive hand. The light was unfortunately too poor in the attic to allow her to see much but as best as she could discern the inscription read,

"Matthew James Livingston, age 5, and Charles Edward Livingston, age 3" followed by the date, "July 20, 1921,"

"Matthew and Charles Livingston," she said aloud, realizing they could very well be the sons of her great grandparents and most likely were. These two might have grown up to become her unknown great uncles.

She knew the Livingstons had other children because if she was assumed correctly her grandmother had been the sister of these two boys and had originally been from Schuylkill County. However, she didn't know how many other children, if any, the Livingstons may have had. She knew back in the early part of the twentieth-century people tried to have big families because often illness or some other tragedy would result in an early death for young children. Plus, if the place were operated as a family farm, Livingston would have wanted many children to help with the chores, especially boys.

Stephanie felt a chill run down her spine and she suddenly sensed she was being watched. She slowly turned and looked about the attic but could see nothing out of the ordinary lurking in the dark shadows. She saw the portrait of Dwight and Marie standing along the back wall of the attic wrapped tightly in its protective tarp and tied securely. She suspected at some point in her research she might once again have to unwrap the portrait to study it in more detail.

Then, whether having been a trick of the poor lighting a breeze in the attic through a crack or simply her own overactive imagination, Stephanie thought for the briefest of moments, she had seen the surface of the canvas tarp covering the portrait rustle ever so slightly. When she looked at it more intently the movement didn't return. She'd have sworn it moved.

She assumed by the strange feelings she was experiencing she may already have stayed too long. Stephanie decided to take the large stack of pictures to the loft where she could begin cataloging them in a better lighted and less gloomy setting.

Stephanie reached down and closed the lid of the box setting her stack of photos on top of it. She carefully stood up on legs which had all but fallen asleep and then bending over, she pushed the large box across the dusty attic floor, getting it as close to the door as possible for Jason to move later.

She thought back to how uncharacteristically angry she had been with Jason and she had been so grateful he said he was finally putting his family first again. She felt ashamed that she had begun to suspect he might have become involved with another woman. How could she have thought such a thing?

Standing up straighter, slightly out of breath, she saw stars flashing in front of her eyes. Then she thought she saw something out of the corner of her eye something moving along the shadowed back wall of the room. She knew there could be nothing back there except for the wrapped portrait of the Livingstons and that old dressing mirror.

Shaking her head, Stephanie picked up the stack of photos, switched off the light, closed the attic door, and went back to her loft studio.

27

THE COLD NOVEMBER winds howled outside as Stephanie intently scrutinized the ever-increasing mountains of documents and photos, making annotations in the margins of the typed pages of certain items she felt were of significance. She'd occasionally stop and enter some information on her laptop. Then she'd return to the pile of documents which had spread to cover the entire area that had once been her desktop. Likewise, her drawing board once used to create beautiful illustrations, now was covered with a large piece of butcher paper containing a scribbled version of a family tree.

The children's book she had set down over a month earlier lay somewhere beneath the mess completely forgotten. The previous week had been the time she had originally designated to revisit the book for final proofing before sending it on to her publisher. But that week and come and gone as did this week without a thought. The fact was she could scarcely even remember writing the book in the first place.

She was currently dressed in a pair of baggy gray sweat pants which were stained with paint, coffee, food, and God only knew what else. Her shirt was an oversized pink sweatshirt sporting similar stains and on her feet were a tattered pair of threadbare bedroom slippers. This had been her standard work outfit for the past week or more and even she was starting to notice its pungent aroma as it was getting a bit ripe and was in desperate need of spending some quality time in the washing machine.

But even so, her condition didn't seem to matter. Stephanie's hair looked like hadn't been combed since she got up that morning or even the previous morning. If asked she wouldn't have been able to tell anyone the last time she had bathed or showered. Her eyes, which were sunken behind dark circles, had the wild gaze of intensity bordering on mania.

The family history was all she thought about. And what was worse, it was all she cared about.

On those rare occasions when she left her loft long enough to speak with family members it had been in short, clipped and often barely intelligible half-sentences and the topic always seemed to contain names or snippets of information about one of her recently discovered ancestors. She spoke of them as if she knew them personally as if they were friends or acquaintances she had known all her life. She also discussed them as if everyone else in the family should know these strangers as well. Each week she seemed to decline steadily, becoming further absorbed.

She seemed to be driven by some strange force, one far beyond her control. She was likewise too frenzied to eat and had lost well over twenty pounds during the past six weeks.

To say her family was concerned was an understatement. However, Jason was at a loss at how to deal with it. The family was still new to the area and Jason didn't feel close enough to anyone at work to share such intimate concerns about his wife. He sensed he was putting off the inevitable by not calling for some type of professional help, but he so wanted to find a solution to this problem on his own without seeking outside intervention.

He had called Stephanie's brother Chuck the previous week and briefly explained about his concerns. Both Jason and Stephanie had been so busy over the past several months they had unfortunately not kept in touch with Chuck and his family. Jason was surprised by the cold vibe coming over the phone line from his traditionally jovial brother-in-law. Jason did his best to smooth things over with Chuck who agreed to stop by on the weekend to check on his little sister.

With Stephanie as indisposed as she had become much of the house cleaning was now handled exclusively by Mrs. Franks. Jason had changed the woman's work status from one or two days a week to five days. She even occasionally stopped by on Saturdays as well. Connie was responsible for cleaning the entire house except for the loft area which was a place Stephanie now insisted everyone including the family avoid. The only exception was Sammy and that was simply because he took his naps regularly in the loft bedroom while Stephanie worked. The rest of the time he just sat quietly staring at the television in an almost catatonic state.

Had she been in a normal frame of mind Stephanie would have become concerned by this change in his daily routine. She would have been both ashamed by her lack of concern and horrified by the reason for his lethargy.

At Jason's further request Connie Franks had also taken over the responsibility of preparing dinners for the family as well as school lunches for the two oldest children. On Friday night when Connie had to leave early, Jason would often order pizza or Chinese food from local restaurants and have it delivered in time for dinner. If there were not a sufficient amount of leftovers, he would also order out on the weekends. This had been going on for more than a month and Jason didn't know how much longer he could allow it to continue. He tried to be as supportive of Stephanie as she had been of him over the past summer but her strange absent-minded behaviors were really concerning.

In the loft, Sammy sat on the floor in what had become his usual manner staring at some mind-numbing children's video Stephanie had left playing in the DVD player. The fact was he wasn't aware of the program. Even if the TV had been turned off, he wouldn't have noticed the difference.

The young boy's mind was elsewhere a million miles away in a magical land where every young child's imagination would love to travel. It was a wonderful world of candy cane trees and lollipop flowers. It was a place of vibrant colors, amazingly pleasant smells and a never-ending array of delicious tastes.

However, below the surface of this idyllic landscape evil lurked. The incredible land of wonderful childhood pleasures was a lie, a falsehood, a sham, projected into the young boy's mind by the ghastly specters inhabiting the property.

When he napped, his mind also traveled to that same special place of childhood wonders. This was the reason he seemed to nap for such long periods; he had no desire to wake up and leave the miraculous land. When Jeremy, Cindy, and Jason came home the spirits lifted the diversion and Sammy was back to his normal persona never remembering a thing.

Jason was no longer spending long hours on the job and was home every evening and on weekends. But then again, he had to be since Stephanie had all but abandoned her family. It seemed to him at times as if she were becoming someone else entirely.

Now hard at work in the loft, Stephanie looked closely at the screen of her computer where she had typed a version of the almost completed family tree. When she began the project, she only had a few names listed: her and her family; her brother Chuck and his family; her parents and her uncle Emerson; and her great-grandparents, Marie and Charles Livingston.

However, during the past several weeks, she'd been quite successful at completing her side of the family tree. The private investigator Emerson hired had done an incredible job of compiling his data. She learned from the report the investigator's name was Jake Malone.

She looked carefully at her family tree on the computer screen examining it for what must have been the thousandth time. Her side of the tree started at the top with the Livingstons and ended with her present family. It also displayed the dates of birth and death for those who had passed away; at least those whose dates could be confirmed.

She likewise had completed most of Jason's family tree back to his grandparents and although she had identified his great-grandmother, she was unable to find anything about who his great-grandfather might be. This was quite frustrating. It was like she had a puzzle and the final piece was missing. She knew this single missing bit of information was the thing bothering her the most. But for the moment she decided to put that particular missing link out of her mind and go back to reviewing her own side of the family tree.

28

DURING HER RESEARCH she discovered the Livingstons, Dwight Charles Livingston and Marie Louise O'Hara Livingston, had produced three offspring, two boys and a girl. The family tree notations for the parents read:

Dwight Charles Livingston — born on July 23, 1890; died
    December 19, 1922
Marie Louise O'Hara Livingston — born June 6, 1892; died
    December 19, 1922

Stephanie was troubled by the fact both of her great-grandparents died on the exact same day. Nor was she able to miss the date of their sons' deaths:

Matthew James Livingston — born June 12, 1916; died
    December 19, 1922
Charles Edward Livingston — born July 2, 1918; died
    December 19, 1922
Sarah Louise Livingston — born August 15, 1920; died October
    16, 1975

Stephanie wondered what might have happened to cause the deaths of four family members on the same day. It also bothered her that that December 19, the day they all died, was the same day Sammy had been born . . . only it had been eighty-six years earlier.

Sarah Livingston, the only child to survive, had been the grandmother she had never known. Sarah passed away the year before Stephanie was born. She realized as she read the entry how close her family lineage had come to ending on that fateful day in 1922 when four of the five members of the Livingston family somehow perished. Whatever tragedy had befallen the Livingston family must have somehow spared the toddler.

"She was only as old as my own little Sammy." A cold chill raced down her spine as she shivered thinking about the young child Sarah. She couldn't imagine her own baby boy growing up without his family. How horrible that must have been for her grandmother.

Stephanie had recently made an additional notation to the section on Sarah Livingston when she had found a note among the piles of paperwork explaining how Dwight Livingston's younger sister, Amelia Livingston Miller had taken young Sarah to live with her and her family in Ashton, eventually adopting the child and raising her as her own daughter. The girl had taken the surname Miller and as an adult had moved to the suburbs of Berks County. Sarah had no memory of Dwight and Marie. So any connection to the Livingston name and history all but died with her adoptive parents.

Continuing to follow the family tree downward, Stephanie read the next entry; the one indicating when her grandmother married her grandfather.

Sarah Louise (Livingston) Miller married Stephen Edward
    Washburn June 8, 1943
Stephen Edward Washburn — died May 15, 1968.
The couple had two sons

This was how the Washburn name entered the picture. The next entry on the tree showed the births and deaths of her father, her mother as well as her uncle Emerson.

Emerson Charles Washburn — born August 7, 1945; died April 12, 2012

Nathan Edward Washburn — born September 3, 1948; died July 20, 1994

Marie Stephanie Jacobs — born August 18, 1949; died July 20, 1994 (wife of Nathan)

There it was again, another coincidence. Stephanie couldn't help but notice the strange twist of fate in how the Livingston family not only lost four relatives in one day but then many years later her own parents died on the same when struck by a drunk driver.

She again wondered about the original Livingston family tragedy and what might have happened. She followed the chart further downward finding the listing for both herself and her brother, Chuck, under her parent's names.

Charles David Washburn — born February 17, 1973

Stephanie Sage Washburn — born June 12, 1976

She looked again at her brother, Chuck's name above hers. "Charles" had been part of the male family members' names since Dwight and perhaps earlier. Had they been aware of Dwight Charles and the rest of the family lineage she might have understood yet somehow the name Charles had nonetheless traveled down three generations. It was yet another coincidence. She looked at the next entry.

Stephanie Sage Washburn married William Joseph Sanders on June 2, 1998

Cindy Marie Sanders — born December 12, 2001

Stephanie and William divorce March 22, 2003

She hated having this entry in her family tree because of the bad memories it dredged up, but she knew if this were to be an accurate historical representation, she had to post the bad right up there with the good. This was especially true since someday Cindy might want to conduct her own research and trace her father's genealogy back several generations.

Then she looked at the final piece of her side of the tree, her marriage to Jason and the birth of their son, Samuel.

Stephanie Sage Washburn Sanders married Jason John Wright
(born May 22, 1974) on May 16, 2009
Stepson Jeremy John Wright — born October 21, 1999
Samuel Jason Wright — born December 19, 2010

She hesitated again for a moment seeing Sammy's birth date. How strange it made her feel realizing the date of his birth matched the date of the mysterious Livingston family tragedy.

She moved her view over to Jason's side of the family tree and starting with Jeremy's birth traveled back through Jason's first marriage and then continued to work backward in time.

Jason John Wright married Sarah Cynthia Jones June 4, 1996
Jeremy John Wright — born October 21, 1999
Jason and Sarah divorce on April 13, 2006

Jason John Wright — born May 22, 1974
Cheryl Elizabeth Wright — born July 25, 1976; died July 25, 1986

There were several other strange coincidences. Sarah Jones Wright, Jason's first wife, had the middle name Cynthia and Stephanie had named her own daughter Cynthia. His ex also had the first name Sarah which was Stephanie's grandmother's first name. Perhaps this coincidence was just another random happenstance and didn't really possess any particular significance whatsoever.

Then Stephanie thought for a moment about Jason's sister, Cheryl. She died when Jason was just twelve years old and she was ten. She apparently had some rare form of bone cancer and fought the valiant fight for several years until finally succumbing to the disease on her tenth birthday. Jason often talked about his sister and recounted many fond memories for Cindy and Jeremy. He tried to stress the importance of family and having siblings. This was especially important in the blended family situation they had created. She followed the tree back further.

> Edmund Walter Wright — born September 8, 1946; died
> January 3, 2005
> Married to Linda Celia Jensen — born March 15, 1947; died
> February 26, 2007

From discussions with Jason after they had met, Stephanie learned his father Edmund, had died the year before Jason and Sarah were divorced. He had a massive heart attack at home and was gone before the ambulance arrived. Jason had been visiting at the time and had seen everything. It was quite traumatic for him. His mother had been suffering from dementia prior to his father's passing and had to be placed in an assisted living facility where she eventually simply faded and died.

Stephanie followed the family tree back to the last few entries she had been able to locate for Jason's family.

> Walter Stephen Wright — born November 29, 1919; died April
> 11, 1973
> Elizabeth Jane Jefferson — born May 22, 1921; died July 2,
> 1982
> Walter Stephen Wright married Elizabeth Jane Jefferson on June
> 21, 1944

This is where Stephanie had hit a dead end. She could find nothing more about the Wright side of the family. She found no information on Walter Wright's parents whatsoever. She suspected his father might have been an immigrant and perhaps had a completely different name upon his arrival. He might have taken the name Wright upon landing in the United States to make him sound more American, as so many immigrants did in those days. She could only guess, as there were literally no records and no information about him whatsoever.

She had a little bit more luck with the grandmother, however. Elizabeth Jane Jefferson in that she was able to identify Elizabeth's mother but was unable to identify her father.

Agatha Jane Jefferson — born August 3, 1897; died 19??

That was pretty much the end of it. She had no idea when Agatha died or who her husband was. Stephanie suspected Jefferson might be her married name as the concept of having children out of wedlock in those days was virtually unheard of. But if there was a Mr. Jefferson there was not a trace of it recorded anywhere. Nor would she locate Agatha's maiden name.

Stephanie looked across the room and saw Sammy sitting slack-jawed staring at the television, a steady stream of drool dripping from his lip. She could smell the foul stench of his soiled diaper. She suspected the boy might end up with a severe rash if she didn't tend to him soon. She knew she should go to him, but she also knew she was almost finished with her work. She was so close. She just needed to find out the final piece of the puzzle.

The problem was she had been through every single piece of information in the box from the investigator Malone and had exhausted her Internet resources as well, but she knew she couldn't rest until she solved this final part of the story.

Stephanie looked one last time into the empty box. She had no idea what prompted her to do so. It was one of those strange feeling she sometimes had, an obsessive-compulsive type of situation which suggested if she just looked one more time maybe there just might be something she missed. She knew it was an exercise in futility as the box had been empty when she checked only a few moments earlier. But she couldn't stop herself from looking inside the box one last time.

However, instead of seeing an empty box she found an old, tattered yellowed envelope lying in the bottom. She couldn't believe her eyes. Stephanie was certain the box had been empty. She reached down into the box and withdrew the envelope hoping against hope to find the final answer. She found much more than she had bargained for.

29

STEPHANIE SAT STARING at the strange envelope in her quaking hands. Where had it come from? She was certain it hadn't been in the box previously. She was reminded of that day almost half a year ago when she held another envelope in similarly shaking hands; the day she received notice of her inheritance. But she sensed the information in this envelope wasn't going to be a letter notifying her of impending good fortune. Still, she had to open it. She had to know what was inside.

The envelope was really a brand-new manila envelope the same type she had been using to catalog her discoveries since the start of the project. However, it appeared to her to be old, yellowed, and tattered, as if to suggest it might have come directly from one of her ancestors. And in a true and very horrifying sense, it had. The illusion of the aged envelope had been planted in her mind. The entities needed her to finish the story and wanted her to discover the horrible truth them to complete the final step of their unholy scheme.

Stephanie gently slid open the top flap of what she saw as a brittle envelope carefully and gingerly folding it backward in order to withdraw its contents. What she found was a letter several pages long which appeared to be written in longhand in an elaborate calligraphic style. Like the envelope, the paper appeared to be an ancient and fragile type of yellowed stationary stock, likely expensive in its time and was personalized with a watermarked "L" which, she assumed, must stand for Livingston.

As Stephanie stared down at what was actually several blank sheets of modern typing paper, she began to read the contents of the mysterious ancient document; written in words only she could see.

From the personal journal of Marie Louise O'Hara Livingston Nov. 16, 1922.

Stephanie was caught off guard for a moment.

"Today's date is November 16, 2012," she said aloud in amazement. "It is exactly ninety years to the day from when this entry was made." Her heart thudded with both anxious anticipation as well as an unexplainable sense of impending dread. She read on, driven by a thirst for knowledge.

Dwight must think me some sort of fool. He believes I am unaware of what he had been doing behind my back and with whom. While I stay at home raising his three children he is out gallivanting with his whore; that immoral sow, that depraved vixen who goes by the name of Agatha Jefferson.

Stephanie stopped in her tracks. That name Agatha Jefferson. She realized where she had seen that name before. She went back to her computer screen and reexamined Jason's side of the family tree. Her stomach sank with revulsion. She was right. She wished to God she was mistaken but she was not. Agatha Jane Jefferson had been the name of Jason's great-grandmother the one for whom she couldn't locate a husband. Could this be the same Agatha Jefferson, Marie Livingston had written about? She didn't like the direction this letter was heading; no, not in the slightest. Her stomach felt as if it might heave at any moment.

He claims to be working late, to be busy conducting his
business dealings far into the evening, but I am no fool. I
know better. The devil's business is what he is up to I say.
Spreading his demon seed about the county with his harlot
is the only business in which he participates. Sharing a bed
with that Jezebel, that is his supposed important business.

"Oh my God!" Stephanie said aloud in bewildered amazement. "What in the world was going on? Was Jason's great-grandmother sleeping with my great-grandfather? Is that what Marie is saying? Could that have been possible?"

Stephanie recalled how the lawyer Mason Armstrong had mentioned; since both sides of their family had been from Schuylkill County there might be a chance they were distantly related several generations back. She thought he was just trying to be funny or clever but perhaps he had unknowingly been right. Or maybe he had seen the letter she now held in her hands and he had known about everything. She was uncharacteristically grateful the lawyer was dead. At least she wouldn't have to face him in her shame.

She never counted on discovering something as unsavory as an extramarital love affair let alone a love triangle involving ancestors from both sides of their families. She hadn't believed such things happened back in the early 1900s. But then she realized such types of illicit relationships were going on since the dawn of time. Although disgusted by what she read she was driven to learn more. She looked down at the blank paper and continued to read the message Marie Livingston wanted her to read.

But I am not the fool Dwight makes me out to be. I
have heard the women in the marketplace speaking in hushed
whispers as I walk by. They all laugh at me behind my

back. They enjoy my pain because we are wealthy, and they are but the wives of poor coal miners. They seem to take pleasure from what has happened as if it somehow brings me down to their low social level. I have overheard snippets of their conversations, bits and pieces, enough for me to be able to piece together the sordid mess. I have found out about her, Agatha, about what she has been doing with my husband and about their bastard daughter as well.

"Bastard daughter?" Stephanie exclaimed. This story was getting worse by the minute. Now she wondered if the daughter about whom Marie was speaking was some other daughter or could it actually have been Elizabeth Jane Jefferson, Jason's grandmother. Could her grandmother who had survived the Livingston tragedy and Jason's grandmother have been half-sisters? It was impossible for Stephanie to comprehend.

Oh, yes. I have learned the horrible truth and I would be dishonest if I didn't say the knowledge has vexed me to the point where I am struggling with my own sanity. Each day that I am forced to reside in this house with that ungodly fornicator knowing his illegitimate offspring lives in town, just a few miles away, knowing others in the community have been aware of his indiscretions and are ridiculing me behind my back, the more I feel myself losing touch with reality. And why would that seem so strange? Why should I want to try to live a normal life bearing the burden of this knowledge? Why should I not just let my mind go? Why not just stop fighting this inevitable creeping madness? I suppose should speak to someone. Maybe I could talk to our minister, but what in the world would I say to him? After all, he too is a man. He would most certainly side with Dwight and blame me for not providing for my husband's manly needs. Oh, dear God I am beside myself with anguish.

Stephanie's eyes welled up with tears. The language Marie used in her journal was so heartfelt and so incredibly painful to read she felt as if she, Stephanie, were feeling the very same pain and sorrow. Stephanie was reminded of how several months earlier Jason had been working so many late nights and she had briefly wondered whether or not he might have been having an affair, perhaps with someone at work. Although she had put the idea all but completely out of her mind, she now recalled the pain she felt in the pit of her stomach at the very thought of him cheating on her. Had it been true she might have suffered from the exact same feelings.

My heart has been broken and now I can feel my mind is rapidly on its way to shattering as well. I know I must do something but I know not what that might be. I am not proud to say I have actually considered killing both Dwight and his harlot. I have had fantasies of slitting their throats with a butcher knife and listening to their final breath bubble and gurgle from their open wounds. I have dreamt of watching the light leave their eyes as they slipped away in death. I have even imagined kidnapping and drowning their little bastard, Elizabeth Jane in the river like a sick kitten and perhaps someday I will.

"Elizabeth Jane?" Stephanie exclaimed horrified. It was as if reading the name of the child in Marie's letter made it official. The bastard girl Marie referred to was Jason's grandmother. Stephanie and Jason really were related. And although any relative might be considered distant it was still too close for Stephanie to feel comfortable. To make matters worse Jason's great-grandmother had been a shameless slut, not only throwing herself at Dwight, a married man but allowing herself to bare his illegitimate child as well. Then the woman had the audacity to parade the little girl around town proudly like there was nothing wrong and as if she had every right to do so. She shamelessly allowed all of the women in Ashton to see the result of her immoral actions.

Stephanie was becoming furious as she thought of the shame and humiliation Marie must have felt at being subjected to such an outrage. Marie was obviously a proper woman, a woman of high breeding while Agatha was likely nothing more than a common tramp. What sort of woman would allow herself to behave in such an unacceptable manner? And to think this slut, this whore, was Jason's great-grandmother! Stephanie was starting to realize had she been Marie she too might have wanted to seek revenge for the injustice. She too might want to drown the illegitimate child in a river as Marie had suggested. With extreme uncertainty, Stephanie read the next section of Marie's journal entry.

Drowning seems like a fitting end for such an immoral blemish on a righteous society. Miraculously I have somehow managed to hold onto enough of my shattered mind to prevent myself from turning my murderous thoughts into foul deeds. I can still comprehend if I were to take such an action; I would likely spend the rest of my life in prison. Perhaps someday when my mind has become completely lost I will no longer care. I can only hope then I will be able to act without any such moral or rational considerations.

But for now I have to think of my children, Dwight's children, my two sons and daughter. My Sarah Louise is the spitting image of me. She is my sweetheart and my joy. She is my precious own little girl for certain so much like me I now prefer to imagine she was conceived without the benefit of Dwight's accursed seed. She looks nothing like her father. She acts nothing like her father. In fact, she IS nothing like her father. She is like me and only like me.

"My grandmother," Stephanie said quietly. "My grand-mother looked just like her mother." Stephanie thought back to how she herself had resembled Marie in the portrait which had originally hung in the living room and which now was stored in the attic. "We all must look similar. We must all look like Marie." Stephanie recalled her own mother and how much they resembled each other as well. Stephanie read further.

My boys, on the other hand, Matthew and Charles, they are so very much like their father. In fact, they look and act so much like their father it sometimes frightens me. It is almost as if they are not just his sons but copies of himself. And now since learning of Dwight's sinful treachery, I have begun to wonder what will become of these two boys when they grow to be men.

Do they have more than appearance in common with Dwight? Will they too someday grow up to break the heart of the women they profess to love? Will they lay with wanton women and father bastards like Dwight has done? Will they subject their wives to shame and humiliation as I have been subjected? I suspect they probably will. They both look so much like their father. They idolize him, imitate him and want to be just like him. I would have to assume their fate will lie on a similar accursed path as their father's.

What was Marie saying? If Stephanie originally didn't like the tone of the journal, she liked it even less now. Once again, her stomach turned but this time in anticipation of what sort of unspeakable direction the journal entry might take.

I must do something to punish Dwight for what he has done to me but what that will be I still do not yet know. I can barely find the strength and presence of mind to write this account, let alone to plan my revenge. My mind wanders constantly, never able to stay on one subject for very long. I seem to think in short random bursts and from the reactions of those with whom I have interacted of late I suspect my speech might also have become just as erratic. I see how they look at me and how they all talk about me when they think I am not noticing. It is like they all know I am going mad and as if they are all in it together against me; all waiting for the madness to take control.

Perhaps I already am mad and if so then all the better. Because if I truly am insane then these horrible thoughts of revenge and violence I have been having are not my fault. If I can't stop these thoughts and if I can't control them how can they be my fault? Maybe I am a danger not only to others but also to myself. Maybe I should be locked away somewhere, in a place where I cannot act on my unspeakable thoughts.

But what if I were to act on them would it be my fault? Of course not. The blame would lie entirely at Dwight's feet. He is the guilty party here not I. I am quite certain people would all say he was the one responsible not me. He is the one who had lain with the harlot. He is the one who fathered the bastard child. He is the one whose activities would have been responsible for driving me mad. How could that possibly be considered my fault? Who would blame me? No one, I suspect. They would say Dwight brought all of it upon himself by his immoral actions. They might even honor me for my courage in the face of such adversity.

They might try to lock me up or even hang me for my actions but what would I care? My life as I once knew it is over so what would be the difference? It would still be better than living with the shame of what has happened to me and being helpless to strike back. I am certain if I am locked away I would miss my lovely, little Sarah, but God help me; I do not believe I would not miss the boys. No, not one bit. I would not miss seeing their father's face reflected in theirs, his eyes in their eyes, his sinful actions in their future actions. I know that is a most horrible and un-motherly thing to say but the more I think of it the more sense it begins to make to me. Those two are more his boys than mine.

A cold chill ran from the base of Stephanie's skull to the bottom of her spine to read such insane ravings. Marie may have believed she was losing her mind, but Stephanie was certain the woman's mind was long gone by the time the letter was written. She couldn't imagine thinking such evil thoughts about her own little Sammy. True, he did look exactly like Jason and he idolized his father. In many ways, he acted just like Jason, but he was his own special person. She couldn't imagine herself thinking as Marie had thought but then again neither had she gone through the mental anguish Marie had suffered. Perhaps such trauma caused one to think irrationally and allowed those ideas to seem rational. Stephanie hoped she'd never need to find out for herself. She read on.

I know such a statement might sound cruel, especially since the boys sprang forth from my own womb, but they are just so much like him, like their horrible lecherous father. I know I shouldn't think like that. They are not just his boys but they are my boys too. I love them. But God forgive me I hate Dwight so. And I want to hurt him in a way he will never forget.

I must think further on this. My mind is swimming in a river of befuddlement. I am unsure of which of my thoughts are real and which are fantasies. I know what I must do but it is in direct conflict with what my mind is telling me I should do. I now know how to hurt Dwight. I know now how to break his heart as he has broken mine. But I can't do it. Yet I know I must do it. I will do it but not today. God help me I need to rest. I need to think clearly. I hate what Dwight has done to me. And I hate the rambling wretch he has caused me to become.

That was where the letter ended. Stephanie looked off into the distance as if in a trance thinking about what he had just read. She set the papers down on the floor next to her and once again they were no longer the aged stationary adorned with calligraphy but was a stack of modern typing paper completely blank.

Stephanie reviewed the newly typed family tree and compared the names once again with those she read in the letter. As strange as it might seem to her it was true Dwight Livingston was not only her great-grandfather but was Jason's illegitimate great-grandfather as well. They shared a common ancestor and although distantly, they were essentially cousins.

In Marie's letter, she had said how much her boys looked like Dwight and her daughter looked like her. Stephanie remembered again how much she and Jason resembled the portrait of Marie and Dwight. Then she began to recall how often people commented on how they both made such a perfect couple, how good they looked together, or how much they looked as if they were meant to be together. Some people even went so far as to say they looked more like brother and sister than husband and wife. And now she had discovered the reason why; they actually were related!

She began to wonder if she would have discovered this information early on in their relationship; would she still have gotten involved with him? She assumed she wouldn't have under fear of potential birth defects in their offspring. But Sammy was not deformed nor did he suffer any mental deficiencies. He was a perfectly normal child. But then again . . . Sammy wasn't exactly a perfectly normal child, was he? No. He was special, very special. She recalled how he was overly sensitive to things that for most children went unnoticed. Stephanie thought how he had reacted much differently than their other kids when he stood staring out into the field where the dear carcass lay rotting. He had been smiling and repeating the word boys, repeatedly.

"Boys?" Stephanie said. "He had been saying, boys. What had he been seeing?" She thought once again of Marie's journal entries about her two boys and about how those two boys, as well as Dwight and Marie, had all died on the exact same day.

She had to find out what happened back then.

From inside the mirror, Marie watched unseen. She was becoming anxious with anticipation seeing the plan finally beginning to take shape. Now there was just one more thing Stephanie needed to see today.

Stephanie looked once again into the envelope which she thought was empty and was surprised to find a folded piece of yellowed newspaper buried deep near the bottom of the envelope. It was strange she hadn't seen it before when she had found Marie's letter.

To any other onlooker, the "article" from the newspaper would have looked like a clipping from the previous day's daily newspaper. But to Stephanie, like the letter, it appeared ancient, yellowed and tattered.

The front-page article was dated December 21, 1922, and was from the *Ashton Daily News*. The headline screamed in bold letters *Murder-Suicide Claims the Lives of Four Family Members.*

30

"**M**URDER-SUICIDE?**"** Stephanie exclaimed, "Oh, my Lord!" She looked back to make sure she had not alarmed Sammy with her outburst but saw he was still sitting lethargically in front of the television screen. She didn't even notice the screen was completely blank. Instead, she refocused on her documents and began reading the details of the story as reported in the mysterious article. She had been familiar with modern-day, big-city newspaper style; short and to the point with a little flourish. The article from the box read more like a pulp fiction story than a newspaper article. Perhaps it was because that style of writing was something accepted in small town turn-of-the-century newspapers or maybe it was because nothing so horrendous had ever occurred in the area before. Either way, she was surprised by the tone of the narrative writing style.

The bodies of four local family members were discovered in the early afternoon hours on their small farm located just a few miles outside of Ashton. Although Ashton constables are investigating the occurrence, unofficial reports suggest the unpleasant incident might possibly have been a case of murder-suicide.

An unidentified informant close to local authorities told the Ashton Daily News the bodies of Dwight and Marie Livingston, ages 32 and 30 respectively, were found on the floor of their bedroom. Mrs. Livingston appeared to have been strangled to death by her husband who was found with an apparent self-inflicted fatal knife wound across his throat. Two separate knives were found at the scene. One was an unused kitchen knife, lying on the bedroom floor. The other blade was an ivory-handled straight razor apparently belonging of Mr. Livingston which was found covered with Mr. Livingston's blood lying next to his dead body.

"Ivory handled straight razor?" Stephanie exclaimed recalling the antique razor Jason had found in a cigar box in one of the dresser drawers in the master bedroom. He had been quite surprised to find it in such good condition and assumed Emerson Washburn had used it. Jason now used that razor to shave daily. Was it the same one? She hoped to God it wasn't.

Stephanie thought about the journal entry she had just read from Marie Livingston and how the woman had said she wanted to slit Dwight's throat with a kitchen knife. She also recalled how Marie had wanted to kill Dwight's lover and then drown their illegitimate daughter in a river. But according to what the article read Dwight may have actually slit his own throat. Although disturbed by the facts unfolding before her eyes, Stephanie needed to know more.

Mr. Livingston was found on the floor in a seated position with his back resting against a wall cradling his dead wife's body in his lap. She was said to have been found dressed in an evening gown and covered with Mr. Livingston's blood which had flowed down from her husband's mortal wound.

This scene seemed strangely familiar to Stephanie. It was as if she had seen it played out before, perhaps in a movie.

Sometime later police discovered the bodies of the Livingston's two sons Matthew age six, and Charles age four, near an open well on the property. Cause of death was presumed to be drowning.

Details are unsubstantiated at this time and it is unknown if the drowning was accidental or if either Mr. or Mrs. Livingston may have killed them. Until more evidence has been gathered sources said all the police can do at this time is speculate based on what they have seen.

Our source close to the authorities said the police are considering the possibility Mrs. Livingston may have drowned her sons as her arms were covered with small scratches of the type one would receive from a struggling child. It was further suggested Mr. Livingston might have returned home, found the boys floating dead in the well, recovered their bodies, and then confronted her in their bedroom where he apparently strangled her for her part in the foul deed.

The Livingston bedroom door was found broken and dangling from a single remaining hinge indicating the husband must have broken it down. If the above scenario is accurate then one could speculate Mr. Livingston, overcome with remorse for his own vile actions in the murder of his wife, may have cradled his wife's dead body and slashed his own throat with his straight razor.

"Oh, my God!" Stephanie said as the tears welled up in her eyes and began to stream down her cheeks. Her breath was coming in short hitching bursts and a buzzing began to ring inside her head making her feel as if she might pass out. Her worst fears had been realized. No. This was far beyond her wildest imaginings. Her great-grandmother Marie Livingston must have lost her mind upon learning of her husband's treachery and killed her own two sons in some misguided attempt to get revenge against him. Why or how the woman could do such a thing made no sense to Stephanie although she had to assume Marie had not been in control.

The bodies of the Livingston parents were discovered in the early afternoon by Mrs. Amelia Miller, sister to Dwight Livingston. Mrs. Miller said she had been returning the Livingston's youngest child, daughter Sarah Louise Livingston age two, who had been spending the night with the Miller family. Mrs. Miller then sent her carriage driver to the town of Ashton for help. Mrs. Miller, a resident of the town of Ashton was stricken with grief over the tragedy and provided only one comment. She said, "This is so incredibly horrible, so unthinkable. Thank God I had Sarah with me or she might have been part of this awful tragedy as well." Mrs. Miller has assumed temporary custody of her niece.

"This is unbelievable!" Then she began to think again about the things she had learned about her family, about Jason's family and was quite certain the newspaper had gotten the story correct. Stephanie sat for a moment in silence trying to absorb all she had discovered.

From inside the mirror hanging on the back wall of the loft, Marie Livingston stared out with wild and insane eyes glowing madly with her sick pleasure. She had accomplished what she needed to do but that was still not enough. She needed the woman to feel her pain to experience the events as if she had lived them herself. This wasn't only important, but it was essential for the next part of the plan to evolve.

Marie waved one of her fingers and once again a series of sparkling white lights flew and encircled Stephanie's head, sending her into a trance-like state.

She was no longer sitting in her loft; she was sitting in the formal living room of the old farmhouse decorated in a fine Victorian style. She immediately understood she had become Marie.

It was early morning on December 19th, 1922 and Marie had arranged for her sister-in-law, Amelia Miller to come and take her daughter Sarah to stay with her and her husband overnight. Marie wanted to have Sarah out of the house and if things went the way she planned to have a place for the child's future care.

Amelia loved little Sarah. And as of yet, her own marriage had not produced any children so she treasured any time she could have alone with the child. Marie knew Amelia would love her like her own no matter what happened.

That morning Amelia arrived by carriage When Marie opened the front door for Amelia, Sarah ran to greet her hugging her legs.

"Hello, Marie," Amelia said lightly grasping her sister-in-law in an obligatory but not heartfelt embrace, "I trust all is well with Dwight and the boys."

"All is as well as can be expected I suppose," Marie replied cryptically. She didn't intend to discuss any of the marital problems she was having especially with her husband's sister. Besides, Marie suspected if half the town of Ashton knew of Dwight's philandering then it was likely Amelia did as well.

"Where are Dwight and the boys?" Amelia asked with what Marie perceived as an odd tone in her voice.

"Dwight is away for the day on business and should be arriving later this evening. The boys are out in the fields playing and doing whatever it is boys do."

"Those boys are adorable," Amelia said. "They remind me so much of their father when he was a boy."

Marie twitched slightly and replied, "Yes." Regaining her composure, she said, "I'd just been thinking the very same thing. The boys adore their father and I wouldn't be at all surprised if they grew up to be just like him."

When Amelia heard this the look in her sister-in-law's eyes didn't project pride. Instead, Marie appeared disturbed by the idea of her boys growing up to be like their father. Amelia couldn't comprehend this as she loved her brother and was proud of the way he provided so handsomely for his wife and children. In Amelia's opinion, Marie should worship the ground he walked on.

"Well, then," Amelia said after a few moments of awkward silence. "I suppose we should be on our way. We will see you tomorrow late morning then. Say hello to Dwight and the boys for me. Tell them I'm sorry I missed them." With that, Amelia and Sarah entered the carriage, and the driver headed down the lane back to Ashton.

Marie replied, "I certainly will." In her mind, however, she knew by the time Amelia returned with Sarah the boys would be dead and hopefully, their father would be as well. Her own future would be uncertain, but she suspected the rest of her life would be either spent rotting away in prison or dangling from a rope. That would be up to the courts.

The scene in Stephanie's mind changed to dusk later that same day. Marie was staggering toward the back of the property where a large well stood. It was round, constructed of large fieldstones and stood about three feet high.

As she approached the well each of Marie's hands held tightly to the tiny hands of her sons, Matthew and Charles. The boys seemed to sense something was very wrong as they were struggling to break her tight grasp.

"Mommy, stop," Matthew whined. "Where are you taking us? Please, Mommy, we're afraid. Please stop, Mommy. We'll be good. We promise."

Charles didn't speak; he just cried and held onto his favorite stuffed bear, egged on by the terror in Matthew's pleading voice. The futile begging fell upon deaf ears. Marie was too far-gone to succumb to the pleas of the terrified boys, Dwight's boys as she now thought of them. She had a mission and no force in could stop her. As she dragged them, she mumbled incoherently, "Just like your father. You look like him. You act like him. Someday you will end up being whoremongers just like him. Not if I can help it. Oh, no. Not if I can help it."

Dwight had constructed a cover for the well out of timber to prevent the children from accidentally falling in. The trap door of this cover was always kept closed and secured with a lock the key for which he kept high in a cabinet in the kitchen. A fully-grown adult could have leaned into the well and with a bit of stretching could touch the top surface of the water. However, small children would never have been able to escape its depth nor scale its slippery sides. Marie had come out earlier in the day with the key and opened the door.

When she reached the side of the well, she stopped for a moment. Then without a word of explanation, she lifted Charles in, his screams following him into the icy water below. His stuffed bear flung out of his grasp and fell onto the frozen meadow near the well. Then Marie bent and using both hands lifted Matthew. He fought, scratched, and clawed at her arms in a futile attempt to get free of her grasp but his only freedom came during those few seconds as he was hurled to meet his brother.

Marie stood at the top of the well looking down at the boys, and screamed maniacally, "He made me do this! Your father made me do this! You're both like your father! Just like your whore-loving, worthless father! You will never get the chance to do to anyone what he did to me!"

From below, she heard the boys' cries and pleas for help but stood above watching them without an ounce of sympathy. If she had a last-minute change of heart, she could have saved them, but rational thought was gone. The boys soon came together and hugged each other in a final attempt to get warm before eventually succumbing to the frigid December temperatures and drowning in each other's arms.

"Just like your father," she said breathlessly. "The both of you. Just like your father. And soon he'll be just like you. Dead. Just like both of you."

Later, Dwight Livingston slowly made his way up the roadway that led to his house from the main road. His Ford Model T chugged and sputtered noisily up the frozen drive, occasionally slipping and sliding as plumes of smoke and steam billowed around it. Dwight had been one of the first people in the area able to afford a motor vehicle and as such was probably fonder of this possession than just about anything else he owned. As he approached the house, he saw some activity out in the back of his property near the well. In the bright moonlight, he could see a woman in a white nightgown.

Marie turned when she heard her husband's vehicle approaching in the distance and decided she'd better head back to the house. She glanced over and saw Dwight leaving his Model T and walking across the meadow toward her. She hurried away, trampling Charles' stuffed toy into the slush and mud as she did. When she was about a third of the way to the house, Dwight had made it about half the distance to the well. He saw Marie storming back toward the house. At first, he was going to call out to her to let her know he was home, but he realized something felt very wrong.

Dwight noticed the top cover of the well was removed. Only he or Marie knew where the key for the well was kept. He looked back at Marie and saw she didn't have a bucket or any means of carrying water. So why was she at the well if not to get water? As he approached the well, he saw something on the ground smashed into the ground. In an instant, he recognized it as the stuffed bear he had recently brought home for little Charles.

Using his walking stick for support, he began to hurry toward the well, hoping not to find what he already suspected.

When he got to the well, he bent down and picked up Charles' toy then headed straight for the opening. The boys knew not to play near the well and the boys always obeyed his requests. There was absolutely no way they would have come this close to the well without either he or Marie bringing them here. With dread building deep in the pit of his stomach, Dwight peered unwillingly down over the side of the well where he saw his two beloved sons entwined in a last embrace of death, bobbing in the water below. Without hesitation, he leaned as far as he could into the well and grabbed onto the water-soaked coats of both boys. Pulling with all his might he lifted their cold, still bodies from their icy tomb and laid them as gently as possible on the meadow grass. Their ice glazed bodies seemed to glow iridescent light blue in the moonlight making them look like angels.

Dwight fell to his knees near his dead sons and began to scream and cry his heart out. Near the house, Marie turned upon hearing Dwight's wails and stood for a moment with pleasure watching him fall to pieces over the bodies of his boys. She walked into the house, through the kitchen, and along the way picked up a long butcher's knife. She would be ready. When Dwight came for her, she would be ready. Then she walked slowly up to the master bedroom.

31

STEPHANIE CONTINUED TO stare out into space in her hypnotic state, watching the events of that horrible night play out on the movie screen of her mind. She was no longer Marie; she was now Dwight, seeing the scene from his perspective and reliving the thoughts and feelings he experienced.

Dwight slowly tried to stand up on wobbly legs looking back toward the farmhouse. He saw Marie looking out at him for just a moment as she approached the kitchen door. He wanted to call to her, but his voice caught in his throat when he saw her face, that horrible expression. In the rising moonlight, he saw her smiling at him. Not the one he'd known and had fallen in love with so many years earlier, though. It appeared more like a hideously bizarre grin; one radiating a twisted, insane rapture.

What was wrong with his wife and what in the name of God had happened to his boys tonight? Had she found them dead in the well and lost her mind with grief? God knew he was barely able to hold onto his own sanity over it. But why in the world had she been wearing such a hideous grinning expression at such an unimaginable time?

Dwight had assumed at first some type of terrible, yet innocent, accident must have occurred. He assumed she might have mistakenly left the top of the well open. He thought perhaps the boys had disobeyed his orders and had accidentally fallen into the opening. Perhaps Charles had fallen in and Matthew had climbed in to try to save him. It was a gutwrenching tragedy, but he was certain it had to have been an accident. Perhaps Marie had heard their cries for help and had come to the well in a futile attempt to try to rescue them. He wanted to believe that was so; he needed to believe it. But he couldn't because deep down inside, he already knew the truth.

After seeing the insane look on his wife's face as she glared madly out at him from the kitchen doorway, he had no choice but to accept the truth.

The boys' own mother had been deliberately responsible. He tried to force the thought away, but it continued to push its way to the forefront of his mind, and he had no choice but to accept it.

With growing anger, Dwight began to make his way through the meadow grass, wet with snow. He stumbled clumsily along the uneven ground, using his walking stick for support. When he got closer, he saw his and Marie's bedroom come alive with the bright glow from several lanterns. He saw Marie's shape passing behind the sheer curtains covering the windows as she moved about, lighting one lantern after another. It all seemed sinister and surreal.

By the time he reached the backdoor of the house, the bedroom appeared to be ablaze with light. He saw the silhouette of his wife standing at the window looking down at him. He couldn't make out her facial features in the shadows but assumed she still wore that mad grin.

He remembered how strangely Marie had been acting over the past several months, how distant and cold she had been toward him. Now that he had taken the time to think further about it, he realized she must have been in the throes of a mental decline. If he was honest with himself, he knew he was likely responsible.

Might it be possible she had somehow learned about Agatha and his illegitimate daughter? He had always been concerned such a day might come, but he never thought finding out would drive Marie to the point of insanity and murder. He mentally cursed the gossiping old biddies of Ashton from whom Marie had likely overheard the truth.

But then again, he hadn't really been discrete himself, had he? In fact, he had been quite arrogant and flagrant about his indiscretions. He had allowed himself to be seen in public with the mother as well as his child. Now in hindsight, he realized just how foolish he had been. Marie was always a strong woman. He should have realized she'd never have tolerated his philandering.

Dwight understood Marie knew everything there was to know about him, his strengths as well as his weaknesses. Therefore, she knew how to hurt him. She knew where to strike the blow to bring him to his knees. She understood how much he loved his two boys and how much they idolized him. But could she really have murdered her own flesh and blood as some sick attempt at revenge?

Suddenly Dwight thought about their youngest child, their daughter, Sarah.

"Oh my God!" he thought, stopping in his tracks. Where was Sarah? What had happened to Sarah? Had Marie killed her too? Surely, Marie couldn't have thrown Sarah into the well too, could she?

Forgetting about his wife for a moment, Dwight turned and looked back toward the well trying to decide if he had missed finding his daughter's body floating in the bottom because of his shock and confusion. Reflected in the moonlight, he could see the glistening wet bodies of his two dead sons, Matthew and Charles. He considered returning to the well to look for Sarah, but such a rescue would certainly be futile. If Sarah were truly in the well it was far too late for anyone to do anything to help her. She'd likely have been the first to be thrown in. His heart broke with sorrow and his gut clenched with revulsion.

His rage returned to a level the likes of which he had never known before. He was going to get the truth from his wife. He was going to find out what had happened to his children.

Dwight plowed through the kitchen door and as it flew open, windowpanes shattered. The broken shards tinkled to the floor sounding like tiny musical instruments. In the back of Dwight's mind, the sound reminded him of the high-pitched, melodic laughter of children, his children; his now dead children. Marie would surely pay for what she'd done.

Stephanie squirmed slightly in her seat, a disturbed expression forming on her face as the scene played out in her mind.

At first, she had become Marie. Then she had become Dwight. Now she seemed to have become separated from both, seeing things as a bystander. She understood the madness that possessed Marie as well as the fury that fueled Dwight. And of course, she knew it would end in a disaster.

Stephanie saw Marie standing before a full-length mirror, the same one that was now stored in the attic of the farmhouse. She watched Marie's reflection look down at her hands, covered with deep scratches. The blood from them had dried. The front of her white gown was stained with small smears of blood.

To Stephanie's surprise, Marie picked up a large hairbrush and began delicately stroking her long tresses, never taking her eyes from the eyes of the woman in the mirror. It was as if she was locked in a gaze with a stranger and was completely fascinated. The bizarre look of calm and the insane, inappropriate smile never left her face, even when the door to the bedroom exploded behind her.

32

IN A SHOWER of splinters and shattered wood, Dwight Livingston burst through the bedroom door. His business suit, which once hung neatly from his muscular frame, was now in disarray. He still held tightly to his walking stick with its wolf-head ivory handle, but now he gripped it less like a means of support and more like a weapon. In the bright light of the oil lamps, Stephanie was amazed at just how much Dwight Livingston resembled Jason, although she had never seen Jason wearing such a look of fury. It was as if she was watching a movie drama in which she and Jason were actors playing the roles of the Livingstons.

Dwight's eyes brimmed with tears and were wild with rage as he stormed into the room. His breath hitched heavily in his chest as he struggled to ask, "What the hell did you do, Marie? What in the name of God did you do to our boys?"

Marie slowly turned away from the mirror and looked directly into her husband's eyes. Her calm and relaxed demeanor took him by surprise. His wife smiled and replied, "Me? I did nothing, my husband. It was all your doing."

"M . . . m . . . my . . . my doing?" Dwight stammered. Then his anger returned. "Of what do you speak, woman? Was it not you who killed our children?"

She hesitated for a moment but then admitted with no apparent signs of regret, "Yes, Dwight. I carried out the deed. It needed to be done. I was the one who drowned your boys in the well, but it was entirely your fault. The boys . . . They were so, so much like you. They worshipped the ground you walked on. They looked like miniature versions of you. I had no doubt that if I didn't take some sort of action if I allowed them to grow into men, they each would surely have become the same kind of unfaithful whoremongers."

"B-but," Dwight sputtered. He took a breath and began again. "But why, Marie? Why would you murder our two innocent babies?"

"Not our babies, Dwight. *Your* babies," she shot back. "They may have come from inside of me, but they were the result of your rotten demon seed, the fruit of your damnable loins. And what do you care, anyway? You'll just go out and find another one of your trollops and make another baby, or maybe two or three more. For all, I know you already have a dozen other little bastards running about besides that little bitch I learned about. Oh yes, Dwight, those boys were more yours than mine, and because they were, they needed to die, just like you must die."

With that, Marie pulled the butcher knife from behind her back and held it in front of her, determined to stab her husband to death, to allow him to join his demon-spawn offspring. She thrust the knife toward his stomach.

But Dwight was faster than she had anticipated. Before she had a chance to strike, he slammed the handle of his walking stick into the side of her skull. Marie collapsed to the floor in a heap in front of the mirror.

Dwight was on top of her immediately. He reached down and wrapped his strong hands tightly around her throat, squeezing with all his might. His eyes blazed like fiery embers in his skull, glowing with a level of insanity that seemed to surpass his wife's. He continued to grip Marie's throat ever-tighter as her eyes bulged wildly from their sockets. Stephanie could see blood begin to trickle down the woman's neck where Dwight's fingernails dug deep furrows into the flesh of her throat. He throttled her back and forth as her head bobbed helplessly until Stephanie heard the woman's neck break with a sharp crack. A moment later, Marie Louise O'Hara Livingston's body lay dead on the floor.

Dwight sat on the floor weeping and cradling the dead woman in his trembling arms. As he sat sobbing, Marie's corpse shifted slightly, and her arm flopped down with a sickening thud.

As Stephanie watched in horrified silence, Dwight reached slowly into his suit jacket pocket and withdrew a long ivory-handled straight razor. The same razor, she knew now, Jason had found. From the newspaper article she had read, Stephanie knew what happened next. She wanted to turn away in horror but was forced to watch the terrible tableau unfold in front of her.

Dwight slowly and calmly lifted the straight razor to his left arm and made several deep horizontal cuts across his wrist. Blood pumped from the wounds and streamed onto the body of his dead wife. It trickled along the length of her arm and eventually began to puddle on the floorboards. Some of the blood beaded on the surface while the rest of it seeped down into the cracks.

A moment later, Dwight brought the bloody razor up to his throat and sliced a gaping wound from just below his left ear over to his right. He seemed unable to feel the pain. With his head raised and his throat extended, the incision split open like a cavernous, fleshy mouth, exposing all of its musculature insides and allowing blood to pour down his arms and the front of his suit, drenching Marie's body with gore. From her vantage point, Stephanie bellowed a silent scream; she couldn't stand to see any more.

A split second later, Stephanie found herself standing in the field behind their property. It was early in the morning on an overcast winter's day and a heavy fog seemed to enshroud everything around her. She saw a woman standing on a rectangular area of the property behind a low wall of stones. She was dressed in a long heavy black woolen coat and wore a matching dark fashionable hat and scarf.

The area looked familiar to her; as if she had seen it before and believed something significant might have happened there. Stephanie turned to her left and saw the familiar hexagonal shape of the spa building in the distance and understood she was standing at the back of her property near the spot where her family had stood staring on the first day they had come to see the house. She wondered how she had gotten outside and why she was at the back of her land.

She looked again at the spa building, noticing how much different it looked when it had first been constructed. Stephanie heard a sniffling sound and saw the woman standing behind the low wall was crying. She turned slightly in Stephanie's direction and Stephanie immediately recognized the woman as Amelia Miller, Dwight's sister. From behind Amelia's legs, a small girl dressed in winter coat and hat, Sarah Livingston, stepped forward slightly and looked down at something on the ground behind the wall: a small family plot with two fresh graves. Stephanie also noticed other gravestones scattered about, but their inscriptions were weathered away making them illegible.

Focusing on the two newer stones, Stephanie read the inscriptions on what she knew to be the boys' graves. Each of the stones had an identical inscription below the dates. Stephanie could barely make them out through the morning fog: "Taken From Us Too Soon by The Hand Of Evil."

Then Amelia spoke, "Poor little Matthew and Charles. That miserable witch did this to you and all because of the misdeeds of my own brother. He was so very wrong in what he did, and he should have been made to pay for his indiscretions. But there was no reason you two innocents should have suffered for his mistakes. Although I couldn't have stopped your father and his sinful ways, perhaps I should have tried harder to dissuade him. I will be sorry for the rest of my days for what happened to you." Then the woman wept openly. Little Sarah clung silently to her leg.

"But don't worry boys," Amelia sobbed, "I promise you with all my heart I'll take good care of your little sister. I will raise her as my own child. I can only hope you boys have found peace on the other side."

Sarah raised her head, looking at something else in the graveyard. Stephanie followed her gaze and could see two shapes forming in the morning mist. Her breath caught in her throat; as she realized what she and Sarah were seeing were the images of Matthew and Charles Livingston. Amelia didn't seem to see the manifestation, as she showed no signs of reacting.

The boys stood side-by-side, still dressed in their night-clothes, holding hands looking directly at their sister. Their pajamas appeared sodden. The boys were pail as milk and their large, hypnotic staring eyes were sunk deep in their heads, surrounded by dark circles. They seemed to still be covered in a thin skin of ice, which gave their mottled flesh the slightest blue glow. Sarah looked out at them with a beatific smile and silently mouthed "boys."

Stephanie flashed back to the first day they had come to the property and recalled that same expression on Sammy's face as he stood in front of this same plot of ground, wearing that very same expression and mouthing that same word. Sammy was special; both Stephanie and Jason knew that, but they hadn't known why. Now Stephanie could see her own grandmother as a two-year-old seeing with the same sight-beyond-sight. She understood where the gift had originated. Sammy was part of her and Jason and they were both descendants of Dwight Livingston.

Stephanie heard Amelia's voice once again. She was still speaking to the boys.

"Over there is where we put your parents. I am heartsick that I forced you to lie in the same ground with strangers, but I could not allow those two heathens to be buried on the same hallowed ground. You are better off finding your way to paradise together without your parents, especially since I doubt they will be joining you. I suspect they will be spending their eternity in Hell. At least that is my personal wish for them."

The two boys turned slowly together and looked at Stephanie. Their dead eyes, now gray with the film of lifelessness, seemed to stare a hole in her. The older boy, Matthew, raised his hand and pointed in another direction. He opened his mouth as if to shout. Stephanie felt a vibration building inside of her head and a steadily louder howl. Reaching a crescendo, Stephanie feared her eardrums might shatter from the unearthly cry. Matthew's gaping maw, surrounded by purple-blue lips, continued to howl until Stephanie thought she would lose her mind.

Then the noise abruptly stopped, and Stephanie was no longer standing in the family graveyard. She was in the spot where Amelia had pointed.

"I ordered special gravestones for them," Amelia said aloud. Stephanie was surprised to find not only had she been transported miraculously to this new location, but so had Amelia and Sarah. At first, she thought Amelia was speaking to her. Then she thought perhaps to young Sarah. Finally, she concluded Amelia was speaking to no one in particular.

"I have to admit," Amelia confessed, "I was a bit generous with Dwight's inscription." Stephanie saw his stone read "Devoted Husband, Loving Father, Tragically Taken In The Prime Of Life."

"I know he was anything but a devoted husband; however, he was a loving father. He was also my brother, so I chose to be kind and forgiving on his final message."

"Marie's grave, though . . . I wanted to make sure the world would know exactly what type of horrid creature she was." Amelia paused and then read the inscription aloud: "May Her Wretched Soul Rot In The Bowels Of Hell For Eternity."

Amelia straightened and said, "I pray by all that is holy, to the Father, the Son, and the Holy Ghost, Marie's soul does just that. In fact, if I could have but one wish, it would be that both Marie and Dwight Livingston must share eternity in damnation together, miserable in each other's company until the end of time. I would ask Dwight be given dominion over her and she would spend her time as his slave. I know that's not the Christian thing to wish, but those two lovely little boys are dead because of the sins of both of their parents. They deserve some type of retribution for their suffering."

Looking down at the graves, Stephanie saw something she couldn't at first quite comprehend. Something appeared to be slowly rising up from each of the freshly dug graves. She looked over at Sarah and saw she, too, was staring down at the earth, mouth agape, and terror on her face.

Before their shocked eyes, images of Dwight and Marie Livingston slowly rose up from the graves. They were dressed exactly as they had been on the night of the murder-suicide: Marie with her blood-stained, white nightgown and Dwight with his gore-covered business suit. Marie held her head at an odd angle as if something was not quite right with her neck, and the front of Dwight's gaping neck wound still trickled with blood.

Stephanie suddenly found herself back in her loft work-space, feeling as if she had just awoken from a disturbing dream. Although she couldn't recall the details, she remembered the majority.

This was her family's tragic secret and their shame. And she realized this disgraceful heritage was Jason's as well. Now, their union and Sammy's birth completed the family circle of blood.

Stephanie remembered feeling something was wrong with all the apparent good fortune. She should have believed the old saying "too good to be true." Now her family was living on the very same property where her great-grandparents and family had died so violently.

She had to let Jason know what she discovered. She had no idea what they'd do next, but she was sure when Jason learned the whole story, he'd think of some way to deal with it.

She took the blank sheet of typing paper in her hands, still seeing the hand-written letter from Marie. Likewise, the article from a recent local newspaper still looked to be the aged story from the *Ashton Daily News*. The envelope also continued to appear old and tattered as Stephanie placed them both back inside. Then she tucked it delicately under her arm and walked over to where Sammy sat staring at the blank television screen.

Stephanie bent down, picked up her son and began cleaning him in preparation for heading back to the main house. As she did so, she caught a glimpse of Sammy in the wall mirror and was surprised by how much he was beginning to look exactly like Jason. He always had looked like his father, but now he was beginning to lose his baby looks and the resemblance to Jason was becoming more pronounced. Stephanie thought about the picture of the two Livingston boys she had found earlier decided to check sometime to see if Sammy resembled them. She suspected the similarity would be amazing.

"Oh, Sammy," she said with an odd tone, not quite sounding like herself. As if noticing the resemblance to Jason for the first time, she mumbled, "You're so much like your father." Then she walked back toward the main part of the house.

Inside the mirror, there was a hideous rumble of merriment as the creatures from the world of the damned cheered over what they had accomplished; their time of entrapment between worlds would soon end. They would finally have a way out, and in their place, Stephanie and Jason Wright would remain to serve out their eternal sentence.

33

JASON LOOKED AT Stephanie as if he were trying to make sense of the ramblings of a crazy woman. He had just returned home from work and was hanging his jacket in the foyer closet. The kids were busy playing in the family room. He gave them his customary greeting and could see Connie Franks in the kitchen preparing dinner.

He assumed Stephanie would still be in her loft working on her infernal project as usual. He was surprised to see her sitting at the dining room table paging through a thin document that she held in trembling hands. She fidgeted in her seat looking extremely anxious. She briefly looked up from her page and catching his eye, she frantically signaled him. He sat next to her, noticing another day had passed without a shower.

"Jason!" she said in a whispered voice fraught with agitation, much more so than he had ever seen her before. "Jason! You have to see this. It's unbelievable!"

Her eyes bulged wide, perhaps appearing worse when paired with her gaunt and haggard-looking face. She seemed to have aged five or more years. The sight of her made Jason think of photos he had seen of World War II death camp survivors. She was out of control and he knew he would have to take some drastic action very soon.

"Steph?" he asked with apprehension. "What in the world is going on with you? You look like you haven't showered in days."

"Nothing's wrong, yet in a way, everything's wrong. Don't you see, Jason?" Stephanie replied, dismissing the hygiene question. "I don't need any help. Not from you, not from anybody. You don't have to worry about me. I'm fine. In fact, I am better than I've been in a long time. But that doesn't matter. All that matters is this. Look, look at this."

Stephanie showed Jason the printed copy of the family tree she had developed. Jason had to lean back a bit to escape the rank smell of Stephanie's foul breath. He wondered with great displeasure when she had last brushed her teeth. Trying desperately to maintain his focus, he reluctantly looked at the document.

It was the exact same copy she had asked him to examine every night for the previous several weeks. Each time she added a name, or a date, or some other insignificant tidbit of information, she'd show it to him acting as if she had discovered some rare and priceless treasure. He always tried to react with feigned enthusiasm, but he was honestly sick and tired of hearing about it. What had started out as a harmless little project had somehow evolved into a full-fledged obsession bordering on mania.

Jason glanced briefly at the document, not actually paying any attention to it, and with unplanned sarcasm, he asked, "Ok, honey, what new incredible historical fact did you discover? Your grandfather was once a physician's assistant? Your great-grandmother had a long-lost cousin named Bertha who knew someone who knew someone who once knew Abe Lincoln? I can hardly wait to hear the news."

He hated hearing the cynicism in his own voice, but it had been an exhausting week, both at work and at home, and he was stressed to the point of breaking. The last thing he wanted to do listen to these wild ramblings.

When Stephanie saw Connie Franks was paying too much attention to them she stood abruptly and grabbed Jason's. She led him into the hallway, past the family room, and finally up the stairs and down the hall to the master bedroom. Once inside Stephanie shut the door and directed Jason to sit on the edge of the bed.

He sat quietly, holding the family tree document while Stephanie paced back and forth. He could see something was building up inside of her. She held a manila envelope in her left hand while repeatedly opening and closing her right hand in a fist. A change seemed to have come over Stephanie and Jason saw another person entirely.

Through clenched teeth, she finally responded to his sarcasm in the kitchen. "Don't you dare speak to me so condescendingly! I may be a bit involved in this research project but I am not insane. In case you haven't noticed, I've been working myself ragged trying to find the final piece of this historical puzzle and I finally found it today. The missing link, the thing causing me so much frustration, ended up coming from your side of the family tree, not mine. So shut up for a minute, and listen to what I have to tell you."

Jason was taken aback. She had never reacted like this and he was unsure if she was simply overwhelmed by something she discovered or had finally gone over the edge. There was a fire burning in her eyes he'd never seen.

He cautiously replied, "I'm sorry. I shouldn't have been so smart. I know how important it is to you. Please forgive me."

For a moment, Stephanie stood glaring at Jason with a wild rage. He was genuinely concerned for the first time that she might pick up a sharp object and use it against him. She had never made him feel that way before. Fortunately, he saw her anger fade, replaced once again by her excitement about her discovery.

"Well," she began, pointing to the first of two typed sheets of paper he held, "remember how I told you how my great-grandmother and great-grandfather, Marie and Dwight and their sons Matthew and Charles, all died on the same day?"

"Yes," Jason replied. "We assumed something like a fire or illness or some other such tragedy must have killed them." Jason thought uneasily about the day two weeks earlier when Stephanie discovered the documents and led her to that discovery. At that time when she had told him, he acted as if it was news to him. He couldn't risk Stephanie learning about what he had found or how he had destroyed and buried the headstones so many months previously.

Back then, he felt he was doing what was best for Stephanie and his family, but now that she had become so involved with her family history, he was certain she would be furious with him if she knew he destroyed the headstones. In hindsight, he realized perhaps he should have simply left the stones where they were.

He considered digging up the pieces of broken tombstone and spreading them around in the tall grass. If he did that, then he could act as if he stumbled upon them. Stephanie would assume they'd broken over the years naturally or at the very least, by some vandal. They could then look for the rest of the pieces together eventually completing their reconstruction. Maybe he'd still want to do this in the spring after the ground had thawed but that seemed years away now.

"What actually happened?" He tried his best to sound interested, but he suspected the story would be a bad one.

"It's much worse than what we could have ever imagined," she said and began to tell a tale of tragedy so eerily detailed and realistic that it seemed like she'd been there.

"Oh, my God! What are you saying?' Jason interrupted. "And how could you possibly know all these details?"

Stephanie ignored him continued with her story of how Marie had killed the boys then Dwight had killed her.

"Unbelievable!" Jason exclaimed. "I can't imagine such a thing." Now, however, many things suddenly began to make sense to him; the way the two boys' headstones were separate from their parents and the cryptic inscriptions on their tombstones. He was overcome with sadness for his wife, having to discover such a horrible secret.

34

"**OH, BABY, I'M** so, so sorry," Jason said, as tears began to well up in his eyes. He reached out to take Stephanie in his arms, but she resisted. She seemed neither upset nor overwhelmed by the information. Instead, she wore the excited look of someone who had made a miraculous discovery.

"Jason, look at me. I'm fine. And in case you didn't notice, I'm not a baby, so there's no reason to treat me like one."

Stephanie began to pace rapidly, gathering her thoughts before finally turning to Jason to tell him the rest of the story.

"There's more, Jason. And I'm sure you're not going to like it."

Jason slumped back sitting on the edge of the bed. He didn't know how much worse it could be, but he braced himself for more tragedy.

"Members of your family played a major role as well!"

"What? My family?" Jason exclaimed. "You just said the tragedy was a murder-suicide involving your great-grandparents. What does that have to do with any of my relatives?"

Stephanie said scornfully, "Tracing your family history back before your grandmother has been a major stumbling block for me. As you know, your family, like mine originally came from Schuylkill County." Jason nodded his agreement and said, "Yeah, we both know that but what–"

"I was finally able to discover your great-grandmother's name. It was Agatha Jefferson, but I hadn't been able to locate any information on her husband. I naturally assumed there would be a Mr. Jefferson somewhere."

"Of course, there would be," Jason replied with certainty in his voice. "Did you find out anything about him?"

Stephanie hesitated for a moment then said, "Agatha never married or had a husband."

Jason stood stunned for a moment, a look of confusion on his face. "She had to have a husband Steph. I had a grandmother, so there had to be a great-grandfather in the mix somewhere." Jason sounded like he was becoming defensive, sensing where the conversation was likely heading.

"Jason. Your great-grandmother was never married. She had your grandmother illegitimately, out of wedlock."

"What? You're not serious!"

"There's an even more shocking twist to the story."

"More disturbing than finding out your grandmother was a bastard?"

"Your great-grandmother, Agatha Jefferson, and my great-grandfather, Dwight Livingston, had an affair. Your great-grandfather and my great-grandfather were the same person."

"The same person?"

"Yes, Agatha Jefferson was Dwight's mistress. Marie Livingston found out about the affair and the illegitimate daughter and the knowledge eventually drove her insane. Then, to get back at Dwight, she drowned her two sons."

"But why would she kill her own sons?" Jason asked with a weak voice.

"Dwight loved his boys incredibly. In Marie's damaged mind, it must have seemed logical that by killing them she would be killing Dwight emotionally. Dwight was so furious by what Marie did, he confronted her in their bedroom, this very bedroom, and he strangled her to death. Then, when the reality of what he did hit him, he slit his own throat and died on the floor with Marie cradled in his arms. This was the unknown family tragedy, Jason. This was my family's dark secret. And now it is our shared dark secret."

Jason stood by the side of the bed, shaking his head in disbelief and looking down at the floor imagining the two dead bodies. "I just can't get my head around all of this Steph. I can't believe such a thing is possible. And if it were true, that would mean we're distantly related. How did you find out all of this?"

"I found out about the affair from an excerpt from Marie's personal diary, and I learned about the murders and suicide from a newspaper article from 1922." She held up the manila envelope. "I have them both right in here."

Jason reached to grab the envelope from Stephanie's hand, wanting to see the proof himself, but she pulled it away from him.

"Easy! This stuff is almost one hundred years old. Be careful."

Jason realized something was very wrong with his wife. He wasn't looking at an ancient envelope but a brand-new manila envelope. However, he understood he probably shouldn't upset her. He took a deep breath and stood still for a moment, calming himself.

"I'm ok now. I just want to read the letter and the article."

"Ok," Stephanie said as she carefully opened the manila envelope and slowly withdrew the three blank sheets of crisp white printer paper. She delicately sat them down on the side of the bed, one next to the other as if she were handling century-old documents from the national archives. Jason watched her with disbelief. Then she reached into the envelope again and withdrew the newspaper article, gingerly setting it next to the blank sheets of paper.

"Read them and know the truth, but be very careful. I haven't had time to laminate them or protect them yet."

Jason looked at Stephanie then looked back down at the blank papers and the recent newspaper article. He looked at Stephanie again. For a moment, he hoped this might be some sort of strange joke on her part, but she had never been prone to doing such things before. By the look in her eyes, she wasn't joking. Stephanie really believed the papers were ninety-year-old, hand-written notes from Marie Livingston and that the newspaper article was from that era as well.

He wasn't certain what he should do next. He was confused and worried sick about his wife's mental state but also relieved to discover everything she had just told him was most likely untrue, a figment of some delusional fantasy. He didn't know if he should try to explain to her that she was imagining everything or simply play along with her. If he tried to tell her the truth, she'd likely become angry and perhaps he might push her further over the brink of insanity. But if he said nothing, he might be helping to fuel her delusions.

"Well? Look at them."

"Um, ok. Just give me a minute," Jason said as he turned and bent over the bed. In that instant, he decided it might be best to play along. He knew now he was going to have to seek professional help. He didn't know how he would get Stephanie to talk to them, but things had obviously gone too far.

He pretended to peruse the documents, his hand clasped behind his back, careful not to touch them. As he did, he tried to estimate just how much time it would take to read a hand-written document so Stephanie would believe he was actually reading something. When he got to the "end" of the final blank sheet he turned slowly to look at Stephanie.

She was standing next to him, observing him and nodding with an I-told-you-so look on her face. "See? Now read the newspaper article."

So he did. It was a lot easier to pretend with the newspaper article as it was an actual printed document. The article was about a local woman who had written a historical book and had donated a copy to the Ashton Public library. Jason could sense Stephanie standing behind him, watching.

"See? Murder-suicide. Marie killed the boys and Dwight killed her and then himself, all because of his affair with *your* great-grandmother."

Jason thought as he continued to read. He assumed any newspaper article would not have gone into anything such as an affair or illegitimate child and would only report cold-hard facts.

After "reading" the article, Jason replied, "It just so awful. But the article doesn't say anything about any affair or illegitimate child."

"Of course not! They'd never print such a thing! But you can plainly see it in Marie's journal. She knew about the baby and about your great-grandmother. You can tell by her erratic writing it was slowly driving her crazy."

Jason had to be extra careful how he proceeded from that point. "But, Steph, just because Marie suspected something doesn't mean it actually happened. She may have imagined the whole thing."

"It most certainly was true, Jason," Stephanie retorted. She couldn't understand why Jason was in denial. The facts were right there. "Didn't you read what she wrote about how she heard all of the local women gossiping about Dwight and Agatha? What more proof could you possibly want?"

But there was nothing spelled out on those blank pages. Whatever Stephanie believed she had read, Jason thought, was all in her own mind. He had no idea how those thoughts had found their way into her head.

He was doing his best to restrain his anger. He wanted to shove the pages in her face and scream these were blank pages of modern printer paper, that there is no letter from Marie! But he knew he couldn't be the one to do something so terrible to the woman he loved with all of his heart. When he spoke of Marie's hallucinations, he was actually speaking about Stephanie's, but he couldn't bring himself to confront her directly about it.

"Look, Steph. I'm willing to accept what you told me about the murder and suicide, but the rest I can't accept without more solid evidence." He wondered to himself if it were possible to do a blood test and determine if he and Stephanie were distantly related. He believed it could be done. That would surely provide proof, assuming he really wanted to know.

Behind the couple in the shadows, the mirror above their dresser began to ripple slightly and a thin, bony finger covered with gray shriveled flesh extended and pointed directly at Stephanie.

Suddenly, Stephanie said, "Well, then, maybe we will have to arrange to have a blood test to see if any of this is true. That should be proof positive."

Jason was shocked to hear her repeat what he'd been thinking. Was she reading his mind? Or . . . it was like . . . someone else was putting the ideas in her mind. Jason suddenly felt as if someone was watching him. He quickly turned around and thought he saw some slight movement in the shadows near the mirror on the dresser. If it had been there, it was gone now.

"Maybe we should," he said. "Or maybe a DNA test. One of those should confirm or deny all of this."

"We can schedule something sometime soon. For now," she said, "I have to go back to the loft and type Marie's journal entry into my genealogical document and scan the newspaper article as well. These are probably some of the most important discoveries of my entire project."

Jason was curious about what Stephanie would end up typing. He realized once she finished, he would be able to, at the very least, read what Stephanie believed she had seen. Once he could see that he might be better able to counter any argument she might come up with.

"What about dinner?" Jason asked, trying to distract her from her obsession.

"I'm not hungry. There's too much work to be done."

And with that, she carefully picked up the papers, gingerly tucked them back into the manila envelope and headed for the door. When she had passed through the doorway, she turned and looked back at Jason with kind concern saying, "Look, Jason, I know this might make things a bit weird, us being related and all but I want you to know it doesn't have to change a thing between us. No matter what our lineage, we're not Dwight and Marie Livingston; we are us. All of this is . . . it's just history. You and I can still be the same, right?"

Jason gave his best, most convincing smile to his deranged wife replying, "Yeah, um, you bet, Steph. You and I are fine, and our family is fine as well. You're right. Get back to your work. I'll see you later at bedtime."

But Jason knew things weren't fine. Things were so far away from fine that he wondered if they could ever be fine again. His lovely wife had suffered some sort of mental breakdown and he had to do something about it.

35

I T WAS LATE Wednesday afternoon of December 19. It was young Samuel Wright's second birthday and just a week before Christmas, but one would never know it by looking around the Wright home. There was no Christmas tree, no decorations, and no suggestion of the upcoming holiday. Likewise, there were no plans to celebrate Sammy's birthday. A rift had developed between Stephanie and Jason and the couple had found it difficult, if not impossible to have a civil conversation. They only spoke when it concerned the kids.

Stephanie sat at her computer, carefully reviewing and editing her almost completed document. It was far more than a document, however; it was an actual book, a detailed history of both sides of her and Jason's families starting at the present and going back to their great-grandparents. The work was not only made up of text but of photos, charts, and scanned images of family members dating back almost one hundred years. It had taken her months of dedicated time and energy to compile everything, and she was probably prouder of it than of anything she had ever done.

It was not a typical family history, laden with facts and statistics, but was an emotional account of the tragedy that had befallen the Livingston clan. It read like a novel, its story told with all of the passion required to allow the reader to experience exactly what had happened on that eventful day. It also explained how Stephanie inherited the property and discovered the tragic family secret. She had made a point of not glossing over any unpleasant details.

Stephanie knew, in Jason's opinion, it was nothing more than a work of fiction. He wouldn't accept the fact his great-grandmother had played such a crucial role in almost destroying Stephanie's side of the family. But whether he believed her account or not was of no consequence to Stephanie; she knew the facts.

The book also contained the text of the newspaper article from December 20, 1922, as well as from Marie's journal entry. Before Jason and Stephanie had stopped speaking, he had asked to read these transcriptions. He said it was to refresh his memory.

As she watched him read, it almost seemed like it was the first time he had seen the words. After he was finished, Jason still refused to accept what the journal entry stated. He even had the nerve to lie outright and claim the original papers she had shown him containing Marie's journal entry were not brittle old parchment written in Marie's hand but were actually blank sheets of modern printer paper. She couldn't believe he would lie so blatantly and make such an outlandish claim. This desperate act on his part made Stephanie begin to wonder whether she really knew Jason at all. The Jason she believed she knew and loved would never have lied to her or tried to convince her to believe such an outlandish story. Her Jason was accepting and supportive.

When Jason read her account of the Amelia Miller incident, he was shocked to discover the areas Stephanie described had matched exactly to the places where he had found the fallen tombstones. His stomach sank when he saw she had even included sketches depicting the grave markers complete with the inscriptions. Jason had no idea how she could have known this.

Stephanie now stood at her computer screen looking closely at the various scanned pictures of her ancestors now on display. She would sometimes enlarge them to see more specific details. She was fascinated by what some might consider simple things, such as wallpaper patterns and clothing material textures. For example, without a magnify-ing glass, most people wouldn't have been able to see the monogrammed "DCL" on Dwight's cufflinks. But Stephanie did and found those details spellbinding.

She had studied Marie's expression in the scanned pic-ture of their wedding portrait. Stephanie was struck with a feeling of melancholy to see how happy Marie had looked in the picture. She was quite certain this had been the happiest day of young Marie's life and knowing the marriage would end so tragically only served to further sadden Stephanie.

"Such a waste," Stephanie said. "Such a God-awful waste."

The original portrait was no longer stored in the attic but now hung proudly on the wall in Stephanie's loft. It didn't bother her anymore how the eyes seemed to follow her wher-ever she moved in the room. In fact, this made her feel as-sured as if her great-grandparents were watching over her and guiding her. From deep inside the mirror, the ghost of Marie Livingston watched unseen, occasionally sending out mind control to keep Sammy locked in his world of imagina-tion and to keep Stephanie focused on her work. She was also gradually instilling a new reality in Stephanie's brain.

There was a foul stench of urine and feces permeating the room because the boy was unknowingly sitting in a pile of his own filth that was leaking from his saturated dia-per. Stephanie's complete immersion into her project had delayed the start of potty training by several months and that was just fine with her. It was much less trouble to slap a diaper or training pants and plop him down in front of the television. She usually remembered to check on him periodi-cally, but even that responsibility had fallen by the wayside. She knew she'd have to make sure he was presentable by dinnertime as she did every evening although she suspected Jason wouldn't be home for dinner again tonight.

There were also a number of other things Jason had done that Stephanie found confusing. Shortly after she had shown him Marie's journal, Jason brought some man home for dinner. He claimed the man was a friend of his and was a doctor of some sort. Stephanie had never heard Jason mention him and she had an odd feeling there was another reason for the man's visit. She felt like the so-called friend had been studying her a bit too intently, perhaps being more of a doctor than he was Jason's friend, asking her a lot of personal questions that she felt were inappropriate and quite intimate. He also seemed to be far too interested in learning about her research.

On more than one occasion during the dinner, Stephanie had looked over at Jason attempting to convey her displeasure, but he didn't seem to notice.

The bizarre evening made Stephanie feel paranoid, but what else was she supposed to think? How did that expression go? It's not paranoia if everyone really is out to get you.

However, one positive thing that occurred in previous weeks was her brother Chuck, started visiting them on weekends. She was happy to reconnect with him as they had temporarily lost contact since the family had moved. Stephanie had worried Chuck resented her receiving the inheritance, but now she saw he held no hard feelings about it. She had to admit though, much like Jason and his doctor friend, Chuck had been acting a bit odd around her.

Sometimes he seemed a bit too quick with his compliments and encouragements, especially about her project. Like everyone else, he seemed to be weighing his words at times when speaking to her. Chuck was usually more direct when he spoke; he was her brother after all. She wondered if her brother had been talking to Jason and his doctor friend.

Yet, other times Chuck seemed to be genuinely supportive. Once, when she felt exceptionally trusting, Stephanie had even shown him Marie's letter, not the transcript but the original letter and he had appeared quite surprised. She noticed the way he looked at her was similar to the way Jason had looked at her and she was afraid he might not believe what he had read any more than Jason had. But he told her she was doing great and important work for the family and couldn't wait to have his own personal copy of the book. He said he was anxious to see the project finished so she could take some time to get some much-needed rest.

Stephanie was unaware that Jason had already debriefed her brother about her deteriorating condition. Jason had told him about the alleged ancient documents and the message they supposedly contained. Since he had been prepared, Chuck was able to pull off a relatively convincing performance while pretending to read them. He had then surprised Stephanie by volunteering to take Jeremy and Cindy back home with him on occasions for sleepovers on weekends when she needed time to work. She always kept Sammy home during these outings however, since he was not yet potty trained.

The kids now were off school for their Christmas break and Chuck's work was on a holiday shutdown. Earlier that morning, he had stopped by to pick up the two older children for another overnight visit, a special middle-of-the-week excursion. He planned to bring them back the next afternoon. Stephanie was certainly grateful for the time alone to finish her work.

Despite the fact it was Sammy's birthday, Stephanie had allowed the kids to go. Had she been thinking rationally she might not have permitted it, but she felt the uncontrollable need to be alone with Sammy. And since Jason was at the office and was likely going to be working late once again, it worked out. Connie Franks had the week off for Christmas, so tonight Stephanie would have to throw something together for her and Sammy. She wondered about how things had become so bad between her and Jason. On several recent occasions, Stephanie had confronted Jason, and each interaction had ended badly.

"Jason, I need you to be home," she had said. "I'm making great progress on my family history book, and I'm almost finished. I could use the extra time to work on it."

"I know, but I've been neglecting my own work for the past several months to be home. Now I need to get back to taking care of my own job. After all, it's what keeps us in food."

"Here we go again, you and your precious job. It always about that, isn't it? What about me and my project and what about my needs?"

"I know how important this is to you, but we have bills to pay."

"What about the inheritance?" Stephanie said gawking at him as if he had forgotten. "Look at this place, Jason. We're rich!"

"No, we're not rich and you know it. We put most of it into college funds for the kids. Don't you remember? And the rest of the money has dwindled away over the past six months. Bringing on Wilbur and Connie Franks full-time was expensive and so was the master bedroom remodel. Those two things put a hefty drain on our funds and now that most of the money's gone. Our day-to-day expenses fall on my shoulders. I'm not complaining Steph, but I do need to keep my job.

"As you may or may not recall, I got a new boss a month ago and he's looking to make a name for himself. This guy, Bill Bostwick, is not as easy to get along with as Tom Mc-Clellan was. He's counting on me to make him look good and when Botswick called me into his office and accused me of not being a team player and not putting in the same amount extra hours he's forcing others to put in, well, I had little choice. I had to start working later or risk losing the only source of income we have."

"But you're not home some nights until eight, nine, or even ten o'clock, Jason. How am I supposed to get my family history finished if you're not home to support me?"

"Maybe you should dig out that children's book you finished and send it off to your publisher. You know he's dying for it. He thinks it'll be a big seller and if we're lucky, it will be. We certainly could use the money."

"Children's book?" Stephanie asked curiously, and Jason could see she had forgotten about it. He started to wonder if she could even recall writing it.

Jason looked at her with frustration and said angrily, "Steph, you have to get something through your head once and for all. We need my job. We don't need to have your stupid family history finished. It's a hobby! It doesn't earn us a damned dime. Get a friggin' grip on reality here. It doesn't matter right now!"

Now Stephanie sat at her desk tapping her pencil irritably at the recollection of that encounter. Who did Jason think he was? He had no right to speak to her that way, no matter how tired or overworked he might be. They had never discussed that outburst again. Usually when they argued, they always apologized. This time though, he didn't even bother.

Recounting the various arguments she had Jason had since then, Stephanie realized he really didn't care at all about her project. All this time he had been humoring her, acting as if he was interested. She also knew Jason didn't believe her story about Dwight, Agatha, and Marie, even though she had shown him the proof.

She began to wonder about Jason's doctor friend again. Had he really been a friend or had Jason brought him around to study her? Maybe he was thinking about accusing her of being mentally unstable. Maybe he was gathering witnesses to testify against her. Could he be trying to find a way to have her declared insane? Could he be scheming to have her deemed incompetent and institutionalized so he could take control of her fortune?

In the back of the loft, Marie Livingston was smiling a rotten-toothed grin inside the mirror. The plan was almost complete. Stephanie believed exactly what the spirits wanted her to believe. And today was the day. It was the ninetieth anniversary of that terrible night. When the plan was completed, she and Dwight would be free of their purgatory and Jason and Stephanie Wright would take their places among the damned for eternity.

36

STEPHANIE GREW ANGRIER and more irrational by the second. She recalled how Jason had tried to convince her they were almost cash broke, but she knew that was impossible. She was sure they really were wealthy, and she was certain they had more money in the bank than what Jason had told her. After all, they lived in a mansion and had Mrs. Franks to cook and clean, as well as her husband Wilbur to do yard work. Common people couldn't afford such a luxury. Why Jason would lie?

She tried to remember exactly how much money the lawyer said she had inherited. The estate document was somewhere in the loft, but the area was such a mess. Jason had said the cash in their estate was only about three-quarters of a million dollars, but she was certain the figure was much, much higher than that; at least several million. Yes. That made perfect sense to her. She even thought she could recall the lawyer telling her there was at least ten million dollars in cash available to her. And now the more she thought about it, that figure was probably more like twenty million dollars, maybe more.

In the mirror, the image of H. Mason Armstrong appeared in the pulsating, liquefied glass. Stephanie couldn't see his visage in the shadows. Had she been able to, she would have been horrified at the gaping hole in his chest. Wormlike creatures crawled freely from the massive wound, both dribbling down the front of his suit coat and creeping up onto his gray, mottled face where they burrowed deep into the thin flesh of his cheeks.

The ghost of Armstrong was focusing on sending thoughts and false memories into Stephanie's already confused mind, convincing her she had inherited great sums of money and that Jason was trying to steal it from her.

"Yes, that explains it!" she said aloud. That was what Jason was up to. If he could get enough people, especially those with credentials, to say she had lost her mind he might be able to take control of her twenty-five million dollars. But why would he do such a thing? They had joint bank accounts, so Jason already had access to her money. So what was the real reason for his treachery? Didn't he love her anymore? Would he do such a horrible thing just to control her money?

Maybe the idea of getting his hands on her thirty million dollars was enough to make Jason betray her. Yes, he might be inclined to do so if the amount of money was as high as she now remembered. Yes, yes, he might do that for thirty-five million dollars.

In the mirror, all the specters now stood together: Dwight, Marie, Armstrong, Emerson Washburn and the charred remains of Jack Moran. They were all connected now, and all had something to gain from what would occur this night. Each of them was doing their best to control the delusions.

Suddenly, it was instantly clear to Stephanie. She knew why Jason wanted to have her declared insane and wanted to steal her money. It wasn't just for the money alone; it was also for another woman. Jason was obviously having an affair just like his illegitimate great-grandfather Dwight Livingston had done. Perhaps it was with someone at work. Most likely that woman from the accounting group who had been practically throwing herself at Jason all the time. Yes. That had to be it.

"That bastard!" Stephanie exclaimed aloud. Sammy still sat silently staring at the blank TV screen, lost in the spirits' fabricated world in his urine-soaked, waste-filled, foul-smelling diaper.

Jason was probably screwing that home-wrecking slut from the office, maybe right now. Stephanie imagined them going at it like two rutting beasts on his office desk. He and his bimbo would steal her forty million dollars. Jason must have been planning this for months, slowly putting his list of witnesses together. He had probably been banging that bimbo since back when he first took the job. Brainless tramps like that always go after the bosses who seem to be on the fast track to success, no doubt hoping to be the trophy wife. Stephanie had suspected as much earlier, but now she was certain.

Inside the mirror, the hideous specters were concentrating, pooling their thoughts and projecting them out at Stephanie. She was theirs now and she would do whatever they wished.

As if experiencing an epiphany, Stephanie straightened.

"She must be pregnant!" Overcome with panic, she paced manically, trying to determine what she would do next. She understood now how Marie Livingston felt. Jason was Dwight's illegitimate descendant and like his great-grandfather before him, he had found his own cheap whore to impregnate.

Behind her in darkness, the specters continued their volley of thoughts to Stephanie.

Stephanie was now totally convinced of Jason's treachery. He was going to pay for his sins, just like Dwight. Thoughts of Marie's revenge played out in her mind and she knew what to do.

She looked over at Sammy on the floor in his soiled diaper, watching the blank screen. She now understood why two older kids were with Chuck. The glass in the mirror pulsated more rapidly than ever as the specters pressed hard against the surface, preparing to make their way out into the world of the living. The vile thoughts streamed toward Stephanie.

As Stephanie looked down at Sammy, she noticed how much he looked exactly like Jason. He looked even more like Jason than Jeremy. Sammy definitely had the Livingston family features which meant he had the Livingston family blood, the blood of adulterous whoremongers. Why hadn't she noticed it before?

"He looks just like his father," Stephanie said with a flat monotone voice. That voice was the voice of Marie Livingston. Stephanie looked down at Sammy and said, "He loves his father. He idolizes him. Someday he'll grow up to be just like his father. Yes, someday he'll find a whore of his own to impregnate and will break his loving wife's heart. It is the Livingston way, the Livingston destiny."

Stephanie looked at the calendar hanging on the far wall and then looked down at the hypnotized form of her son. With an evil smile, she said, "Happy birthday, Sammy."

Across the loft, the mirror on the wall was rattling off its hooks. Soon a gray, withered hand with yellowed split fingernails eased from the glass. Next, another followed and soon the hideous head of Marie Livingston with its wild and greasy hair slid out.

The surface of the mirror began to ooze from the confines of its frame and cling to the walls, the floor, the ceiling. It formed a film of mercurial liquid, flowing outward like fingers spreading every direction.

Then the unspeakable creatures of the netherworld began to crawl forth from their land of the damned along the silvery surface, careful not to touch the world of the living. Soon they would be able to do so, but not just yet. First came Marie Livingston who crept out of the rippling glass, still dressed in the blood-splattered nightgown she had worn the night she died. Her gray-filmed eyes still held the look of insanity. As she clung to the wall on the glistening pool of glass, her movements appeared jerky and erratic.

A moment later the charred remains of Jack Moran followed, moving upward and clinging to the ceiling like a giant blackened spider. H. Mason Armstrong and Emerson Washburn were next, creeping out and taking their positions along the wall while staring with hatred at Stephanie. It was clear they were all focusing their attention on her.

Finally, two gnarled hands emerged from the mirror, one gripping each side. A moment later, the form of Dwight

Livingston, master of this damned cadre, leaped out of the darkness and stood upright in front of the mirror, floating inches above the floor. The other specters flew from their perches and hovered behind their master. Marie and Washburn stood directly behind Dwight while Armstrong and Moran took their place in the rear. They said nothing but remained standing, looking at Stephanie who was lost in thoughts projected by the spirits. Her ravings were becoming louder as she paced wildly waving her arms and screaming epithets about Jason and his many women.

Sammy's glassy eyes began to flutter in a sign of waking. The energy required to maintain Stephanie's mania meant the creatures could no longer support the boy's illusions.

He could hear his mommy yelling and sounding very angry. Sammy turned to look at her to see what was wrong and stopped.

He saw something bad, something really bad.

There were people, bad people, standing near the back of the room. They were really, really scary. They were scarier than any scary thing he had ever seen. The scary man in the front looked sort of like Daddy but not Daddy. He remembered that scary man from the picture Mommy kept where she worked. The man had really scary eyes with dark rings around them. And the scary man had a big cut across his neck. Sammy thought it looked really yucky.

There was a lady behind him, and Sammy didn't like her either. He remembered her from the first day they came to the new house. She was the scary lady in the glass who had made him cry. And right next to her he saw the other man he didn't like. Sammy remembered his name was "Armsong." Sammy didn't like "Armsong" before and he didn't like him even more now. He was really scary and yucky now. Sammy didn't want "Armsong" to see him, so he closed his eyes, but when he opened them again, "Armsong" was still there.

The men in the back scared Sammy the most. He didn't know them, but the one man looked like the burned-up guy he saw in the burned-up car outside the house a while ago.

The scary people made Sammy's belly hurt worse than hearing Mommy yelling. Why was she yelling so loud? Sammy didn't like it. He felt like he was going to cry really bad until he saw something that made him forget about crying.

Between Sammy and the scary people, he saw shapes where there wasn't anybody before. Sammy recognized them.

"Boys," he thought. They were the same boys Sammy had seen in the field a long time ago. Sammy forgot about the boys because he never saw them after that one time, but now the boys were back. Maybe they came back to play with him.

Sammy liked these boys. They weren't scary like those bad people. They didn't even look the same as they did when Sammy saw them before. They didn't look sick or tired anymore. Now they looked clean and they had a bright yellow light all around them. The light made Sammy feel good in his tummy and made him not want to cry. The boys were wearing suits like Daddy wore to church, but they were all white and shiny with the bright light.

Sammy was surprised to hear some words in his head. It sounded like the two boys talking and saying the same words. But the boys' mouths weren't moving. Sammy never knew people who could say words inside his head. Sammy thought that was fun. He liked this game and he tried to see if he could make words in their heads too.

"Hi, boys," Sammy thought. The boys smiled at Sammy and then he heard two voices say, "Hello, Samuel."

Samuel? Who was Samuel? "Me Sammy," he thought. "Not Samuel."

The boys said together, "Sammy, listen carefully to us. Do not be afraid."

Sammy wasn't afraid of the boys at all. They were nice boys. He had been afraid of the scary people, but now he couldn't see them because of the bright light, and that was ok with him. In fact, he had almost forgotten about the scary people. He thought, "I'm not scared. You are good boys."

"Yes," the boys replied. "We are good boys, and we are here to help you. Those bad people want to hurt you and your mommy and daddy. They are making your mommy think bad things and they are going to make her do something really bad to you."

Sammy thought this was silly. His mommy loved him and would never do anything bad to him. The boys were mixed up. Mommies were good, not bad.

"You are right, Sammy." he heard the boys say. "Your mommy *is* good, but those bad people are making her not good. We can't stop the bad people. We can see them, but they can't see us. Only your daddy and mommy can make the bad people go away. You have to get your daddy to come home right away."

"Daddy help," Sammy thought as he silently formed the words with his mouth. "Daddy help," he mouthed.

"Yes. That's right, Sammy. Can you say the words, 'Daddy help?'" the boys asked. Sammy knew he could say those words and many more. He was two. He knew lots of words now. "Daddy help," Sammy said quietly.

The boys said in Sammy's head. "That's really good. Do you know how to say 'please'?"

Sammy thought for a moment and mouthed the word please, but it came out sounding like "peaze."

"Good, Sammy," the boys said. They turned and looked toward the place on the floor where Stephanie's purse lay. It was overturned on its side and her phone was visible.

Sammy heard a scraping sound and saw the boys moving their hands. His mommy's phone slid across the floor stopping right in front of him. The front of the phone lit up and Sammy could see all the little pictures on the screen. He knew a lot about Mommy's phone because she sometimes let him play with it. She had some fun stuff on her phone. Sammy liked the cat that said stuff back to him. He could say a word and the cat would say it back in his silly cat voice. And sometimes the cat farted. Sammy loved that. The cat farts always made him laugh.

Sometimes he pushed the picture of Daddy by mistake and then he would hear Daddy talking through the phone.

"You must get your daddy Sammy. You must say 'Daddy, help me, please' until your daddy comes home. Can you do that, Sammy?"

"Mommy said 'no touch.'"

Then the boys said, "We promise. It's ok this one time. Only Daddy can help you and Mommy. Only Daddy can make the bad people go away. Daddy must come home. You must talk to Daddy, Sammy. You're two years old today. You're a big boy, Sammy. And big boys can do this."

The undead floated across the room toward the large rear windows which were hidden by a wall of closed curtains. They paid little attention to Sammy, as he no longer posed a threat to them. They couldn't see the two Livingston boys, but the boys were aware of their every move.

They told Sammy, "You must do it. You must get your daddy to come home. If not, you will die. Do you know what it means to be dead?" Their question made Sammy feel very scared in his tummy. Sammy knew about dead stuff. He had squashed bugs and made them dead. He saw the dead deer in the field with all the bugs. If that was being dead, he didn't want to be dead. He didn't want bugs and birds eating him.

He looked down at the lighted face of his mommy's phone and saw the little picture of his daddy. The boys were telling him in his head to call his daddy. His mommy was screaming and shouting all kinds of bad stuff, a lot of words he didn't know and had never heard her say before. Sammy didn't know what to do. He didn't want to be a bad boy, but he really wanted his daddy to come home. He took a deep breath, sighed, and then reached down and pressed his daddy's picture on his mommy's phone.

He could hear the phone begin to ring as he waited to hear his daddy's voice. He knew what he would say. If he did that, Daddy would come home and help him to not be dead and help Mommy too. Daddy could make the bad people go away. The boys told him so.

Across the room, Dwight Livingston lifted his withered arm and pointed it at the back wall of the loft. The drapes flew open revealing a panoramic view of the rear of the property. The yard was awash with moonlight. Dwight approached the windows and began saying something silently while looking out into the yard.

The ground near the back of the property began to tremble and the ground began to rise. Within moments, there was a large round hole that rapidly filled with icy, cold water from an unknown source. The dirt around the hole began to mold itself into a cylindrical shape resembling stone and mortar while maintaining the texture and color of the soil. The well that had claimed the lives of Matthew and Charles Livingston almost a century earlier, had returned, and it waited for its next victim.

37

JASON WAS AT his office desk deeply engrossed in a series of charts and spreadsheets, the results of the same project he'd originally been assigned during his time at the Lancaster division of his company. Now, almost seven months later, he was in the implementation phase and things were not progressing as closely to plan. Because of the special nature and complexity of the products being run across the machine, it was becoming a challenge to make the numbers he had forecasted.

The result was a lot of heat from his new manager. Jason was sure the project would eventually be a winner, but the ramp-up time was longer than they had anticipated, and he'd been forced to return to his schedule of working long days and weekends.

He missed his family. He worried about Stephanie. He hated the long hours and if he were to be perfectly honest with himself, he hated his job. Part of him wished he could get fired so he'd be forced to take the initiative to either find another job or start his own consulting company. He'd allowed Stephanie's inheritance and the chance for a promotion to cloud his judgment; hell, they both had. Now in hindsight, their decisions seemed to have been way off base.

Jason was startled by the vibration, then ringing of his cell phone in his shirt pocket. It was almost 8:30 at night. Surely, any call he might receive on his personal cell had to come from home. And that could only mean something was wrong. He saw it was from Stephanie's cell.

Jason was apprehensive about answering the call. In fact, he couldn't remember the last time Stephanie had even bothered to call him when he was working late. He suspected it had to have been many weeks. He had no idea why Stephanie had chosen to call him this time, but he suspected she must have had a good reason. As the phone rang again, Jason began to worry more about a family emergency with the kids. He knew Jeremy and Cindy were staying with Chuck overnight, so he assumed things were fine with them. Otherwise, he would have heard directly from his brother-in-law. Putting all apprehension aside, he pressed the button to answer the call.

Jason cautiously asked, "Hello? Steph? Honey? Is everything ok?"

He listened carefully and thought he could hear breathing on the other end of the phone, as well as strange indistinguishable noises in the background.

"Steph? Is that you? Is everything all right?" Still, the breathing continued, and the strange noises grew louder. It sounded like a woman shouting. The strange quality of the voice made Jason's stomach constrict. He began to sense danger.

Jason assumed Sammy had accidentally called him again. Perhaps the background noises were simply one of his cartoon shows. He listened for the young boy's breathing on the other end.

"Sammy? Hey, baby boy. Is that you, sweetie? Are you calling Daddy again?" Jason said with the hopes Sammy might respond. Then Jason heard something that made his stomach knot up all over again. His precious Sammy said in a small voice, one obviously filled with fear, "Daddy. Help me. Peaze."

"Sammy! What's wrong?" Jason said terrified, trying desperately to sound calm as he stood and began putting on his winter coat.

"Sammy? Please put Mommy on the phone," Jason pleaded. "Can you please get Mommy, sweetie?"

Again, Sammy said, "Peaze, Daddy. Help me." Then the boy began to whimper. That sound of terror in his young son's voice drove a spike of pain deep into his very soul. It was then Jason more clearly heard the shouting in the background, realizing for the first time it was Stephanie. She sounded like a lunatic. Keeping the phone in the crook of his neck, Jason finished putting on his coat and he hurried out through the main office area. Those of his staff who were working late watched him leave with concern.

He skipped the elevator and as Jason ran down the stairs, taking them two at a time, he could hear Stephanie shouting words like "whoremonger," "bastard child," and threats like "he'll die for this."

Stephanie's mind must have finally broken and now his son was alone with her. He had to get home as soon as possible. He jumped into his car and sped out of the parking lot. He knew he could be home in less than ten minutes, but he hoped it would be enough. The last thing he heard before the phone went dead was the voice of his little boy crying "No, Mommy! No! Peaze!"

38

STEPHANIE WALKED BAREFOOT across the frozen field between the garage and the spa toward the menacing resurrected well. In her spellbound state, she was oblivious to the frigid conditions around her, including how her feet ached from the ice-covered grass. The area glowed brightly in the motion-activated security lighting, giving the icy ground an otherworldly appearance. Under her right arm, she carried her son who was kicking and screaming fiercely, trying in vain to escape. He had no idea what was happening, but he knew the woman carrying him was not acting anything like his mother.

Behind the well, Stephanie saw the assemblage of undead beings waiting for her. In her entranced state, it didn't faze her that she was staring at five dead creatures.

She recognized Dwight and Marie Livingston, as well as her former lawyer. She also saw Emerson Washburn from photos she had found during her research, although in his emaciated condition made him barely recognizable. She had no idea who the fifth being was, but it didn't matter anyway. The wretched thing was barely more than charred flesh pinched tightly over blackened bones.

Some of the water had bubbled up over the top of the well, coating the circular dirt structure with a layer of shimmering ice before dropping back down to its normal depth. The resulting feature resembled a beautiful ice sculpture of a well.

Stephanie looked down at the boy she was carrying under her arm. She was confused about his identity. Once moment she thought it might be someone named Samuel. A moment later, she thought he was one of Marie's Livingston's sons and she was Marie, not Stephanie. Next, she thought he might be one of her cheating husband's bastard children. She even believed for a moment the boy might simply be an inanimate doll.

It was as if she was living in a dream world. Perhaps that was why she didn't fear the hideous creatures or couldn't concretely identify the thing in her arms. Perhaps in the dream, she believed she was having, nothing was real.

One thing she did know was it was her job to bring this thing under her arms to the well. Stephanie thought she was supposed to sacrifice the thing to get revenge on her unfaithful husband, Dwight. No, she thought. Her husband's name was Jason and Marie's husband was Dwight.

Now she wasn't sure who she was, let alone who her husband might be or if she even had one. What she did know was what she had to do. Once the thing she carried was placed in the well, everything would be all right.

As Stephanie approached the well, Marie Livingston raised her arms high in the air and began speaking in a loud and unearthly voice.

"We have waited for this night for almost a century. Dwight and I have been unwillingly bound together in death because of a curse placed upon us long ago by his sister, Amelia.

"In this unfortunate union, he is in the role of master and I am his servant. I present this information at the behest of that master. Neither of us is content in these roles and we have tried to find a way to free ourselves. We watch others live their lives while we wallow in anguish.

"We have finally found a means to break those bonds and we must sacrifice the life of the one who can complete the circle of blood. And those who gave life to him must also die as Dwight and I did so many years ago.

"Samuel Jason Wright, born on this day, December 19, must die by his own mother's hand. The child's father will murder his wife before succumbing to remorse and taking his own life. This was how it happened so many years ago and how it must happen again tonight. The ceremony of the blood circle must be carried out before midnight."

"Stephanie Sage Washburn Wright, present the child, Samuel Jason Wright, for submergence in the sacrificial well."

Stephanie lifted Sammy directly in front of her. For the first time since leaving the loft, she looked into his eyes. Those eyes pleaded with her not to hurt him. They changed something inside her; she started to feel like herself.

Stephanie looked over and saw the dreadful mob of beings and she understood who they were and what their horrible plan was. She looked back at Sammy and then held him tightly to her breast whispering, "Oh, Sammy. Oh, my sweet baby boy. Mommy loves you so, so much. I promise I would never do anything to hurt you."

Stephanie looked defiantly at the ghost of her great-grandmother and shouted, "I now know who I am, and I know who and what you are! I know my husband Jason is a good man and not like your unfaithful husband, Dwight. He would never do such a thing to me and I would never ever lift a finger to hurt either Sammy or Jason. So give up your plans and go away because I will never help you."

Marie Livingston let out an ear-splitting wail of anger and frustration. Dwight turned and looked angrily at Marie to indicate she had failed him. Marie suddenly bent over screaming as if suddenly racked with incredible agony.

"You know what you must do woman," Dwight bellowed at Marie in a voice like thunder. "You must do what she cannot do. You must complete the circle of blood, no matter the cost."

Marie stood upright to the best of her ability and Stephanie could see the look of fear on her face. She was terrified of Dwight. She pointed an unsteady hand at Stephanie, summoning all her strength. Stephanie felt herself lose control of her limbs. She held Sammy out in front of her again and his eyes filled with renewed terror. She wanted to set him down and tell him to run away, but she was powerless to do so. It was apparent that Marie was now in control of Stephanie's body. Then, one shuffling step at a time, Stephanie began to walk closer to the well. She tried to fight against the force but was helpless to do so.

"I told you the circle had to be completed," Marie screamed, "and it must be! If you won't willingly kill the boy yourself, then I'll force you. Your beloved Jason won't know the difference. He'll find you with the body, mumbling like a mad woman and he'll assume you murdered your son. Then he'll kill you and finally take his own life. It is how it must be."

Resist as she might, Stephanie continued to shuffle forward, tears streaming and freezing down her face in the frigid air. She would rather die herself than let anything happen to Sammy, but she couldn't stop herself.

"I command you to throw the boy into the well and kill him," Marie bellowed.

From somewhere in the darkness behind her, Stephanie heard a voice shout, "The hell you do, you rotten old bitch!"

39

JASON RAN FROM the shadows out into the light. He pointed an accusing finger at the phantom Marie Livingston and shouted, "No! No more! Get away from my family!"

Startled by Jason's outburst, the ghost lost her control over Stephanie. Then the creature realized there was more to her losing focus than simple shock or surprise. There was something about this man, Jason Wright, which had instantly depleted her strength. Stephanie turned and with Sammy tightly against her chest, stumbled back toward her husband. Jason wrapped his comforting arms around them.

"Steph! Honey! Are you all right?" he asked struggling to sound calm and reassuring.

She replied tearfully, "Y-yes. Now I am, thanks to you." Then she pressed her head against his shoulders and cried in his arms, "Oh, my God. Jason, what's happened? What's wrong with me? I can't seem to remember anything, just bits and pieces. It's like I just woke up from a bad dream."

Jason kissed her forehead and said, "Shhh. Steph. Don't worry. I'm here now. I don't really understand all of this, but I swear I won't let anyone or anything hurt you or Sammy."

"Mommy cwy," Sammy said, obviously concerned about his mother.

"Yes, Sammy," Jason said steadily, "Mommy is crying, but she won't cry anymore because her big man Sammy is here to protect her from those bad people."

Then Jason looked directly at the unearthly gathering of demonic spirits for the first time, taking in the details of each of them. The ungodly sights he saw would be burned into his memory for as long as he lived whether that was sixty more years or sixty more seconds. And Jason understood his life could very well be over in minutes.

Jason's first instinct was to take his family and flee as far as possible, never looking back. But such an action would be futile. These creatures, these demons, had controlled and manipulated events not only locally but over distance as well. He had no idea how far they might have to run to escape, assuming they could escape at all.

Anxiety took Jason in its grip. No, he would have to face the horrible, undead, unholy beings or else he and his family could never hope to be safe again. He was going to have to find a way to permanently drive them back into the hell from which they came . . . or die trying.

"Jason John Wright," Dwight Livingston roared, "you must bring the woman, Stephanie Sage Wright and the boy Samuel Jason Wright, to us. I command it."

Jason felt a tugging sensation inside his skull; he could feel the force of the specter trying to influence his own body into doing its bidding. But Jason apparently had an unknown power of his own because he was still in control of his actions. He could also tell by the strange look appearing on Livingston's face that he was equally surprised to discover he couldn't control Jason.

"Steph," Jason said, "I have an idea. And I think I'm right, at least, I hope I'm right. Listen, no matter what you hear or see, try not to be afraid of them. I think that might be part of the secret of how we can beat them. I think they live on the fear and the hatred of others. That's why they tried to pit us against each other. They need us to be at odds. I suspect with the three of us here together and combined as one force they can't beat us."

Stephanie looked perplexed for a moment and then said, "I think you're right. I can feel them trying to take back control of me. But they can't seem to do it. When it was just me, they could, but now I don't think they can."

"Keep fighting them. We can beat them together. I know we can. We love each other and nothing is stronger than that. I'm sure of it."

"You will bring the bitch and the child to me now!" Dwight shouted, his form was twitching and moving erratically, as were the rest of the creatures. Jason could see something was now very different about the ghosts; something was happening to them, but Dwight still tried to assert his control.

"You will do as I command, or I will order you all to rip out your own eyes and swallow them while we watch with pleasure!"

Fueled by newfound confidence, Jason pointed his finger at Dwight and shouted back, "Screw you, Livingston. Any powers you believe you have are useless against us. We are a strong and unified force of unconditional love and you can do nothing to harm us. You've existed without love for so long you've forgotten its power. We don't fear you."

Then Jason decided to push even harder, "My wife's soul is pure, my son's soul is pure, and so is mine. And together we are immune to your ridiculous commands.

"We may have the blood of Dwight Livingston flowing through our veins, but we have souls that are uncorrupted. And you don't have the power to separate us ever again. You're the murderers, not us. You've failed miserably. You didn't count on the power of our love. You can do nothing to harm us when we are one."

Jason shouted one taunt after another, and he could tell the more he showed his strength and lack of fear the more disturbed the spirits appeared to get.

Then the ghosts began to howl in agony. They continued to twitch and gyrate. Jason shouted at the group of hell-spawned demons, "I, Jason John Wright, illegitimate great-grandson of Dwight Livingston, with the strength of my family's love, now possess the power. And I command all of you miserable creatures to return to whatever corner of Hell you have arisen from. Leave me and my family alone forever."

The specters were now contorting and screaming as Jason's words hit them like a barrage of bullets. Fresh blood began to ooze from each of the creatures' old wounds.

Then the sound of a thousand buzzing insects emanated from the opening of the well as an enormous dark swarm of black flies flew from the pit, encircling the creatures bored deep into their fresh weeping sores.

One of the insects flew close to Jason's face and before it flew away, he saw it clearly in all of its horror. The thing's body was similar to the type of fly Jason had seen many times around garbage or dead animals; a mix of blue, green, black, and other colors gave the impression of an oil slick on a puddle. Its legs were double the length of a normal fly and appeared to have long, talon-like claws on the ends of tiny humanoid fingers.

Its hideous face was by far its most disturbing feature, resembling a balding old man with wispy, gray hair; segmented insectile eyes; and two long, ram-like horns curving back from the forehead. Its mouth was much too large for its head and overflowed with hundreds of long, pointy needle-like teeth. That single second of observation seemed like an eternity to Jason and he was relieved when it returned to the swarm, obviously not interested in either he or his family.

Armstrong twisted from side to side, bellowing in agony. The hole where his heart had once been was black with the carnivorous insects and was increasing in size as thousands of chomping mouths devoured him from the inside out. Likewise, the gaunt form of Emerson Washburn twitched and convulsed as the tiny creatures filled the gashes in his chest, lapping up his oozing fluids. Some had zeroed in on the area between his legs and were chewing on the dangling threads of the musculature which was all that remained of his severed genitalia.

All around them, the ground began to tremble, and the family found themselves in the middle of an earthquake. Then before his eyes, Jason saw the well begin to change shape. The ice holding it together began to melt and the wall crumbled back to soil. Instead of its original round shape, it took on the shape of a massive slit, looking like God had taken a giant ax and cleaved a gash in the earth. Steam rose up all around the crevasse, the earth becoming hot and molten.

Jason could smell something foul and sulfurous from inside the crevasse. Pools of lava bubbled followed by occasional bursts of flames. Soon the flames were larger, almost twenty feet high as the ground continued to shake.

Jason wasn't even close to prepared for what happened next. Long, flaming tentacles sprang out of the opening whipping like a nest of vipers. One of the whipping lava lariats wrapped around Dwight Livingston's throat and began pulling him toward the hole. Dwight screamed and howled, trying desperately to fight it off. An instant later, another rope of molten lava wrapped around his arms and legs and pulled him down into the bubbling cauldron. Just before he disappeared, Jason witnessed the specter's head separate from his body, as did his arms and legs.

Jason heard a woman scream and saw Marie Livingston entwined in the fiery filaments, which melted the flesh from her ghostly body while simultaneously dragging her contorting form toward the volcanic pit. Her hair was ablaze and burning like a torch. She looked directly at Jason, as if pleading for help when her eyeballs exploded, and a swarm of black insects streamed out. Likewise, her scream vomited a swarm of buzzing pestilence.

The charred skeletal remains of Jack Moran were face-down, clawing and digging at the earth trying to escape the ropes of flames wrapped around its ankles.

Within the next few seconds, the rest of the horrible beings were likewise pulled down into the flaming portal. Jason couldn't think of anything but Hell that was capable of the carnage he was witnessing. The earth continued to shake so violently Jason found it almost impossible to remain upright.

After a moment, Jason heard a small burst behind him. The natural gas line that connected the main house to the spa building had ruptured.

With the conflagration of fire billowing from the crack in the earth, Jason knew he only had seconds to get his family to safety. He turned and tried desperately to lead Stephanie and Sammy away from the imminent explosion. But before they got more than twenty feet, the spa building blew up, sending deadly debris of flaming rock and timber flying high into the sky.

40

THE PRESSURE FROM the blast knocked Jason, Stephanie, and Sammy to the ground as a storm of flaming debris began plummeting down toward them. Despite his shocked condition, Jason managed to make himself a human shield, covering Stephanie and Sammy with his own body. He prepared himself for what was to come, determined to use his last breath to save his family.

He heard the fiery rubble of stone and rock fall around him and gritted his teeth in anticipation of the agonizing pain he knew was coming. To his surprise, however, he felt nothing. He heard sizzling sounds from above and cautiously lifted his head to try to see what was happening. All around them the formerly frozen meadow was ablaze as fiery debris continued to rain down. Yet the small area around them remained untouched.

"Jason? What's happening? Why aren't we dead?"

"I don't know, Steph. None of the stuff seems to be landing anywhere near us."

"Look!" Stephanie exclaimed pointing upward. She still was lying on the ground but had rolled over on her side. About ten feet above them, the raining pieces of burning debris miraculously stopped midair, sizzled, and then turned to ash. The ash slid down a giant translucent dome that glimmered with millions of tiny sparkling lights. The large structure completely covered them. "Look at it, Jason! What in the world is it? Where did it come from?"

Sammy sat up and pointed to a place in the meadow about thirty feet away and said, "Boys."

Jason and Stephanie followed his gaze and saw two bright, glowing forms of light which seemed to be roughly shaped like two small boys. The brightness of their iridescent forms was almost impossible to look at directly. Through squinted eyes, shielded by his hand, Jason could make out a stream of luminescent particles extending from the shimmering beings linking them to their mysterious protective dome.

"Boys help," Sammy said. "Boys help call Daddy. Boys help Sammy."

Then, before Jason and Stephanie had a chance to grasp the significance of what was happening, they heard another incredible explosion, even greater than the first. They whipped around to see their beautiful renovated farmhouse mansion blasted into flaming rubble before their eyes. The shock wave from the blast shook the earth below them. The translucent dome wobbled from the blast but still maintained its shape. As before; the fiery remnants flew everywhere setting the remaining out-buildings ablaze.

"Oh, my God, no! Everything we own. Our house, our clothing, our furniture, it's all gone." Stephany cried.

Jason's stomach sank with the frustration of the loss. But he realized, compared to what they had just managed to escape, the burning buildings and all of their earthly possessions were just things.

"Don't cry, Steph. All of that was just stuff. We can worry about it tomorrow. Right now, all that matters is we're safe and alive." He knew Stephanie agreed with him, but he also knew it was natural to grieve for the loss of their belongings.

In a few minutes, the rain of debris stopped, and Jason saw the translucent sparkling dome begin to dissipate and fade away. In the distance, the two glowing boys stood quietly, arms at their sides.

"Go see boys," Sammy said as he squirmed in Jason's arms. They stood together and Sammy led his parents to the light, carefully walking between the flaming remnants. Now they all could clearly see the Livingston boys in detail. They were dressed in bright white dress shirts and white pants but were barefoot.

Stephanie stepped forward and said, "Matthew, Charles, thank you so much for protecting my family. You saved our lives."

The two spectral shapes stood looking at her but said nothing.

"Had you lived, I'm sure you would have grown to be fine men and I would have been proud to have had you as great-uncles. God bless you both."

After a few seconds, slight smiles appeared on their cherubic faces, looking upward as if hearing someone calling to them. Then they began to dissolve as Stephanie had seen the dome dissolve. Next, two long streams of effervescent particles streaked up onto the heavens.

"Bye-bye, boys," Sammy said.

Jason and Stephanie looked about the burning buildings, the billowing smoke, and the debris-strewn patches of burning meadow.

"What now?" Stephanie asked, staring around in stunned confusion.

"Well," Jason replied, pulling out his cell phone, "now I guess we call 911."

EPILOGUE

"**W**RIGHT Industrial Consulting, Jason Wright speaking," Jason said into his desk phone. "No. Sorry. I have don't have a need for anything at the moment, but I'll keep you in mind. Thank you and goodbye." He hung up the phone and thought, "Salesmen! Well, I suppose they have to earn a living too."

He had found since setting up his own business and working from his home office, he seemed to be getting a lot of cold calls from a variety of salespeople. This was probably because he had been doing a lot to promote his business.

"I put myself out there to try to gain some name recognition. I have to assume it's working by the number of sales calls I've been getting. Too bad most of them aren't from potential clients."

As he was about to return to the project on his desk, he stopped for a moment and found himself once more reflecting back on how much had happened. And how much had changed over the past six months since that unbelievable night.

After the fire department had managed to get the blaze under control and the gas company had capped the leak, he, Stephanie, and Sammy had been taken to a hospital in the city of Yuengsville to be treated for shock as well as minor cuts and abrasions. The rescue workers were amazed the three had even survived the carnage. When they had arrived on the scene, the workers found them aimlessly walking toward the main road, down the driveway as a conflagration equivalent to a war zone could be seen burning behind them. One rescue worker described the sight as appearing like three survivors escaping from Hell.

Jason had been carrying his son in one arm while his other was secured tightly around his wife. The fire trucks had proceeded up to the home site while the ambulance crew looked after the family near a large rock in the driveway, which bore the inscription "Fallen Stones."

None of the Wrights seemed to have had much of a recollection of what actually happened. Somehow, they'd managed to survive a gas explosion that had destroyed every single structure on the property. Even the in-ground swimming pool and patio area as well as Jason's car in the driveway had been blown to bits.

Later, Jason called Chuck from the hospital to check on Jeremy and Cindy. He wanted to be sure the specters had not done anything to harm them. When he heard they were ok, he quickly told Chuck about the explosion and asked him to keep the kids for another day until he and Stephanie could get some details worked out. He knew it would take months until their lives even came close to returning to normal, but he figured he could at least get them settled into the hotel as a temporary measure by the next day.

The property was a total loss. All that remained of any of the building was rubble. Luckily, their homeowner's insurance eventually settled at three million dollars for their loss.

After what they'd been through, Jason and Stephanie both decided it would be best to move back to Berks County and begin again with a fresh start. Jason quit his job at the Ashton facility and pursued his dream of starting his own consulting business. He already had several lucrative client contracts and since he had managed to leave his old job on good terms, the Ashton factory management agreed to become one of his clients.

He and Stephanie built a brand-new home in Western Berks County in a new upscale subdivision on a two-acre lot. The home didn't compare in opulence to the one which was destroyed, but that was just fine with them. Jason had a home office from which he could run his business and Stephanie had a small studio she could use to write her books. The kids each had their own bedrooms; there was a large family room and an in-ground pool in the backyard.

Stephanie's latest book was doing amazingly well in a very tough market. Fortunately for her, about a week before the fire, Jason had sneaked into her loft in the middle of the night and found her book and illustrations buried under a stack of papers. Jason packaged everything and then sent it to her publisher. The night of the disaster when he had suggested that she send the book, it was already on its way. He knew she would never send it on her own. About a month later, a galley proof of the book arrived at the apartment where they were temporarily staying. Jason surprised Stephanie with it one night while having dinner at their favorite restaurant.

He was delighted by her tearful reaction. He hadn't seen her so happy since their wedding day or the day Sammy was born. She had assumed it burned up in the fire. Stephanie was so inspired she immediately began working on her next book. She had also been doing numerous book signings, readings, and interviews with magazines, newspapers, and blogs, as well as television and radio.

Stephanie no longer had any desire to recreate her family history and told Jason perhaps it would be better if the kids didn't know about their ancestors. Maybe in a hundred years or so one of their descendants might take an interest and begin researching anew, but she didn't want to record what she knew or what they had been through. She thought once again that everything happened for a reason. All of her research material was destroyed in the fire and so perhaps it was meant to be destroyed.

She and Jason almost never discussed the events of that horrible evening, hoping perhaps time might erase the memories. Nightmares sometimes returned, and there would be little they could do to stop that, but they could opt to not discuss it while awake.

Sammy seemed to have completely forgotten about it, or maybe it was his child-like resilience; he simply found a way to block it out and that was just fine with his parents.

Since Emerson Washburn's will required they not be permitted to sell the property and must keep it in the family, Stephanie thought of a way to put the land to work, making at least some money for them. She asked Jason to hire a contractor to remove the debris from the property. Then, since the gas line was capped at the highway, she had them dig it up and eliminate it. They destroyed the foundations of all the buildings as well as the pool and filled in the holes, re-tilling the entire forty acres to make it perfect for farming. Then they contacted local farmers and found several interested in leasing the land. The income from the lease was not much, but it made Stephanie happy to know the land, which had once caused so much sorrow, was being put to good use.

Now, Jason decided to check over the latest proposal he had prepared for one of his potential clients. He reached over and removed the paperweight. He picked up the weight and smiled knowingly as he turned it about in his hand. It was a flat, irregular-shaped piece of stone, about two inches thick.

To the casual observer, it looked like a piece of marble or granite. The back of the paperweight was smooth, but the front bore a partial carving which resembled half of an angel's or cherub's face. It was the type of engraving one might find on the tombstone of a very young child.

Jason picked up the report and placed the stone back on the stack of documents, smiling once again.

Lawrence Knorr's Original Ideas for "Circle Of Blood"

(Remember unless you want some of the story spoiled, wait to read this until you finish the book.)

This Stephen King-style thriller starts with a young family with children moving onto a farm in upstate Pennsylvania.

An old family plot is discovered on the property in a copse of trees in the middle of the property

Meanwhile, the children begin to experience ghostly encounters from ghost children and a ghost mother.

The mother, who had been working on the family genealogy, decides to research the (long ago) former owners. (relatives)

She discovers a tragedy—first determining this family all died around the same time—tracing from census records to burial records, wills, and newspaper accounts.

She also discovers there is a genetic connection between the woman and herself.

Ultimately, an old letter is found in the county archives describing how the mother killed all of her children, drowning them in a well.

The husband came home, discovered this, killed his wife, and then himself.

The mother begins to lose her mind, and sets out to repeat history . . .

But, will the husband get home in time?

Will the spirits prevent her?